CHRISTOPHER BUSH
THE CASE OF THE DEAD SHEPHERD

CHRISTOPHER BUSH was born Charlie Christmas Bush in Norfolk in 1885. His father was a farm labourer and his mother a milliner. In the early years of his childhood he lived with his aunt and uncle in London before returning to Norfolk aged seven, later winning a scholarship to Thetford Grammar School.

As an adult, Bush worked as a schoolmaster for 27 years, pausing only to fight in World War One, until retiring aged 46 in 1931 to be a full-time novelist. His first novel featuring the eccentric Ludovic Travers was published in 1926, and was followed by 62 additional Travers mysteries. These are all to be republished by Dean Street Press.

Christopher Bush fought again in World War Two, and was elected a member of the prestigious Detection Club. He died in 1973.

CHRISTOPHER BUSH

THE CASE OF THE DEAD SHEPHERD

With an introduction
by Curtis Evans

DEAN STREET PRESS

INTRODUCTION

THAT ONCE vast and mighty legion of bright young (and youngish) British crime writers who began publishing their ingenious tales of mystery and imagination during what is known as the Golden Age of detective fiction (traditionally dated from 1920 to 1939) had greatly diminished by the iconoclastic decade of the Sixties, many of these writers having become casualties of time. Of the 38 authors who during the Golden Age had belonged to the Detection Club, a London-based group which included within its ranks many of the finest writers of detective fiction then plying the craft in the United Kingdom, just over a third remained among the living by the second half of the 1960s, while merely seven—Agatha Christie, Anthony Gilbert, Gladys Mitchell, Margery Allingham, John Dickson Carr, Nicholas Blake and Christopher Bush—were still penning crime fiction.

In 1966--a year that saw the sad demise, at the too young age of 62, of Margery Allingham--an executive with the English book publishing firm Macdonald reflected on the continued popularity of the author who today is the least well known among this tiny but accomplished crime writing cohort: Christopher Bush (1885-1973), whose first of his three score and three series detective novels, *The Plumley Inheritance*, had appeared fully four decades earlier, in 1926. "He has a considerable public, a 'steady Bush public,' a public that has endured through many years," the executive boasted of Bush. "He never presents any problem to his publisher, who knows exactly how many copies of a title may be safely printed for the loyal Bush fans; the number is a healthy one too." Yet in 1968, just a couple of years after the Macdonald editor's affirmation of Bush's notable popular duration as a crime writer, the author, now in his 83rd year, bade farewell to mystery fiction with a final detective novel, *The Case of the Prodigal Daughter*, in which, like in Agatha Christie's *Third Girl* (1966), copious references are made, none too favorably, to youthful sex, drugs and rock and roll. Afterwards, outside of the reprinting in the UK in the early 1970s of a scattering of classic Bush titles from the Golden Age, Bush's books, in contrast with those of Christie, Carr, Allingham and Blake, disappeared from mass circulation in both the UK and the US, becoming fervently sought (and ever more unobtainable) treasures by collectors and connoisseurs of classic crime fiction. Now, in one of the signal developments in vintage mystery publishing, Dean Street Press is reprinting all 63 of the Christopher Bush detective novels. These will be published over a period of months, beginning with the release of books 1 to 10 in the series.

Few Golden Age British mystery writers had backgrounds as humble yet simultaneously mysterious, dotted with omissions and evasions, as Christopher Bush, who was born Charlie Christmas Bush on the day of the Nativity in 1885 in the Norfolk village of Great Hockham, to Charles Walter Bush and his second wife, Eva Margaret Long. While the father of Christopher Bush's Detection Club colleague and near exact contemporary Henry Wade (the pseudonym of Henry Lancelot Aubrey-Fletcher) was a baronet who lived in an elegant Georgian mansion and claimed extensive ownership of fertile English fields, Christopher's father resided in a cramped cottage and toiled in fields as a farm laborer, a term that in the late Victorian and Edwardian era, his son lamented many years afterward, "had in it something of contempt....There was something almost of serfdom about it."

Charles Walter Bush was a canny though mercurial individual, his only learning, his son recalled, having been "acquired at the Sunday school." A man of parts, Charles was a tenant farmer of three acres, a thatcher, bricklayer and carpenter (fittingly for the father of a detective novelist, coffins were his specialty), a village radical and a most adept poacher. After a flight from Great Hockham, possibly on account of his poaching activities, Charles, a widower with a baby son whom he had left in the care of his mother, resided in London, where he worked for a firm of spice importers. At a dance in the city, Charles met Christopher's mother, Eva Long, a lovely and sweet-natured young milliner and bonnet maker, sweeping her off her feet with a combination of "good looks and a certain plausibility." After their marriage the couple left London to live in a tiny rented cottage in Great Hockham, where Eva over the next eighteen years gave birth to three sons and five daughters and perforce learned the challenging ways of rural domestic economy.

Decades later an octogenarian Christopher Bush, in his memoir *Winter Harvest: A Norfolk Boyhood* (1967), characterized Great Hockham as a rustic rural redoubt where many of the words that fell from the tongues of the native inhabitants "were those of Shakespeare, Milton and the Authorised Version....Still in general use were words that were standard in Chaucer's time, but had since lost a certain respectability." Christopher amusingly recalled as a young boy telling his mother that a respectable neighbor woman had used profanity, explaining that in his hearing she had told her husband, "George, wipe you that shit off that pig's arse, do you'll datty your trousers," to which his mother had responded that although that particular usage of a four-letter word had not really been *swearing*, he was not to give vent to such language himself.

Great Hockham, which in Christopher Bush's youth had a population of about four hundred souls, was composed of a score or so of cottages, three public houses, a post-office, five shops, a couple of forges and a pair of churches, All Saint's and the Primitive Methodist Chapel, where the Bush family rather vocally worshipped. "The village lived by farming, and most of its men were labourers," Christopher recollected. "Most of the children left school as soon as the law permitted: boys to be absorbed somehow into the land and the girls to go into domestic service." There were three large farms and four smaller ones, and, in something of an anomaly, not one but two squires--the original squire, dubbed "Finch" by Christopher, having let the shooting rights at Little Hockham Hall to one "Green," a wealthy international banker, making the latter man a squire by courtesy. Finch owned most of the local houses and farms, in traditional form receiving rents for them personally on Michaelmas; and when Christopher's father fell out with Green, "a red-faced, pompous, blustering man," over a political election, he lost all of the banker's business, much to his mother's distress. Yet against all odds and adversities, Christopher's life greatly diverged from settled norms in Great Hockham, incidentally producing one of the most distinguished detective novelists from the Golden Age of detective fiction.

Although Christopher Bush was born in Great Hockham, he spent his earliest years in London living with his mother's much older sister, Elizabeth, and her husband, a fur dealer by the name of James Streeter, the couple having no children of their own. Almost certainly of illegitimate birth, Eva had been raised by the Long family from her infancy. She once told her youngest daughter how she recalled the Longs being visited, when she was a child, by a "fine lady in a carriage," whom she believed was her birth mother. Or is it possible that the "fine lady in a carriage" was simply an imaginary figment, like the aristocratic fantasies of Philippa Palfrey in P.D. James's *Innocent Blood* (1980), and that Eva's "sister" Elizabeth was in fact her mother?

The Streeters were a comfortably circumstanced couple at the time they took custody of Christopher. Their household included two maids and a governess for the young boy, whose doting but dutiful "Aunt Lizzie" devoted much of her time to the performance of "good works among the East End poor." When Christopher was seven years old, however, drastically straightened financial circumstances compelled the Streeters to leave London for Norfolk, by the way returning the boy to his birth parents in Great Hockham.

Fortunately the cause of the education of Christopher, who was not only a capable village cricketer but a precocious reader and scholar, was taken up both by his determined and devoted mother and an idealistic local elementary school headmaster. In his teens Christopher secured a scholarship to Norfolk's Thetford Grammar School, one of England's oldest educational institutions, where Thomas Paine had studied a century-and-a-half earlier. He left Thetford in 1904 to take a position as a junior schoolmaster, missing a chance to go to Cambridge University on yet another scholarship. (Later he proclaimed himself thankful for this turn of events, sardonically speculating that had he received a Cambridge degree he "might have become an exceedingly minor don or something as staid and static and respectable as a publisher.") Christopher would teach in English schools for the next twenty-seven years, retiring at the age of 46 in 1931, after he had established a successful career as a detective novelist.

Christopher's romantic relationships proved far rockier than his career path, not to mention every bit as murky as his mother's familial antecedents. In 1911, when Christopher was teaching in Wood Green School, a co-educational institution in Oxfordshire, he wed county council schoolteacher Ella Maria Pinner, a daughter of a baker neighbor of the Bushes in Great Hockham. The two appear never actually to have lived together, however, and in 1914, when Christopher at the age of 29 headed to war in the 16th (Public Schools) Battalion of the Middlesex Regiment, he falsely claimed in his attestation papers, under penalty of two years' imprisonment with hard labor, to be unmarried.

After four years of service in the Great War, including a year-long stint in Egypt, Christopher returned in 1919 to his position at Wood Green School, where he became involved in another romantic relationship, from which he soon desired to extricate himself. (A photo of the future author, taken at this time in Egypt, shows a rather dashing, thin-mustached man in uniform and is signed "Chris," suggesting that he had dispensed with "Charlie" and taken in its place a diminutive drawn from his middle name.) The next year Winifred Chart, a mathematics teacher at Wood Green, gave birth to a son, whom she named Geoffrey Bush. Christopher was the father of Geoffrey, who later in life became a noted English composer, though for reasons best known to himself Christopher never acknowledged his son. (A letter Geoffrey once sent him was returned unopened.) Winifred claimed that she and Christopher had married but separated, but she refused to speak of her purported spouse forever after and she destroyed all of his letters and other mementos, with the exception of a book of poetry that he had written for her during what she termed their engagement.

Christopher's true mate in life, though with her he had no children, was Florence Marjorie Barclay, the daughter of a draper from Ballymena, Northern Ireland, and, like Ella Pinner and Winifred Chart, a schoolteacher. Christopher and Marjorie likely had become romantically involved by 1929, when Christopher dedicated to her his second detective novel, *The Perfect Murder Case*; and they lived together as man and wife from the 1930s until her death in 1968 (after which, probably not coincidentally, Christopher stopped publishing novels). Christopher returned with Marjorie to the vicinity of Great Hockham when his writing career took flight, purchasing two adjoining cottages and commissioning his father and a stepbrother to build an extension consisting of a kitchen, two bedrooms and a new staircase. (The now sprawling structure, which Christopher called "Home Cottage," is now a bed and breakfast grandiloquently dubbed "Home Hall.") After a falling-out with his father, presumably over the conduct of Christopher's personal life, he and Marjorie in 1932 moved to Beckley, Sussex, where they purchased Horsepen, a lovely Tudor plaster and timber-framed house. In 1953 the couple settled at their final home, The Great House, a centuries-old structure (now a boutique hotel) in Lavenham, Suffolk.

From these three houses Christopher maintained a lucrative and critically esteemed career as a novelist, publishing both detective novels as Christopher Bush and, commencing in 1933 with the acclaimed book *Return* (in the UK, *God and the Rabbit*, 1934), regional novels purposefully drawing on his own life experience, under the pen name Michael Home. (During the 1940s he also published espionage novels under the Michael Home pseudonym.) Although his first detective novel, *The Plumley Inheritance*, made a limited impact, with his second, *The Perfect Murder Case*, Christopher struck gold. The latter novel, a big seller in both the UK and the US, was published in the former country by the prestigious Heinemann, soon to become the publisher of the detective novels of Margery Allingham and Carter Dickson (John Dickson Carr), and in the latter country by the Crime Club imprint of Doubleday, Doran, one of the most important publishers of mystery fiction in the United States.

Over the decade of the 1930s Christopher Bush published, in both the UK and the US as well as other countries around the world, some of the finest detective fiction of the Golden Age, prompting the brilliant Thirties crime fiction reviewer, author and Oxford University Press editor Charles Williams to avow: "Mr. Bush writes of as thoroughly enjoyable murders as any I know." (More recently, mystery genre authority B.A. Pike dubbed these novels by Bush, whom he praised as "one of the most reliable and resourceful of true detective writers"; "Golden Age baroque, rendered remarkable by some extraordinary flights of fancy.") In 1937 Christopher Bush became, along with Nicholas Blake, E.C.R. Lorac and Newton Gayle (the writing team of Muna Lee and Maurice West Guinness), one of the final authors initiated into the Detection Club before the outbreak of the Second World War and with it the demise of the Golden Age. Afterward he continued publishing a detective novel or more a year, with his final book in 1968 reaching a total of 63, all of them detailing the investigative adventures of lanky and bespectacled gentleman amateur detective Ludovic Travers. Concurring as I do with the encomia of Charles Williams and B.A. Pike, I will end this introduction by thanking Avril MacArthur for providing invaluable biographical information on her great uncle, and simply wishing fans of classic crime fiction good times as they discover (or rediscover), with this latest splendid series of Dean Street Press classic crime fiction reissues, Christopher Bush's Ludovic Travers detective novels. May a new "Bush public" yet arise!

Curtis Evans

The Case of the Dead Shepherd (1934)

"You see, George, it's hard to get excited about a school. You remember my definition of romance [viz., the other person, in some other time, in some other place]? Well, a school is the exception. Now if it were a jail we were going to, or a theatre, or a big store—"

"Or a pub," ventured Menzies.

"Exactly," admitted Travers, "or a pub; then there might have been some sort of thrill." He turned beamingly to Wharton. "I ask you, George, as a man of the world—do schoolmasters and mistresses have souls full of glamour and passion and intrigue? Are they torn by the same emotions that rend people like you and Menzies and—shall we say—myself?"

"That's what we're on the way to see," said Wharton, and grunted.

The Case of the Dead Shepherd

TO WHATEVER EXTENT teachers indeed "have souls full of glamour and passion and intrigue" in real life, they certainly reveal these compelling qualities in crime fiction, where schools, both primary and secondary, have proven a popular setting for murder since that hallowed literary age known as the "Golden Age of detective fiction" (generally defined as the period between the First and Second World Wars). Three years before the 1934 publication of Christopher Bush's singular primary school mystery, *The Case of the Dead Shepherd*, there appeared in the United Kingdom the bluntly titled *Murder at School* (1931), a detective novel by James Hilton, who over the next decade would become famous in English-speaking countries as the author of *Lost Horizon* (1933), *Goodbye, Mr. Chips* (1934) and *Random Harvest* (1941). *Murder at School*--which Hilton, perhaps concerned about his reputation as a serious writer, originally published under a pseudonym--deals with the suspicious "accidental" deaths at Oakington School of two boys, brothers, both of whom were students there.

Possibly reflecting the view that children's schools were really not the proper place for fictional bloodletting, in the United States *Murder at School* was published the next year with its setting decorously concealed under the generic title *Was It Murder?* Yet the school setting proved intriguing to mystery fiction reviewers and readers as well. Writing in 1935, after the runaway success of *Goodbye, Mr. Chips* had led to the reissuing in the US of *Murder at School/Was It Murder?* under Hilton's own name, the American mystery writer and reviewer Todd Downing, in a notice of Nicholas Blake's detective novel *A Question of Proof* (which, like Hilton's mystery, is set at a boys public school and was written by a distinguished man of letters, future poet laureate Cecil Day Lewis), speculated that Hilton's novel had "started a fad for boys school mysteries in the English murder mart." This "fad," however, if fad it was, seems to have pertained as much to co-educational schools as boys' public schools. (Girls' public schools seemingly are less represented in the Golden Age.)

Co-educational schools are the settings not only of Christopher Bush's *The Case of the Dead Shepherd*, but Anthony Berkeley's *Murder in the Basement* (1932), Gladys Mitchell's *Death at the Opera* (1934) and Margaret Cole's *Scandal at School* (1935). Another co-ed murder mystery, a comparative latecomer to the field, is Alan Clutton-Brock's *Murder at Liberty Hall* (1941)--to which, it has been speculated, Clutton-Brock's old public school pal George Orwell may have contributed; while in the following year Leo Bruce (mainstream novelist Rupert Croft-Cooke) published a boys school mystery, *Case with Ropes and Rings* (1941), the author's first of two detective novels with this setting.

Enough of these school mysteries had appeared by 1935 that British Crime Queen Dorothy L. Sayers--who that same year published her famous college mystery, *Gaudy Night*--was moved to query, in a *Sunday Times* review of Blake's *A Question of Proof*, "Why are school mysteries always so convincingly real?" Certainly in Christopher Bush's case the realness, not to mention the grimness, of the setting of his school mystery reflects the many years of his life that the author had devoted to teaching in English co-educational schools, particularly Wood Green School, near Oxford. These were years which, to judge from comments made in his detective novels, the author was rather glad to leave behind him when his writing career had ascended sufficiently for him to do so.

Five years before the publication of *The Case of the Dead Shepherd*, Bush had deprecated, in his breakthrough 1929 detective novel *The Perfect Murder Case* (published when he was still teaching at Wood Green School), the occupation of schoolmastering as "the most unappreciated, unromantic, and unremunerative profession there is." Similar sentiments expressed in *The Case of the Dead Shepherd*--which Bush mordantly dedicated "to THE IMPORTUNATE SCHOOLMASTER who, on the plea that other educational institutions besides the public-schools could do with a few murders, bludgeoned me into writing it"--indicate that Bush's absence from the teaching profession for several years had done nothing to make his heart grow fonder of it. Happily for mystery fans, Bush with his twelfth Ludovic Travers tale channeled his quite discernible disillusionment with his former vocation, which is reminiscent of the character of embittered schoolmaster Andrew Crocker Harris in Terence Rattigan's celebrated public school play *The Browning Version* (1948), into the devising of a superlative detective novel, one which is greatly enhanced by the authenticity of its institutional setting and the authority with which it is conveyed.

The Case of the Dead Shepherd opens with the commencement of an investigation by Superintendent George "the General" Wharton--assisted, as by this time we have come to expect, by his amateur extraordinaire friend Ludovic Travers, and by his cynical medical myrmidon, Dr. Menzies--into the suspicious poisoning death of a schoolmaster at the dismal Woodgate Hill County School. Once the trio, accompanied by Inspector Quick from the local police, arrives on the premises of the depressingly "jail-like" Woodgate Hill ("There was a cold starkness about [the main building], and a repulsive rigidity. Its great bricks and facings of stone were dead and chill even in the damp heat of that tempestuous afternoon."), they soon find themselves presented with yet another most unnatural death --a bludgeoning this time. The second victim is no less than the much-hated headmaster of Woodgate Hill, the splendid-ly-named Lionel Twirt, the titular "dead shepherd" of the title and without a doubt the most reviled person in the school.

The inquisitive Travers learns that the Head had pompous-ly christened himself the school's "shepherd," an appellation viewed with heavy irony by his staff, man and woman alike, as one of their number sourly explains: "He was fond of saying that he wasn't really the headmaster of the school, but a shepherd in charge of a flock. And by the way he used to say it, you gathered that it was the Almighty Himself who had made the appoint-ment." This particular member of the staff dispensed with irony in Mr. Twirt's case and simply referred to the Head--behind his back--as "the bastard." Taking stock of the "repressed, neurotic collection" that the terrible Twirt had made of the staff at Wood-gate Hill, Travers can only exclaim, "My God! What a hole to work in! It's a miracle you all weren't driven insane."

Looking over the Staff Register at Woodgate Hill, Wharton and Travers find that one of the staff members there "had come up to Cambridge from a well-known school," a revelation that induces Travers to wonder "what curious chance" had sent this individual "for a living to a place like Woodgate Hill instead of a public school." Christopher Bush himself had missed his chance to attend Cambridge as a young man and resultantly found him-self for years teaching at a co-educational school, where he be-came entangled in an unsatisfactory sexual affair with another teacher, by whom he fathered a son, the future composer Geof-frey Bush. Disillusionment over lost opportunities and unful-filled promise permeates the novel like a stale smell, and these feelings seem sadly reflective of Bush's own personal experienc-es. Of one of the schoolmistresses at Woodgate Hill, a character witheringly comments: "She thinks she's a gipsy melody, if you know what I mean, and all she is, is a tune on a cracked record."

At another point in the novel, the author damningly observes: "Of all the devastating sights this world affords, that of the flirtatious schoolmarm is surely the most distressing." Were these caustic observations reflective of the author's own failed relationship with his discarded *inamorata* at Wood Green Hill?

At this late date there seems no way of knowing such things about Bush, but what is clear is that *The Case of the Dead Shepherd* offers vintage mystery fans an uncommonly bracing read for a Golden Age detective novel, one in which the darker human passions that in real life can and sometimes do result in murder are not elided by an author concerned only with devising for his readers a clever puzzle. Yet the puzzle in *The Case of the Dead Shepherd*, it should be noted, is an uncommonly fine one, making the novel, in my estimation, one of the more notable works of detective fiction from its Golden Age. "Read it," advised the *Saturday Review* in the US, avowing that "[f]ew current [detective] yarns boast such a clever criminal" and that "[the] sub-plots are diverting."

In the *Sunday Times*, Dorothy L. Sayers praised Shepherd's "ingeniously worked out" plot and "well indicated" characters, concluding that as a whole the novel was "thoroughly engrossing, well written and full of legitimate puzzlement." Sayers, who earlier in life had suffered her own dismal experiences with teaching, like Christopher Bush saw writing detective fiction as offering a blessed escape from the purgatory of pedagogic life, pleading in correspondence with her concerned mother in December 1921:

> Nobody can feel more acutely than I do the unsatisfactoriness of my financial position. I wish I could get a reasonable job, or that I could know one way or another whether I shall be able to make money by writing. . . . If you like, I'll make you a sporting offer—that if you can manage to help me to keep going till next summer, then, if Lord Peter is still unsold, I will chuck the whole thing [detective fiction], confess myself beaten, and take a permanent teaching job.

Happily for Sayers, her first Lord Peter mystery, *Whose Body?*, was published in 1923, launching a great crime writing career and allowing Sayers to avoid the terrible fate of taking a permanent teaching job. In her review of *Shepherd* eleven years later, Sayers wryly observed that "nearly all school murder stories are good ones—probably because it is so easy to believe that murder could be committed at such a place." No doubt Christopher Bush would have seconded this assertion.

THIS BOOK IS DEDICATED
TO

THE IMPORTUNATE SCHOOLMASTER

WHO, ON THE PLEA THAT OTHER EDUCATIONAL
INSTITUTIONS BESIDES THE PUBLIC-SCHOOLS
COULD DO WITH A FEW MURDERS, BLUDGEONED
ME INTO WRITING IT

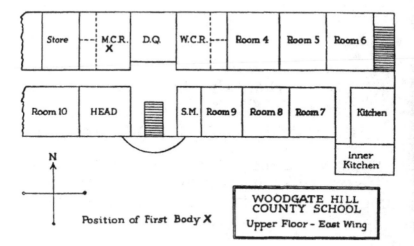

Store	M.C.R. **X**	D.Q.	W.C.R.	Room 4	Room 5	Room 6	

Room 10	HEAD		S.M.	Room 9	Room 8	Room 7	Kitchen
							Inner Kitchen

N

Position of First Body **X**

WOODGATE HILL
COUNTY SCHOOL
Upper Floor – East Wing

CHAPTER I
TRAVERS DEFINES ROMANCE

"ROMANCE," said Ludovic Travers, "is a very relative term. If I were driven to a definition"—he smiled diffidently to conceal the fact that he was bursting to give one—"it'd be this. Romance is the other person, in some other time, in some other place."

Superintendent Wharton frowned in thought, being wary in his handling of Travers's epigrams. And then the telephone went and he grabbed the receiver. His amiable old face with its gigantic, weeping-willow moustache lost its deceptive benevolence and became official. Travers, whose long legs had been stretched out from the only easy chair, sat up and listened unashamedly.

"You're sure it isn't suicide?" A sardonic drooping of the lips. "Well, you're damn lucky to be sure of anything these days. . . . I see. And why shouldn't he have been lugging a book about? Isn't that how schoolmasters earn their money—lugging round books? . . . Oh, I know. . . . Just wait a minute then."

He pressed the receiver to his chest with the elaborate caution that was a humorous part of him.

"Weren't you writing some sort of a pamphlet lately about education?"

"Not a pamphlet, George," Travers reproved gently. "A book. A real book."

"All the better," said Wharton. "And are you busy for an hour or two?"

"Yes—and no," said Travers. In the same moment he thought of a devastating continuation, but Wharton was speaking down the phone again.

"You there, Quick? . . . Right, I'll be along straight away. . . . Say in half an hour."

Back went the receiver, and the table-bell was pushed. When the sergeant had taken his orders and gone again, Wharton began his explanations.

"That was Inspector Quick—O Division, Woodgate Hill. One of the old school of detectives, but not a bad stick in his way. He was called over to see a dead schoolmaster they found there, and thought it was suicide. Now Quick says it isn't." He put on his hat and surveyed himself for a moment in the wall mirror. "If you're ready we'll make a move. Menzies will be down below."

As they went along the stuffy corridor Travers's smile was wasted on Wharton's back. In most murder cases it had been a question of thrusting one's self shamelessly forward, and here was Wharton apparently only too anxious to have at his disposal the very services that had hitherto been a matter of regretful acceptance.

"What's the real idea of wanting me to go to this Woodgate Hill place, George?"

"Don't you know all about schools?" Wharton fired at him. "Besides, dead schoolmasters aren't much in my line."

The car was drawn up outside and old Doc Menzies was waiting. Wharton pointed scornfully at the waterproof the Doc had on his arm.

"What's the idea, Doc? Sleeping out the night?"

"Look up there and you'll see," Menzies told him as they got in.

It was an afternoon of late July, and for an hour the atmosphere had been unbearable with stuffy heat. As the car moved off there was audible above the traffic roar a rumble of thunder.

"Looks as if we're running straight into it," said Wharton, settling into his corner seat.

As he spoke the first heavy drops splashed on the window. Inside a minute the rain was lashing in sheets. Hard on the white flashes of the lightning came the bursts of thunder, so that the three were silent, watching from the windows the drive of the rain that had cleared the streets miraculously of traffic and sent pedestrians in a mad scurry for shelter. And then, as quickly as it had come, the main storm passed. At Camden Town the rain had almost ceased, and at Holloway the sun was gleaming hotly from the tossed, purple sky.

"Quick said it was a co-educational school," said Wharton all at once, in the manner of a man who has been chewing on a mystery. "I reckon that means boys and girls taught together."

"That's the idea," said Travers.

"Then why couldn't they say so?" complained Wharton fretfully. "It always was so in my young days, so why'd they want to go inventing long-winded names for it?"

"Ah, but only in the primary schools," Travers reminded him. "Now they've extended the idea to secondary schools. They have the sexes from about twelve years to as much as eighteen, and they're taught in the same room by masters or mistresses."

"Put me among the girls!" quoted Menzies, and gave Travers a jocular nudge in the ribs. The police-surgeon was as badger-grey as the day when Travers had first clapped eyes on him, and his humour often included such flippancies.

"I take it it's a secondary school we're going to?" said Travers with an assumption of off-handedness.

"Yes," said Wharton. "Woodgate Hill County School is what they call it. On the very edge of the suburbs. And what exactly is a county school, by the way?"

"It's a secondary school in a new or newish suburban area," Travers told him. "In the country there're grammar schools for boys and high schools for girls. A county school is the two in one. Co-educational, as you said."

"What about the teachers?"

"*Staff* is the correct term," said Travers flippantly. "They're graduates of the newer universities principally, with a smattering of Cambridge and Oxford. Usually they work on the specialist system."

"And what's that?"

"That," said Travers, "is an attempt to fit round pegs into round holes. Whereas you, in your young days, were taught every subject under the sun by whoever was your form-master; now each person—master or mistress—teaches one thing only; the things he or she knows best. Mathematics or history or languages, it may be, or science. That means that the pupils sit still in their rooms while the staff wander in and give whatever lesson it happens to be, unless that lesson should require a special room—the chemistry lab., for instance."

"And a very sound system too," pronounced Wharton, as if he knew. Then he subsided into another silence.

Travers fiddled with his glasses. "What's the particular mystery we're supposed to be going to unravel?"

Wharton pursed out his lips beneath the huge moustache, and at such a moment it was easy to see why the Yard knew him—affectionately enough—as the General.

"Well, Quick says there was nothing the man could have drunk the poison out of—no bottle or container or anything. Also he reckons this chap had the best of reasons for not committing suicide. Then there's the little matter of the damn great book he was clutching."

"What book was that?" asked Travers politely. Wharton always dealt out information grudgingly.

"Well, according to Quick, it was like this," said Wharton. "Just before four o'clock a boy went to the masters' room—" He stopped tantalizingly. "That wasn't what Quick called it."

"The masters' common room, perhaps," suggested Travers.

"That's it. Well, this boy went to the masters' common room for something, and there was a master crawling on his hands and knees and just about at his last gasp. He sort of groaned out for the boy to go and fetch some other master—I've forgotten his name—and when this other master and the boy got back to the common room again, the chap was dead. And what he had been holding on to all the time was a perfectly enormous catalogue or something." The General swivelled a crafty eye round at the other two. "What do you make of that?"

Travers smiled dryly. "There're a hundred explanations, George, that'd fit the circumstances. The trouble is we don't happen to know what all the circumstances are."

"That's shirking the issue," said Wharton. "But I should have told you that the masters' common room has a sort of inner room or annexe, and that's where they reckon the poisoning was done—"

"What was the poison?" cut in Menzies.

"Why do you think we're taking you down to see the local man?" asked Wharton, with a tremendous patience. "If Quick's man knew, he wouldn't want to consult with you. All the same, you can bet it wasn't cyanide or anything obvious. Still, what Quick gave me to understand was that the man took the poison while he was in that inner room, and when he knew he was for it, he crawled out to the main room with this damn great book in his arms. You see the point now? He was dying—and he knew it. Then why did he go lugging that book around?"

"Lord knows," said Travers, and began thinking it out.

Meanwhile the rain had begun again, and the car was running steadily through the suburbs. The dingier fringe had been passed and now came more open, tree-scattered districts; their streets washed clean by the same storm that had burst over the city.

Wharton's voice came again. "I noticed your face fell when I mentioned it was a school we were going to," he said to Travers.

"Did it?" countered Travers, and smiled. Then he fumbled at his glasses—a trick that always accompanied any special effort of the mind. "You see, George, it's hard to get excited about a school. You remember my definition of romance? Well, a school is the exception. Now if it were a jail we were going to, or a theatre, or a big store—"

"Or a pub," ventured Menzies.

"Exactly," admitted Travers. "Or a pub; then there might have been some sort of thrill." He turned beamingly to Wharton. "I ask you, George, as a man of the world—do schoolmasters and mistresses have souls full of glamour and passion and intrigue? Are they torn by the same emotions that rend people like you and Menzies and—shall we say?—myself?"

"That's what we're on the way to see," said Wharton, and grunted. Then he tapped on the glass partition, and Travers saw the car was drawing up outside the police station of Woodgate Hill. The chauffeur stepped out into the steady drizzle and had a few words about the rest of the route, and off the car moved again.

In a minute they were away from the busy high streets, with their trams and shops, and were making their way through quiet roads with red-bricked villas. Then those petered out and there was open, patchy country, with yet more villas in course of erection, and men swarming about them like disturbed ants. The road was up, and the car threaded its way between mounds of earth and the piles of stone blocks that would bound the new roads. Then all at once the car turned sharp right, and there before them was the building to which they were bound.

Travers never forgot his first sight of Woodgate Hill County School. In that weird light, through the drizzling rain and against the background of empurpled sky, the building reared itself above the sprawling, indeterminate villas like something grimly forbidding. There was a cold starkness about it, and a repulsive rigidity. Its grey bricks and facings of stone were dead and chill even in the damp heat of that tempestuous afternoon.

"I don't like the look of that place," said Travers. "It gives me the blue horrors, George."

"I've seen jails that looked more homely," said Wharton, and let out a scowl of his own as the car went through the entrance gates.

At close quarters Woodgate Hill County School was indeed a jail-like building. A nine-foot wall separated it from the quiet road, and in front of that was a stretch of bare, bleak, open country. Between the school front and the wall ran a crescent of gravelled drive. At its near end was the boys' entrance, and at the far end, the girls'. Plumb centre of the wall was the main entrance, reserved for visitors and staff. Through this Wharton's car had come, and it drew up before the semi-circular porch and its rows of steps. Just beyond it an ambulance was waiting, and on the steps stood Quick.

But when Travers stepped out of the car, hunching his shoulders against the rain, he became aware of something definitely strange about the front of that school. It was as if he were standing in a drab garden—a kind of lonely pole in an oasis of green. Wharton noticed it too—and then the reason for the strangeness became apparent. The land on which the school was built sloped away to the north. Whereas the back of the building rested on solid earth, the front had been raised upon six foot of pier. And to disguise that hideous six foot of brick, shrubberies had been made each side of the raised porch as far as each wing, so that the building seemed set in a green forest with the drive as a gravelled river. And between that drive and the wall were yet more shrubberies, with tallish trees at the back, so that the wall itself was wholly invisible.

"Here we are then, Quick," said Wharton briskly.

"Nothing new happened?"

"Nothing at all, sir," said Quick, "except that the headmaster seems to have disappeared. He ought to have been back at four o'clock."

He led the way up the staircase that confronted them just inside the porch. Wharton stopped, and sniffed.

"Foul sort of smell here?"

A corpse-like smell, thought Travers, but Quick cut in with a snort.

"It's the smell of ink, sir. You get it in all schools. But what I was going to tell you, sir, was about Flint, the caretaker. We wanted to ask him a few questions, but blowed if he ain't gone off too, and nobody knows where."

Wharton grunted.

"Then there's three or four others here too, sir, waiting to see the headmaster. One of the governors of the school, and a constable the headmaster sent for to be here at four o'clock, and an Indian gentleman."

Words failed Wharton, and he grunted again. Now the party was at the head of the stone stairway, where there was a spacious landing. Quick waved a hand round.

"I don't know if you'd like to get the lie of the land, sir, but that room there that'll look out over the front is the Head's room. This one facing it is the senior mistress's room." He turned his back and waved round again. "This corridor goes right along the building from the head of the boys' stairs to the head of the girls', and the class-rooms open out on it both sides. This room facing us across the corridor is the secretary's room. That one on the right is the mistresses' common room, and that one to the left of it is the masters' common room."

He moved towards that last-mentioned room, and the party followed.

"How'd you come to know all this?" asked Wharton suspiciously.

Beneath Quick's modesty was an abundant, parental pride. "My daughter Daisy is the secretary here, sir. She happened to see the dead man and it upset her, so Mr. Castle kindly thought she'd better go home."

"I see," began Wharton, and then said no more.

The door of the masters' common room opened and a man was all at once standing there. Travers gave a little start, for it was rare that he met a man as tall as himself, and this man beat his six foot two by another good inch. And he had an easy litheness with it. About thirty-five, he seemed, and he carried his height and his clothes with a supple grace. But most noticeable was the jet-black of his hair, and the dark eyes that gave a quality to the clean-shaven face and set it alight with a kind of cynical alertness. The face itself was at the moment flooded with an elusive attractiveness, and the lips drooped with a smile that the shadows made faintly ironical.

"This is Mr. Castle," said Quick. "He's what they call the senior master, so he's in charge till Mr. Twirt gets back."

Wharton thrust out a hand. "How d'you do, Mr. Castle. And who's Mr. Twirt? The headmaster?"

"Yes," said Castle. "Mr. Twirt is the headmaster." His voice was as attractive as himself, and yet it too had some quality of irony about it. Then he drew back and Wharton entered the room.

Across that room there were windows, wet with the rain of the storm and the after-drizzle. Through them one could see the playing-fields, which sloped away to the north so steeply that they were terraced as the school itself was terraced. To the left was a door that led apparently to that inner annexe which Wharton had mentioned, but the eyes that had lifted towards it fell at once to the table in the centre of the main room, and the body that lay uncovered upon it.

"This is him, gentlemen," said Quick, indicating the body. "Dr. Williams I think you know, sir." The local police-surgeon got a handshake from Wharton. In less than no time he and Menzies were whispering over the body, and Wharton's eyes were running round the room and its collection of occupants. On a chair by one of the windows sat a brown-faced gentleman in black suit and turban; a small suit-case at his feet. In another chair was a wizened-looking man with thin hair, straggly beard and scraggy neck. By him stood a constable in uniform, and alongside him were three of Quick's men.

"Switch the lights on," said Wharton to one of them. "July or not, this room's like a cave."

Even when the lights went on, Travers still felt singularly uncomfortable in that room. It was as if the building itself had compressed its forbidding starkness within the compass of four walls. The atmosphere was muggy, with too much of the smell of human breath, and the unnatural light from the electric bulbs gave something of horror to the table and the body that lay on it. And yet, as Travers looked down at that dead body, he felt himself pervaded with some rare particular pity. The dead man's face was pale and his eyes staring, but the fixedness of that terrible death could not hide the quality of the man or the charm of a dead personality. He was a man of medium height, with high forehead and tooth-brush moustache, and about as little like the layman's idea of a schoolmaster as Travers could have imagined.

"You knew him pretty well, I suppose?" He whispered the words to Castle. Somehow it seemed sacrilege to speak aloud in that room and with one's eyes on that table.

"Yes," said Castle. "He was a great chap was Charles."

"Was that his surname?"

"Tennant—Charles Tennant," said Castle, and all the time his eyes had never left Menzies and his ghastly prying-open of the dead man's jaws.

Then Quick's whisper came across the room. "Do you think you might let some of these people get away now, sir? They're only cluttering up the place."

Wharton nodded; turned his back on the table and the corpse and had another look at the waiting oddments by the window.

Quick cleared his throat for the introductions, and began with the man with the straggly beard.

"This is Mr. Sandyman, sir—one of the governors."

Travers—most incredibly ill-mannered—raised a surreptitious eyebrow. His idea of a governor of a secondary school was a splendid personage, lined outside with fine linen and inside with port. But Sandyman looked the spit of a tradesman, and a schemer at that. His clothes were not right, and as soon as he spoke, his voice had a thin, cheap, ugly quality.

"And what are you doing here, Mr. Sandyman?" Wharton asked him. In his official occasions the General was an imposing person. One forgot that hairy adumbration above his mouth, and saw only the dignified bulk of the man, the loftiness of the forehead and the keen, unwavering eyes.

"Well, sir, Mr. Twirt sent word he wanted to see me on most particular business at four o'clock. As a matter of fact I really suppose I'm waiting for him now."

"Yes, but what are you doing in here?"

Castle supplied the answer. "Mr. Sandyman was waiting outside the Head's room at four o'clock so I naturally asked him if he'd seen anything happen that might throw light on—on this affair."

"And did he throw any light?"

Castle smiled, and again there was a hint of irony. "No—unless it's a help to you to say he saw nothing at all."

Wharton nodded. "We can get you if we want you, Mr. Sandyman?"

"Oh, yes, sir." Sandyman was obviously itching to be gone. "I'm on the phone, and Inspector Quick knows all about me."

"That's all right then," said Wharton. "We needn't keep you any longer."

Sandyman hesitated for a moment as if he felt some special words of farewell were expected, but the eyes were no longer on him. As he shut the door, a voice came in on the new silence. The voice was staccato and sibilant.

"May I go now too, please?"

It was the Indian who was standing all at once in front of Wharton; shoulders bent and palms upward like an Oriental who regretfully refuses the bid for the carpet. In spite of the heat he was wearing a black coat tightly buttoned across his chest. Above his sallow forehead his yellow turban looked amazingly dainty. One gathered that his eyes were black as his hair, but they were concealed by horn-rims even more immense than the monstrosities that Travers wore. The tiny straggling of side-whisker by his ears gave an impression of age, and yet he was no more than thirty—if that.

Castle came forward. "Perhaps I can explain. This is Mr. Ram. Mr. Twirt wished to see him at four o'clock and made an appointment to that effect. He was sitting outside the Head's room with Mr. Sandyman, and he says he saw nothing."

"I see," said Wharton. "And now he's waiting for Mr. Twirt; is that it?"

But with his gloved hand Mr. Ram was flourishing a card beneath Wharton's nose; and vaguely irritated as Wharton was, he took it and gave it an official inspection.

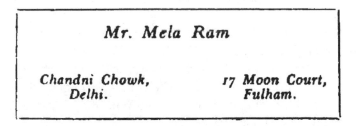

Mr. Mela Ram

Chandni Chowk,   *17 Moon Court,*
Delhi.   *Fulham.*

"Yes, but what did your headmaster want to see him about, Mr. Castle?" persisted Wharton.

"I will explain, please—"

Wharton dismissed him with a magisterial hand, and Castle did the explaining. His smile was now definitely cynical.

"Mr. Twirt is always willing to throw open this school and place his staff at the disposal of any foreign gentlemen who wish to inspect an English educational institution. We've had a Jap or two here, several Frenchmen, a German and a Malay. Mr. Ram was merely coming to look over the school tomorrow, since a friend of his had told him about the place. He obtained permission from Mr. Twirt over the phone, and Mr. Twirt sent him a short note asking him to be here to-day at four o'clock so that he could find out precisely what it was that Mr. Ram wanted to see—and could set the stage accordingly. That is so, Mr. Ram, I believe?"

"Yes, yes!" said Ram. "But I must go now. It is very urgent, please."

Wharton raised his hand reprovingly. "Just a moment, Mr. Ram. There's other people who may have to be seen to first."

It was on the uniformed constable that his eyes had fallen, and the General took a step towards him.

"And what are you doing here?"

"I was sent for, sir," said the constable. "My orders was to report to the headmaster here at four o'clock—and I've been here ever since."

"What for?"

"I don't know, sir. The sergeant didn't know either. The gentleman said over the phone that he wanted someone round at four o'clock."

"That's right, sir," cut in Quick. "No one's any idea what the headmaster wanted him for."

Wharton grunted. "Wanted his bicycle cleaned, perhaps. But what are you waiting for now?" The constable smiled, discerning, no doubt, the kindly heart beneath Wharton's waistcoat.

"That's what I don't know, sir."

"See anything to throw any light on this?"

"Not a thing, sir. I was outside the headmaster's room with the other two gentlemen, till I was fetched in here."

Once more there was an interruption. Ram was spreading out his palms before Wharton.

"I go now, please?"

"Just a minute," said Wharton and waved him aside. There was as yet no particular hunch in the General's mind, but somehow he knew the Indian for something peculiar and unnatural—some vague, suspicious concomitant of murderous feasts;

something whose very cringing laid itself open to closer examination. "You'd better wait till the headmaster comes," he said.

The other cringed still lower. "No, please. I must go now, please. I have important engagement."

"So have a lot of us," said Wharton severely, and turned to the constable again. "The best thing you can do is report back to your superiors and say what's happened."

Then, suddenly, there was the slam of the door and a pattering of feet on the stone stairs. Ram had sidled across the room, suit-case in hand, and when Wharton had turned, had made a bolt. The General stared for a moment, hardly realizing what had happened. Then he let out a holler.

"Hi! Fetch him back here again. One of you men there!"

Quick's sergeant was first at the door and they heard him taking the steps two at a time. Wharton nodded over at the constable.

"All right. You can go now. And if you see that chap giving any trouble, lend a hand to bring him back here."

The door closed on the constable and the room seemed almost deserted. Wharton scowled round at nothing in particular. Menzies straightened himself.

"Any water here?" he asked Castle. "The doctor here and myself would like to wash our hands."

Castle showed them to the basins in the annexe and Wharton followed for a look.

"You said there wasn't anything he could have drunk the poison out of," he said to Quick. "Here's a decanter and a glass, and the water tap to fill it from."

"But there weren't any of his prints on the glass," said Quick. "And if he took it straight out of a bottle, then we've had a hunt— even outside the lavatory window—and we can't find one."

Menzies finished wiping his hands and had a word with his colleague.

"We'll get him away now if you don't mind," he said to Wharton.

"Know what killed him?"

"Not definitely," said Menzies with a shrug. "We rather suspect it was oxalic acid—only, suspicions don't count."

The body started on its road to the mortuary and the room was still more empty. On the table now lay only the contents of the dead man's pockets. Wharton turned them over idly for a moment, and then became aware of the waste of time.

"About this headmaster of yours, Mr. Castle. A very strange thing, isn't it, not being here and having all those appointments for four o'clock? Why, if that clock there's right, it's gone half-past five!"

So subtle was the sneer that Travers alone detected it in the speaker's voice. "Mr. Twirt is a very busy man," Castle said. "His whole life is centred on education—or Mr. Twirt, which is the same thing. Perhaps he's met somebody and they're discussing one or other of the topics."

Wharton shot a quick look at him. Castle was wholly outside the range of even his enormous experience. He wanted somehow to dislike the man, and to irritate him, or goad him—and he was finding the feat impossible.

"You're sure he *is* out?"

"Oh, yes," said Castle. "He said at a quarter past three that he was going out, and word was brought me by the secretary—Miss Quick—that he'd gone out. I have to be informed, in case anything happens while he's away. And as he isn't in his room or anywhere else on the premises, all we can presume is that he's still out."

"He's married?"

"No," said Castle laconically. "A widower—and childless. But he's got the phone at his house and his housekeeper's ringing us if he goes straight back there."

Wharton grunted again. "Incredible, it seems to me—for a public man. But you don't find it so?"

"Oh, dear, no," said Castle calmly. "I've often known him to keep a string of people waiting—particularly after he's been rotating."

"Rotating?" Wharton stared.

"Sorry," said Castle. "Mr. Twirt is a Rotarian, and occasionally attends luncheons and so on. An excellent opportunity to discuss education. A word or two in season—as it were."

Wharton turned away for a moment, pursing his lips. In that suave assistant there was very much that he was failing to fathom. But Ludovic Travers was finding in Castle a man after his own heart. The polished irony, the charmful ease, and the whole of the man had an immediate attraction. And what intrigued him most was not what Castle had let out, but what he was keeping in. As Travers saw it, the irony was merely an outlet, and in telling half-truths he kept clear of utter disloyalty and indiscretion. And the more Travers had listened and watched, the more he had felt in his bones that below the surface of things, within that grim forbidding building and within the souls of those who lived in it, there had been strange stirrings. With his own first glimpse of that mass of cold brick and stone he had seen, too, some repulsive emanation which—as Wharton had said—was the aura of a jail.

The voice of Wharton cut across Travers's romantic wonderings.

"Bring in that boy who saw the man dying."

Castle gently cleared his throat. "I'm afraid he isn't here. He's a young boy—less than twelve—and rather sensitive, and we didn't want him to see or know too much. When I came down with him here and saw Tennant on the floor, I kept him out of the room. But Inspector Quick and I took a statement from him, if you want to see it."

"I think you did quite right," granted Wharton. "Still, let's begin somewhere. Perhaps you'll tell us, Mr. Castle, all you know about this afternoon."

CHAPTER II
THE DEAD SHEPHERD

"WE'LL BEGIN at the important end first," said Wharton. "Why is everybody so sure he didn't commit suicide?"

"He wasn't that kind," said Castle curtly.

Wharton gave his most genial smile. "I see. In other words, there's never a suicide case that isn't expected! No skeletons in the cupboard either! Still, perhaps you'd like to amplify the statement."

"Perhaps I would," said Castle dryly. "You're married yourself?"

"Oh, yes."

"You'd be surprised, when you got home to-night, to find your wife had poisoned herself?"

"I'm not going home to-night," smiled Wharton, "though I'd certainly be surprised enough. But why bring in impossibilities?"

"Precisely!" retorted Castle. "You know your wife, and I don't. I knew Tennant, and you didn't. I knew him at Cambridge and I knew him during the war, and I was chiefly responsible— God forgive me!—for getting him his job here."

"All right then," admitted Wharton, "we'll say it was unexpected. Anything else?"

"He'd just got a job as headmaster. He got the news last week. It's a new school of this type, and not too far away."

Wharton screwed up his lips. "I'm afraid I don't see the argument."

Castle gave a little sigh. "Well, I'll put it like this. By the way, this talk is confidential?"

"Implicitly so," Wharton assured him.

"Very well, then. After twelve years as a hack in a hole like this, Charles Tennant was taking charge of a decent school of his own. Instead of four hundred a year, he'd be getting six—and he'd go on to nine."

"Now I begin to see things," said Wharton. "As you say, why should he do himself in with a prospect like that in sight?"

Quick had been quivering restlessly, and now he broke in. "If you'll excuse me, sir, you didn't actually read that letter we found in his pocket. It's from a cousin—Mr. Castle says—saying him and the dead one were to meet in town to-night."

Wharton read the letter through. "Barnstead, eh? That's not too far? . . . John Something-or-Other."

"John Tennant," volunteered Castle. "I've met him once or twice."

"The dead man was married?"

Castle shook his head. "As far as I know, except for his cousin John, he hadn't a relative."

"They didn't live together?"

"Oh, no," said Castle. "Charles lived in Woodgate Hill. About a mile from here."

Wharton turned to Quick. "Get one of your men off at once to this Barnstead address, and ask Mr. John Tennant to come along."

He waited till the door closed again. "Now about this afternoon, Mr. Castle. Tell us exactly what happened."

"Well, Tennant was off duty," said Castle. "He had what we call a free period from three o'clock to four, and according to the headmaster's interpretation of the term, that meant he ought to have been in here doing a job of work—in this case, correcting examination papers. I peeped in here at about ten minutes or so to four—I'd slipped down from my room to get some papers I wanted—and there wasn't a soul or a sound here then. What I now know is that he was in that inner room."

"What for?"

A most peculiar look came over Castle's face. "Well, there're reasons and reasons. Personally, I don't think it matters."

Travers leaned across to Wharton. "Perhaps you might once more assure Mr. Castle that all communications are implicitly confidential."

"Of course," said Wharton. "Of course!"

"That being understood," resumed Castle, "I might say that men were accustomed to shut themselves up in that inner room to lie doggo. It closes from the inside, and if the Head came bursting in here to find a man to do a job of extra work, he wouldn't see anybody. Meanwhile the man who'd earned his free period could sit safe in there and read the paper or have a rest."

"Yes," put in Quick, who had just come in again; "I've heard my daughter laugh about that."

Castle looked none too pleased at that disclosure. "Then you'd better warn your daughter to be a bit more discreet. Still, about what happened. I was teaching in Room 9—doing a Shakespearean play—when a small boy came rushing unceremoniously in to say that I was wanted here. He saw Tennant was ill, and when I got here, I found him dead; stretched out on the floor where those chalk marks are. The boy had been sent down here by the master who was teaching him to fetch a bundle of papers"—he waved round at the shelves where the piles stood—"and his story is that he saw Tennant sort of trying to crawl painfully over the floor there, as if he'd come through the annexe door. Tennant gasped at him to go and fetch me. All he said was, 'Mr. Castle . . . Castle!'—just like that. The boy was scared stiff, but fetched me, as I said."

"Hm!" went Wharton, and stood for a good minute in thought. His eyes went to the annexe door and lowered to the chalk marks on the parquet floor.

"Do you know why it was you he sent for?"

"I don't," said Castle. "It might have been because, as the Head was out, I was the responsible Head myself. Or what I'm inclined to think now is that he sent for me as his closest friend. I might say I was his only real friend on the staff—if you take the term in the best sense. What I mean is that he and I were the only ones who had all the vital things in common. We understood each other."

"I see," said Wharton. "But wasn't there a little matter of a book?"

"Here it is, sir." Quick brought the book over from one of the small cupboards where he had put it for safety. "You notice that dust on the back, sir, and the prints? That shows nobody handled it but himself."

But Wharton's eyes had not opened at the sight of the prints; it was the book itself that staggered him. It was a huge, cloth-bound tome, weighing best part of ten pounds. And it was nothing but a pre-war catalogue of chemical and physical apparatus! The precise date was 1910.

"He was a science master?" asked Travers.

"Nothing of the sort," said Castle, who appeared as much bewildered as anybody else. "He was hopelessly unscientific. He was the history specialist."

Wharton let out another grunt. "And you say he'd lugged this damn great thing out of that annexe and was dragging it with him across the floor?"

"I found him dead with it in his arms," said Castle quietly.

Wharton nodded. "Very well, then; let's be logical. Let's get down to incontrovertible facts. Tennant knew he was dying, or desperately ill; and he wanted *you*. He wanted to show you something in this book, and if the boy hadn't come in—and he'd have lived so long—he'd have crawled right up to the room where you were. Is that right? And if it is, can you explain it?"

"It sounds logical enough," said Castle slowly "All the same, I say in all sincerity I'd give the very devil of a lot to know just why."

Travers was fumbling at his glasses. "If I might ask the question: just why was this antique catalogue kept at all? It looks hopelessly out of date—especially with regard to prices."

"It just happened to be kept," said Castle. "You see, it wasn't so much out of date before the war. Then during the war it just lay inside there, and since then the men have kept it because sometimes during lunch, or after school, they play a kind of indoor golf on the parquet floor here, and that book—and one or two others we've got—makes a damn good bunker."

"I'll send it along to the Yard," said Wharton, then rubbed his chin. "No, I won't. I'll get a man of mine along here. There's a phone handy?"

"Oh, yes," Castle told him. "In the Head's room, and I've unlocked the door."

Wharton wrote a hasty message for Quick to send. "Now do us a favour," he said to Castle. "Sit down here and have a good look through it. See if there's a secret message or anything marked. Don't think I'm in my second childhood, but try to imagine he was really trying to show you something extraordinary that you might otherwise miss."

He left Castle at it and went through to that annexe. It had two self-contained parts. That on the left was a dark and narrow room, with an electric switch and an easy chair. Shelves ran round the walls, and on them were articles of sports' clothing, and old books, and two putting-cleeks evidently used in that golf game. The lock was self-closing, with the key outside. A man in other words, had only to pocket the key and be safe from interference. As for the rest of that annexe, it consisted of washbasins and a closet. From the closet window, which he raised, Wharton saw the playing-fields, with their puddles which the storm had left and the drizzle was still filling. At the side—middle distance—was what looked like a large tool-shed. At the far end were netting, surround posts which announced tennis-courts.

Wharton went back to the main room, feeling that if anything he knew less about the case than when he had started. Quick had been out again and was just closing the door.

"No sign of the headmaster yet, sir."

"That reminds me," said Wharton, with a click of annoyance. "What about that Hindu? Where's that sergeant of yours that he hasn't come back yet?"

Quick shook his head. "I reckon the Hindu took a taxi or something, sir, and the sergeant's following it up."

Wharton scowled, then once more clicked his tongue. "And what was that about a missing caretaker?"

"Ah, that!" said Quick, as if he were really coming to something. "Mr. Castle suggested that the dead man might have gone along to the kitchen and taken the poison there—if you know what I mean. So Mr. Castle went along to find Flint—the caretaker—and he wasn't there. His wife said she didn't know where he was. All she did know was that Mr. Tennant hadn't been there, because she'd been in the kitchen since three o'clock herself."

"And how do you know he hasn't come back?"

"Because Mrs. Flint promised to send him here as soon as he did come back, sir. She's in her cottage, and that's just round by the girl's entrance, inside the grounds."

Castle glanced up from his careful examination of the catalogue. "I think myself that the Head has taken Flint off somewhere with him and they'll come back together."

Wharton's mouth opened exasperatedly, but no words came. There was the sound of feet scampering wildly up the stone stairs, and the door was flung open. It was Quick's sergeant—and pretty badly rattled. He licked his lips as his eyes went round the room. They stopped at Wharton's.

"The headmaster . . . Mr. Twirt, sir. I found him outside. Murdered, sir!"

Wharton made a move at once. The news was too extraordinary for comment or questioning, and through Ludovic Travers there tingled a new thrill of horror. Outside on the porch steps the sergeant stopped.

"He's lying over there, sir—in that shrubbery."

"What're you waiting for then?" asked Wharton gruffly.

He made his way at once towards the main gate, and just short of it, cut in to the left.

"I found him by chance, sir, when I was looking for that Indian. No one saw the Indian out on the road anywhere, sir, so I thought he might be skulking somewhere."

Wharton's head was bare to the drizzle, and the soaking shrubs drenched his coat as he brushed them aside. Then at an open space the sergeant drew back that the others might see.

On the ground lay the body of a man of below middle height. His grey suit was saturated with rain, and his hat lay just by his head. On the greying hair at the top of his skull was a dark, triangular-shaped blackness where the blood had seeped. By the wall stood a heavy sledge-hammer, with smooth ash handle.

But in that tiny clearing was something else—a slender laburnum tree with its stem askew, and lying on the far side of it, a stout stake. The pictures ceased to be an isolated series and, once the dead man was forgotten, the wherefore of everything seemed plain. The tree had got top-heavy and had heeled over, and someone had brought the stake as a support, and the sledge-hammer to drive it in.

Wharton began snapping orders back over his shoulder. "Quick, get Dr. Menzies on the phone at once and ask him to come here, and see the ambulance comes too. Sergeant, you fetch Mr. Castle." The sergeant's, "He's here, sir," and Castle's, "Here I am," came together.

"Step round here, Mr. Castle, will you?" said Wharton. "Keep in close in case there are footprints."

"There aren't any, sir," the sergeant told him. "All this ground is clay, and it's baked hard as iron with the weather we've had."

"All the better then," said Wharton. "But there's prints now that we've made ourselves. Which proves—" He stopped short. "Mr. Castle, I take it that's your headmaster all right?"

"Yes," said Castle, and kept his eyes on the body.

"And what time did the storm break over here this afternoon?"

"At a quarter past four exactly."

"Right," said Wharton. "Now watch me and see what happens."

He got astride the body and turned it gently to one side. Beneath it the clayey soil was bone dry.

"There you are," said Wharton. "He was lying here dead before a quarter past four. That's why he made no marks when he came in—nor did the man who killed him."

Castle nodded down at the soaked body. "If I might make a suggestion, I'd say he was killed between ten past four and a quarter past."

Wharton stared. "How do you make that out?"

"Well, everybody knew a storm was coming on because it had threatened most of the afternoon. The bell went for afternoon dismissal at four o'clock, and I'd say all pupils who weren't definitely down to play games hurried home as fast as they could go. Between five past four and ten past both ends of this drive were full of pupils hurrying home, and some of the staff would be going out of the main gate."

"I see," said Wharton. "Too many people about, eh? But why not between four and five minutes past?"

Castle smiled. "Some early birds among the pupils dash off on the dot. I also know one master who was actually in the drive there from about one minute past four till about three minutes past."

Once more Wharton was startled. "Why are you so sure?"

"One of the men wanted to get away early," said Castle. "I think you'll find, if you care to question him to-morrow, that he slipped down well before four and got the antiquated engine of his antiquated car ticking over. The car always stands on the girls' side of the porch, in the drive. At four o'clock he'd be down like a streak of lightning, and if his car happened to be still ticking over, he'd be in it and away. That's why I allowed from one minute past four till three minutes past for the drive to be occupied."

Wharton grunted, and in some measure to conceal his respect for the accuracy of the deductions. There was also no little respect for Castle himself, and the calm matter-of-factness with which the statements had been made.

"And how do you account for the hammer?"

"I should say the groundsman brought it here," Castle told him.

"Know where he lives?"

"Certainly. I can have him here in ten minutes if you want him."

"On good terms with the headmaster, was he?"

Castle's lips drooped again. "No better—and no worse—than any of us."

"Like that, was it?" He grunted again. "Well, get him here at once. Inspector Quick will send one of his men if you tell him. You take the hammer, sergeant, and do it for prints. And tell Inspector Quick—"

But Quick was there to speak for himself. He gave a holler to show he had heard, finished his brief conference with Castle, and brushed his way through the wet bushes.

"About that damned Indian," said Wharton. "There seems something fishy to me. Take this card of his and get hold of the Yard. Say I want two men to go to that Fulham address and collect Mr. Ram and bring him here. They're to wait all night—and the rest of the week—if necessary."

Off went Quick, and Wharton became aware of the unobtrusive presence of Ludovic Travers.

"Anything occur to you?"

"Nothing," said Travers. "Except that he appears a rather miserable specimen of a man. Not much like a headmaster."

He was looking down at the rain-sodden figure. Wharton, following his glance, saw something, and stooped to rub his fingers over the cold jowl.

"Didn't shave to-day either. And none too robust a specimen, as you say." He pursed his lips. "Well under nine stone. Age about fifty. Not a nice face either. Sallow and peevish."

"Just one other thing," said Travers. "Why should Castle have excluded from his deductions the possibility of his having been killed *before* four o'clock? I take it everywhere was quiet enough then?"

Wharton's grunt this time was prodigious. He rubbed his chin, then made up his mind. His voice lowered suggestively.

"You go back and have a little quiet chat with our friend Castle. And ask him, too, to have that caretaker's wife sent over. I'd like a look at her."

Travers's eyes opened at that. "Of course. . . . I'd forgotten that. We'd assumed that Flint had gone somewhere with the Head . . . and naturally he hasn't."

"You never know," said Wharton grimly. "They may have gone somewhere together, after all. Someone may have done him in too."

He settled to another examination of the body, and Travers backed through the drizzle and the wet bushes to the drive again. Upstairs in the common room Castle seemed once more to have settled to a methodical examination of that bulky catalogue. Travers came in quietly and watched him for a few moments. Then Castle looked up.

"Any luck?" smiled Travers.

"No," said Castle, and smiled wryly. "Between you and me, I feel rather a fool looking through the damn thing at all. Why should this book have anything to do with sending for me?"

"But why should a dying man hang on to the book at all?"

Castle slowly shook his head. Then he got to his feet. "The only idea I had was a note of some sort stuck between the leaves—and there isn't any." He stretched his long arms and looked as if he were going to yawn. Then he smiled instead. "What's your name, by the way? I mean, it seems too damn silly, calling you nothing."

"Travers. Ludovic Travers."

Castle's eyes opened. "Not the man who wrote *The Economics of a Spendthrift*?"

But on the heels of that discovery came a puzzled look. "If I may ask it, what's a famous author doing here with the police?"

"Ah!" said Travers enigmatically, "that's all part of the mystery. But before I forget it. Why was it you ruled out the possibility of your headmaster's being killed before four o'clock?"

Castle made a face. "No reason at all—except that he obviously said he'd be back here at four. I know him, and I've never known him to have the manners to be in time for an appointment that didn't mean some colossal advantage to himself."

"Clever—but none too logical." Travers straightened his face. "A terrible business, though; and utterly incomprehensible—at the moment. Don't you find it so?"

The old cynical droop came to Castle's lips. "I don't know that I do."

"You mean you know how he was killed?"

"Not at all," said Castle, with supreme indifference. "You asked me if I found his killing incredible—and I don't."

"You know who'd be likely to kill him?"

"Not in the least," said Castle, with the same amused indifference. "I hate death, and murder's a mad and vulgar thing. All the same, I don't find it mad or vulgar or incredible that someone should have provided Woodgate Hill with a Dead Shepherd." His lips drooped again. "Also, between ourselves, I know few people who'd have gone far out of their way to have kept him alive."

Travers winced. The flippancy seemed somewhat out of place, and the irony behind it had some horrible quality of ill-chosen time and circumstance. And behind the words was something he was failing to grasp. And he wanted to grasp it, for it had in it something of that horror and quick repulsion which he had felt at his first sight of that jail-like school.

"Why did you call him a Dead Shepherd?"

Castle's eyes narrowed for a moment. Then he turned and caught Travers's intense look.

"Because it was one of his own pet names for himself. He was fond of saying he wasn't really a headmaster, but the shepherd of a flock. And by the way he used to say it, you rather gathered that the Almighty had made the appointment." He caught Travers's look. "I know it sounds pretty unctuous, but you didn't know the man. He was humbug personified. That was why the staff generally alluded to him as The Shepherd—sardonically enough, as you'll come to understand."

"Yes," said Travers, and shook his head slowly.

"I think I see it. And what was your own pet name for him?"

"For The Shepherd?" said Castle, and raised his eyebrows. "Well, I generally alluded to him as the bastard."

For a moment Travers had that strange feeling of horror. There was a silence while both men thought.

"You hated Twirt like hell?"

"I did," said Castle quietly. "I hated him worse than that. And he wasn't even worth the respect of anyone's hate, and that used to make me hate myself."

"All the same, you didn't murder him?"

"Oh, no," said Castle, and smiled. "I didn't murder him. In any case, you wouldn't use the word *murder* in reference to a man like Twirt." His lip drooped. "One doesn't talk of murdering a beetle."

Then there was a noise from below the stairs. Quite a crowd of people seemed to be there, and Quick was coming up with two women. Then a small group of men appeared, most of them strangers to Travers, at least in that dim light.

"They're bringing up the body," he said to Castle.

The senior master went out to await the procession. "If I might suggest it," he said, "I think you'll find the Head's own room more convenient. The phone's there and you're less likely to be disturbed." He moved on ahead to open the door, while the feet shuffled across the stone floor, and the wet coat of the Dead Shepherd left a damp trail to mark its slow progress.

CHAPTER III
WHY TENNANT DIED

TRAVERS STAYED ON for a minute or two in the common room. He was in no hurry to see again the body of Castle's incongruous Shepherd. Murder to him was a bestial thing, and the untimely dead whom he had to view would beset him for weeks in his dreams. And besides his hesitation to follow the small procession, something else demanded a delay and a pondering. And the object of that pondering was Castle; not as the possible murderer of Twirt—for already Travers knew the supreme impossibility of that—but as a personality so startling and so vital, that the very unexpectedness of him demanded a moment's thought apart.

Everything about the man was attractive. There was something in him that bespoke the first-class brain, and a brain, too, that loved to busy itself with gracious, unremunerative things. He could dominate without obtrusion; his ease of command had no irritation since it was so sure of itself. And yet a man like Castle had almost certainly been driven near to a desperate breakdown by that skimpy, grubby little person of a headmaster. And since there could never have been the same domination of personality in the man who looked more like a down-at-heel clerk than the Head of what some would call a first-rate school, then the cause of Twirt's ascendancy must have laid in the dictatorship of an unassailable position and the mad qualities of obstinacy and egomania which he possessed. Castle had more than hinted that the whole of Twirt's staff would gladly have murdered him, provided, doubtless, that there was no risk. Castle's own hate had been tremendous, there was no mistaking that; for he had spoken with a tense, concentrated venom that was terrifying. So fierce, indeed, had been the hate and the loathing that even when the cause of it was dead, Castle had still no redeeming feature to mention by way of epitaph.

And yet Castle himself had not murdered Twirt. It was not that he had said so himself that made the sureness of Travers's knowledge—the brief contact with the man had made a greater certainty. Castle's hatred lay deeper than mere murder. It was a hatred of the soul—not the body.

Somewhere, then, in all that hate, like figures that appear for a moment out of a swirling fog, Travers saw against the background of that sinister barrack of a school, the forms of two dead men. And both had qualities that were enigmatic. Charles Tennant had been murdered, and he too must have been a man worth the studying, or Castle would not have spoken of him as he had done. As for that other partly known quantity—Twirt; and when Travers began again to consider the Dead Shepherd, he found his feet moving instinctively towards the room where now his body would be lying.

In the corridor he was just in time to see an enormous woman appear for a moment in the door of the secretary's room. Then Quick came out, and Travers heard a fresh young voice call after him.

"Is your daughter better?" Travers asked as they crossed the landing.

"So she says, sir," Quick told him. "I didn't want her and Mrs. Flint to see what's in where we're going, so I sent them up ahead and made out that Mr. Twirt had had an accident."

The headmaster's room was a large one, and it was the most untidy room Travers had ever seen. It announced the mind of a muddler and shuffler. Desk, centre table, side table, and even windows were stacked with papers, catalogues, books and files. But the centre table had been cleared and the body was on it.

Menzies began feeling that contusion on the skull, and half a minute satisfied him. He straightened himself with a sniff.

"That's what did it all right. Pass me that hammer." In a moment he was measuring and noting.

Wharton turned to the sergeant. "Sure there was only one set of prints? Because, if so, we'll have that groundsman in and hear what he's got to say."

The door closed, and he looked across at Castle. "Did I understand you to say the groundsman had a grudge against the headmaster?"

"You didn't," said Castle bluntly. "The Head had threatened him with the sack—that's all." Wharton raised his eyebrows. "And isn't that enough? Are new jobs so easy to find?"

"Maybe not," said Castle. "But a threat of the sack isn't much in this school. Most of us have had it in our time."

"And what's your opinion of him?"

"Vincent? Well, I like him. He's honest and a good worker."

There was a tap at the door, and Vincent came in with the sergeant. He was a youngish man; short, stocky, and intelligent-looking.

Wharton took him over. "You're Vincent, the groundsman here?"

"Yes, sir."

"That the hammer you were using this afternoon?"

"Looks like it, sir."

"Mind if we take your finger-prints?"

"It's all right, Vincent," smiled Castle reassuringly. "Merely a matter of form."

But during the operation the groundsman's eyes fell on that figure on the table. Travers saw his eyes raised furtively to Castle's, and Castle's turn away. Then the sergeant nodded meaningly to Wharton, and there seemed no doubt whose the prints were.

"Now tell us all about the hammer—and what you were doing with it this afternoon." The tone was Wharton's most gracious one.

Vincent looked down for a moment at the cap he was twirl-ing in his fingers. "Well, sir, at a quarter past three it was, I was coming round the boys' entrance with that hammer and a stake because I'd remembered the Head had told me to fasten up that laburnum what the wind had shifted; and just as I come round the drive, sir, he come down the steps and see what I was going to do. Then he told me to leave that job for a bit and go and cut the tennis-courts—"

"Those at the far end of the playing-fields?"

Vincent smiled. "Them's the only ones there art, sir. So when he said that, sir, I didn't want to take the things all the way back to my shed, so I put the hammer and the stake ready by the tree in case I had time to do the job before I knocked off at five; only, I didn't, you see, sir, because the storm stopped me."

Wharton nodded. "And I suppose you can't account for the fact that your headmaster was found dead by that tree, with his skull smashed by that hammer?"

"No, sir." He shook his head resolutely. "I was working on them courts till the storm broke, sir, and two of the prefects was with me all the time. Then we took shelter in my shed till best part of five. What I was going to do, sir, was get up in the morn-ing and finish off them courts to make up for lost time."

"You didn't have a peep in the shrubbery on your way home?"

"I don't go that way home, sir—least, I didn't to-night. There's a back lane up to my hut, sir, where we cart things through. And the hammer wouldn't be taking no harm in the wet."

"I see." Wharton tugged at the ends of his vast moustache. "And you couldn't suggest why the Head went into the shrub-bery?"

There was an awkward hesitancy about Vincent's manner. Again he tried to catch Castle's eye—and Castle avoided him.

"Speak your mind without fear or favour," said Wharton heartily. "Say whatever you think. It's confidential, and no harm'll come to you. Isn't that right, Mr. Castle?"

"Perfectly right."

Vincent made no more ado. "He was peeping and prying, sir—that's what I think. He knew I couldn't finish them courts if I stayed my full time; all the same, he had to poke his nose in to see if there was anything he could find fault with. Probably thought I'd dodged back and fastened the tree up, just to spite him."

Wharton nodded, then gave a pert, sparrow-like look. "And strictly between ourselves, what was your precise opinion of your headmaster?"

"Him, sir?" His eyes narrowed. "He was a dirty bastard, sir—and that's plain."

"Plain enough," said Wharton dryly. "And any particular reasons, have you, for saying so?"

"Yes, sir." What had been bottled up came out in a flood. "He could never give you a job and let you get on with it. He was one of them know-alls; knew more about everything than anybody else. Always sneaking round to see if he could catch you out—him and the caretaker."

"Flint, you mean?"

"Yes, sir. Him, sir. He was always carrying tales, and about the staff as well as me—and Mr. Castle can bear me out."

Wharton grunted. "And I suppose you can't tell us where Flint is at the moment? He seems to have disappeared."

Vincent's eyes opened. "That's funny, sir. Just about four o'clock I see him go into the back lane by my shed. He had his hat on, sir, and he was in a rare hurry."

Wharton turned questioningly to Castle. "Just what's strange about that?"

"The back lane," said Castle. "Flint's cottage is by the girls' entrance, and he should have gone that way. It looks as if he was trying to get away somewhere without being seen."

"Yes, but mightn't he have been going somewhere where the lane was a short cut?"

"The lane merely runs parallel to the boys' entrance," said Castle. "It starts at the road and ends at the shed. It's merely a way of entry for heavy carts or lorries."

"Well, that's clear enough." He turned to Vincent again, and his manner was positively wheedling. "Don't forget that we're talking in confidence. And don't forget that you're not to let a living soul know that Mr. Twirt is dead. And talking of Flint, of course he had no reason to kill the headmaster!"

Vincent gave him a quick look. "Not unless he was afraid of losing a good job."

Wharton screwed up his eyes. "I'm afraid I don't follow you."

"Well, then, sir, I'll tell you something I've never spoke about to a soul. Last Monday it was—two days ago—and the Head come to me all spluttering about them tennis-courts and laying down new turf. So I told him early September'd be the best time; also Flint could give me a hand pulling the heavy roller, as he'd be back from his summer holiday. Then the Head looked at me sort of queer, sir. I don't remember the exact words, but he said I wasn't to count on Flint, because most likely he wouldn't be here then. And soon as he'd said it, sir, you could see he'd let out too much, and he sort of slipped off without another word."

"Most interesting," said Wharton. "And you couldn't guess where Flint was going to when you saw him at four o'clock?"

Vincent shook his head.

"Then do you think Flint was aware of the fact that he was due for the sack?"

Vincent thought hard, then grinned. "I don't know that he didn't, sir. He looked pretty well down-in-the-mouth when I see him this morning."

That was all that was needed from the groundsman at the moment. Then at the very door, Wharton called him back.

"Where did the headmaster go when he left you?"

"Don't know, sir." A peculiar smile. "Though I dare say I could guess."

"Very well, then—guess!"

Again Vincent's eyes sought those of Castle, and this time Castle accepted the challenge.

"I think I know what Vincent means. If you don't mind, I'll explain when he's gone."

Wharton nodded, and out went the groundsman.

"It was a question of discipline, having him answer questions like those," said Castle. "But what he meant was this. During the course of every week in the summer, the whole school goes to the baths for swimming lessons and practice. Wednesdays and Fridays are the afternoons, and there are two relays. That is, a quarter of the school, approximately, went this afternoon from two to three, and were followed by another quarter from three to four. They march in the usual crocodile through the streets, and in charge of them are the members of the staff who would be teaching them if the lessons had been the normal ones of the rest of the year. I'm not too prolix?"

"You can't be," said Wharton. "Make everything so that even a fool like myself can understand it."

Castle smiled. "Very well, then. The chief point is that the staff know that they're not needed there. At least half of them are wasted. The drill-sergeant could easily control the boys and the drill-mistress the girls. The staff therefore resent having to go to the baths and twiddle their fingers, and I imagine they resented it especially to-day—"

"Pardon me, but just why to-day?"

"That means more detail," said Castle. "Still, if you can stand it, here goes. In schools of this type, the grand event of the year is the School Certificate examination, which is practically synonymous with matriculation. It's taken by pupils who are about sixteen years of age, and if they pass the examination, they have an excellent passport for a job. But while the senior pupils take that examination, the rest of the school have our own examination, which takes a whole week. In every subject and every branch of it, there is an hour and a half paper to be written. Now do you see it? Imagine the work the staff have, correcting those masses of papers, and correcting them with extraordinary care, because on the marks a pupil obtains depends whether or not he or she is promoted to a new form next September."

"I quite see it," said Travers. "Instead of the staff being allowed for once to stay here in order to cope with the mass of extra work, they had to sit at the baths and watch the little victims play—so to speak."

"You've got it," said Castle "And you can guess that Twirt knew just what was in their minds. He had the idea that members of the staff who went on that second relay would approach the drill-sergeant or the drill-mistress and try to sneak off home before four o'clock. Therefore Vincent knew—as we all knew—that Twirt was on his way at a quarter past three to make surreptitious inquiries at the baths to see if every one of his staff who ought to be on duty *was* on duty."

Menzies, who had been emptying the dead man's pockets, had paused as if fascinated to watch Castle's face while he made his cool deductions. But no sooner had the speech ended then he fired a question.

"Why isn't he shaved?"

"Because he was bone-lazy," said Castle. "I grant you he rarely went more than two days. Generally he used to shave overnight and make that do—unless he was going anywhere important."

"He had no sense of personal dignity?" asked Travers.

"It wasn't quite that," said Castle. "The man was an egomaniac. What sufficed for him had to be good enough for everybody else."

"What about getting him away now?" asked Menzies.

"Why not?" said Wharton, and nodded for the men to lend a hand. "And what about the other one? Know anything definite yet?"

"The whole thing would have been finished in another ten minutes if I hadn't been called away. It's oxalic acid right enough."

"But that wouldn't have killed him as quickly as that, surely?" protested Wharton, who was no mean toxicologist.

"Depends on his state of health," said Menzies. "His heart was pretty bad. And I'd say he had a thin time in the war."

"He had," said Castle. "His health was reasonable, but he wasn't too robust."

Then there was an interruption. Feet sounded outside, and there was a tap at the door. It was Quick's man, ushering in a gentleman, whom he announced as "Mr. Tennant, sir."

John Tennant looked like a young professional man, with clean-shaven face and neat, dark clothes. But the most noticeable thing about him was the set of his jaw. If ever a man had worked himself into a furious passion and was trying to keep it under reasonable control, it was John Tennant. He gave a hostile glare round the room, but it was to Wharton he addressed himself.

"What's this yam about my cousin committing suicide?"

The plain-clothes man began a quick protest. "I didn't tell you he'd committed suicide, sir. I said he might have done—as far as we knew."

Tennant gave him a glare.

Wharton came over placatingly. "Now, Mr. Tennant, don't get upset. Your cousin didn't commit suicide; you know that."

"I know it all right," said Tennant, none too graciously. "I know a lot of things."

His eye fell for a moment on the body whose head was concealed by the bulk of Menzies. Then he glared at Wharton again.

"Where's the headmaster? I want to see him. I insist on seeing him!"

"See him by all means." Wharton waved a bland hand at the table, and Menzies stepped aside.

Tennant looked, then stared. His mouth gaped. The words came stutteringly.

"But I—I thought—"

"You thought it was your cousin," suggested Wharton.

"Yes." His eyes narrowed again. "Who killed—this one?"

"Who said he was killed?" said Wharton sternly. "How'd you know he was killed?"

For a moment Tennant looked almost frightened. "There's a hammer there . . . and his head looks smashed."

Wharton took refuge in a grunt. "That's nothing to do with it. And suppose it is. What can *you* tell us about it?"

"Nothing. Nothing at all." His manner was astoundingly less aggressive. "I didn't kill him. I'd only just got home from town when your man saw me." He produced a card. "You can get me there any day if you want me."

He was a salesman, it appeared, with Pullingers, the Bond Street jewellers. And seeing him in a reasonable frame of mind, Wharton asked a few questions—and with no result. He could

throw no light on his cousin's death, and that chemical catalogue was to him a profound mystery. But Menzies was in a hurry, and at last John Tennant left.

"That chap knows something," said Wharton, as soon as the
door had closed. "Why did he scowl round at everybody like
that? Why did he insist on seeing the headmaster?"

"In his position you'd have been upset," said Menzies.
"Shouldn't they have been going out together to-night?"

"As for his wanting to see the headmaster," said Castle quietly; "when you've been in this school a few more hours you'll
know that it's perfectly natural to ascribe to him everything disastrous that happens here."

Wharton grunted.

Menzies coughed. "Well, let's get him away, at any rate."

The body was on its way to the ambulance and he was about
to follow, when Wharton remembered something.

"About that other one. What did he take the oxalic acid in?
Or did he take it neat?"

"He took it in a cup of tea," said Menzies. "We were just doing that when you rang."

"A cup of tea!" Castle was staring. He moistened his lips,
then looked at Menzies. "My God! I wonder."

"Wonder what?" said Wharton quickly.

But Castle was already out of the door. Menzies looked
round bewildered, but Wharton was out too. It was the secretary's room into which Castle had rushed, and almost at once he
was out again. The stout woman and Daisy Quick came out too,
and disappeared in the corridor to Wharton's right. Then Castle
came back to the room again.

"I think it's all right." He was smiling somewhat ashamedly,
as if in relief. "I don't know when I've been so scared. I thought
Flint might have been poisoned!" The eyes were staring blankly
at him, and he explained. "He might have drunk some of the
tea!"

"Yes, but what tea?" asked Wharton testily.

There were steps outside, and Quick opened the door to
let in the two women. Mrs. Flint, a heavy-featured woman of

fifteen stone, set a tea-tray down on the table, with a cautious look round the company. Daisy Quick was a pretty blonde of not much over twenty; all competence and good spirits.

"I'll explain about the tea," Castle was saying. "And, Miss Quick, you hear me out. You knew, of course, that Mr. Twirt was dead?"

"Dead?" Her eyes opened wide. She turned accusingly to her father. "You told us he'd had an accident."

"Now don't you go worrying about that," Quick told her. "He did have an accident—and he's died of it."

"I'm not going to see him!"

Quick took her arm. "I know you're not. Pull yourself together and do what Mr. Castle says." He explained to the room. "She got a bit of a shock when that other one died."

"I'm all right now. It was silly of me." But she took the chair which Travers placed, then smiled bravely round the room.

Castle had been making signs to Wharton to get rid of Mrs. Flint. Wharton took the cue.

"No sign of your husband yet?"

She shook her head. "No, sir. What I think is Mr. Twirt sent him somewhere and he's not back yet."

Wharton nodded. "Perhaps you're right. Remember, by the way, and you too, Miss Quick, that nothing's to get out for the moment about Mr. Twirt's death. That's an order." He glanced at Castle to take up the running.

"Who made the Head's tea this afternoon?"

"Why, Flint, sir—same as he always do."

"Did he make any remark to you about it?"

"What remark should he have made, sir?"

"That's what I don't know," said Castle. "And how'd the tray get back to the kitchen?"

"A boy brought it, sir, the same as they always do."

There was a hush while Menzies examined the tray. He tried two licks of a finger that had stirred the tea-leaves. Then he wiped a finger round the bottom of the empty milk-jug. Then he tasted the sugar—and his face screwed up.

"The poison was in the sugar?" fired Wharton.

"It's there still," said Menzies curtly. "I'll get all this lot away. Get your gloves on, sergeant, and take charge."

"The headmaster's sugar was kept separate?" asked Castle.

Mrs. Flint shook her head. "It was just ordinary granulated sugar, sir. We always kept his things apart, though, on a special shelf in the cupboard."

Wharton took over again. He was a shrewd judge of women. Now he was never more sure of anything than that she knew more of her husband's whereabouts than she had divulged. There was about her just a shade too much desire to please, and she had been startled to hear of Twirt's death.

"All right, Mrs. Flint," he told her. "We won't keep you any longer. Let us know the moment your husband comes back."

The door closed on her, and he whipped round on Quick.

"How many ways out of that cottage of hers?"

"Only one, sir—the front gate."

"Right. Put two men on her tail. Watch all night if necessary."

Once more the inquiry was resumed, and Castle began his main explanation.

"Mr. Twirt always had a small pot of tea brought to his room at a quarter past three. The procedure is that Flint knocks at the door, and if there's no answer, he leaves the tray on one of the chairs outside the room here."

"Why couldn't he walk right in?"

"The Head mightn't be in, and then the room would be locked. Flint wasn't allowed to use his own key and come in during school hours. The point, however, is this. If the Head were out, or urgently engaged inside, the tea would stand and get stone cold. One day Tennant said he didn't see why he shouldn't have it himself, and after that—when he was free and he had a shrewd notion the Head was out—he'd take the tray away and drink the tea himself. Naturally that didn't happen often."

"Mr. Tennant knew the Head was going to be away to-day," broke in Miss Quick. "I heard him tell him so."

"Tell us about it," said Wharton.

"Well, I was in my room and my bell went, saying the Head wanted me. Just before a quarter past three it was, and Mr. Tennant was sitting just there, and the Head was at his desk where you are now. They looked as if they'd been laughing about something; then the Head said, 'Anything to sign, Miss Quick?' I said there wasn't, and I was surprised, because he knew there wasn't. He was just showing off. Then he said, 'I'm just this moment going out. Let Mr. Castle know, and remind him about four o'clock.' So I did so, and that's all that happened."

Castle turned to Wharton. "I told you, if you remember, that when the Head went out I was generally warned, so that I might take over. About his wanting me at four o'clock, I don't know precisely what it was for."

Menzies broke in there. "I'd better be going now. But just one question first. Did Tennant take sugar in his tea?"

Daisy Quick gave a little laugh. "He liked it so that the spoon stood upright."

"That's all I want to know," said Menzies, and departed.

Wharton had a question or two to ask.

"About Mr. Tennant taking the tray. How was he to know the Head was definitely out?"

"He'd try the famous encyclopedia trick," said Miss Quick.

Wharton peered questioningly at her.

"In this case here," she explained, "is the *Encyclopedia Britannica*, and it's supposed to be for the benefit of the staff and the senior pupils. If they wanted to consult it, they came in here. If anybody wanted to know if the Head was in or out, he tapped at the door. If there was no reply, then the Head was out, and the door would be locked. If the Head called, 'Come in!' all they had to do was to walk in and say they wanted to consult the encyclopedia. Then the Head would be awfully pleased, because it showed people were enthusiastic about their work."

There was a general smile. "Most ingenious!" said Wharton, and his eyes twinkled. And then the queerest expression came over his face. He half rose, and he turned to Daisy Quick as if he had caught her picking pockets.

"The Head took sugar in his tea?"

She smiled "Even more than Mr. Tennant did."

"And all the staff knew it?"

"Why, of course they did. We were often having teas together—at school functions, and so on."

"Then tell me—and be dead sure you're right." He waved back at the door. "Imagine the tray's outside there. Would anyone else but Tennant touch it?"

She shook her head. "I'm sure they wouldn't."

"Did you ever touch it, Mr. Castle?"

Over Castle's face came an expression of disgust. "I don't think I'd get any satisfaction from drinking Mr. Twirt's tea."

"Right," said Wharton. "And now, Miss Quick, this leaving of the tray was often happening?"

"Very often."

"Right. Imagine, then, you're one of the ordinary staff and you see the tray on the chair outside there. What, precisely, do you think?"

She frowned for a moment. "Why, that the Head is out and his tea is getting cold."

"You wouldn't touch it yourself?"

"Of course not! Besides, I always make one for myself just before four o'clock." She hesitated. "Of course if I knew the Head was out for good, I'd send it to the kitchen by a boy."

Wharton smiled. "That's not the point. We don't want you in your capacity of secretary. Remember that for the purposes of this test, you're one of the ordinary staff, and they wouldn't interfere with the Head's tea, would they?"

She shook her head.

Wharton looked round the room. He had come to his first dramatic moment. He got to his feet.

"Then am I right when I say this? Whoever put the oxalic acid in the sugar had no intention whatever of killing Tennant. *It was Twirt who should have been killed.*"

There was no answer. The statement was a fact as undeniable as that the evening dusk had suddenly come on till it was hard to see the trees from the uncurtained windows.

"Who was Tennant's enemy?" continued Wharton. "Who wanted to kill him? And who could possibly have known that he would take the tea?"

"No one," said Castle. He, too, had got to his feet. "And no one would have tried to kill Charles Tennant."

"Everybody liked him," said Daisy Quick. "You couldn't help liking him. I know he had that row with Miss Gedge, but everybody's had a row with *her*. And she really liked him too—I'm sure of that."

Her lip was beginning to tremble. Castle's hand fell on her shoulder.

"You run away home now. We can do without you here." He smiled at her. "Turn up bright and brisk in the morning."

She dabbed at her eyes, and then without a word made her way to the door.

"What did you want to get rid of her like that for?" asked Wharton suspiciously.

"Couldn't you see she had a blinding headache?" said Castle, giving him a look. "Also there's something I ought to tell you. *That method of killing Twirt has been actually discussed in the masters' common room.*"

CHAPTER IV
WHARTON IS OPTIMISTIC

THROUGH TRAVERS'S MIND there flashed again the face of Twirt—sallow and peevish, as Wharton had said. There, on the table, with the contents of his pockets, was the wet from his rain-soaked clothes. And those clothes should never have been wetted. He should have met Tennant's death—a twisted death on the parquet floor. But as for that statement that the masters' common room had deliberately discussed that way of murdering him, Travers was finding it incredible. Wharton, too, was inclined to discount it somewhat.

"You'll pardon me saying so, Mr. Castle, but how on earth could things have got to such a pass here?"

Castle smiled wryly. "Perhaps I'm rushing too far ahead." Then all at once he got up again and switched on the rest of the lights and drew the blinds, talking as he did so. "The bald statement doesn't content you, then? You'd like me to go into details?"

"I absolutely insist on them," Wharton told him. "The man's been murdered twice, and how're we going to get to the bottom of anything if we don't know every possible motive?"

"I think you're wise." He came over and found a seat.

Quick came in just then with a nod to Wharton to show that Mrs. Flint's tail was being duly sat on.

"Twirt came here during the war," began Castle. "The best men were doing a job of work, and headmasterships were ten a penny. He was pretty plausible at first, so they tell me, and took some time feeling his way. A year or so after I got back he began launching out. Before long it was plain that he was a loose talker, a liar, and generally unscrupulous. But we wouldn't have minded that if he'd let us alone to get on with our work.

"I've told you he was an egomaniac. He had a craving for publicity and for hearing himself speak. He had a high-pitched, objectionable, common voice, and he finally got into the habit of haranguing the school on every possible occasion. That damnable voice of his sounded in people's ears like an electric drill. You'd hear it—and his silly laugh—in the corridors or outside this room, and people would wince or shudder. His voice was a sort of invisible, audible symbol of himself.

"Then he was always beginning new stunts before the old ones could be tried out. Anything for publicity, was his motto. The work of the school would be thrown clean to hell, and when people ventured to protest, he'd say he had a disloyal staff, and threaten them with the sack. The more he gave other people to do, the less he did himself. He shifted practically all of it on Miss Quick and myself, till all he had to do to pass the time was to think of still more schemes, and jaw to anybody he could get to listen to him. If you want to know how much real work he did in a day, I'll tell you in the words of one of our men—young Furrow. 'This is my day's work—that was!'"

He paused for a moment. "Carry on," said Wharton. "I'm enjoying it."

There was no sign of amusement on Castle's face as he carried on. "Well, he made the classes as big as he dared, and he cut down everybody's free periods till they were nearly crazed with work—in school and out. But when the Board of Education insisted that to meet their requirements he should do some teaching himself, he put his name down for some, and then dodged it in the most bare-faced manner. When his classes were actually waiting, he'd pretend he was busy, or had to go out. Then some already overworked member of the staff had to be hustled from a free period to do the job he was getting credit for."

"That's why the men used to hide in that inner room?"

"Exactly, Mr. Travers. And can you blame them? Also he'd trick people into telling tales about their colleagues, and he'd listen to Flint's tales. To sum up, he was the most loathsome little swine I've ever met. Everybody hated him, and even those who feared him and toadied to him, frankly acknowledged that nobody who knew him could have for him the slightest respect."

"I see," said Wharton, and then with a dry smile. "And what were his good points?"

Castle smiled too. "Well, he had the finest gift of the gab I ever knew. Of all the brainless men I've ever run across, he could best live on snippets, and cover up his ignorance, and pick other men's brains and regurgitate the knowledge as his very own. And in his love for himself, he was the most devoted of men."

Wharton gave a special grunt. "Those were his good points, were they? And why didn't you get rid of him?"

"We! Get rid of him!" Castle smiled amusedly. "My dear sir, headmasters don't get the sack except for something publicly scandalous. And everybody outside this school thought him one of the Almighty's choicest marvels. Wait till you read the obituary notices in the local rags! Why, he used to fascinate the nitwits with his chatter. With us he kept within the law, and we were helpless. And we were a damn sight too loyal. Whatever talk there was in the common rooms and threats of rebellions, we couldn't talk to outsiders. Also you can never get perfectly united action from a staff—and that was his real salvation."

"I must say, gentlemen, I can corroborate all that Mr. Castle has told us," said Quick, "though I think people outside were beginning to get wise to him at last. I know my daughter wouldn't hear a word against him when she first came here, and now she's been sometimes nearly off her nut what with overwork and the dirty tricks he plays."

Wharton nodded. "Well, I think I understand the kind he was. Now what about that common room talk?"

"I'll show you first the nature of the talk and the way tales got carried," said Castle. "One day, for instance, Twirt asked the men to stay on after four for one of his damn conferences, and he was late as usual. One of the men said, 'I hope the little bastard has got run over by a bus.' Everybody knew that was too good to be true. However, a day or so later, that man was in the Head's room and the Head twisted the conversation round till he could say to him, with a meaning look, 'I might get run over by a bus, you know, Mr. So-and-so!' Sounds incredible, doesn't it? Yet things like that were always happening. We think Flint heard that particular remark and reported it."

"But how could he possibly have heard it?"

"That annexe wall of the masters' common room is also the wall of a store, where Flint often has to go. I'm sure he leans his ear against it, and then you can hear most things that are said. I've tried it out."

"Most interesting," said Wharton. "Anything else?"

Castle smiled—a warm, friendly smile. "Yes. A bit of comic relief for a change. Charles Tennant had a great scheme. One day we were in the common room and the men were at the eternal topic—how to get rid of Twirt—when Charles suddenly said he'd got it. I may tell you that the senior mistress—Miss Gedge, or Ma Gedge, as she's generally called—is a bitch of authentic pedigree. She's always making excuses to leave her classes to closet herself with Twirt and gossip by the hour. Well, Tennant suggested, and Furrow offered to be his assistant, to wait till Ma Gedge was nicely settled in Twirt's room, and then throw open the door with, 'Oh, Mr. Twirt! I'm ashamed of you. And you, Miss Gedge—and at your age, too!' Furrow was to be at his elbow to swear to the intimacy." He smiled. "When you see Miss Gedge, you'll also see the joke. All the same, I'm not so sure that if Tennant hadn't spoiled the scheme by announcing it in public, they wouldn't have brought it off!"

Even Wharton had to smile. "Well, it has its amusing side. And what about the poison suggestion?"

"That arose when the common room were at the same old topic. Godman—a junior language master—said it would be easy to drop some poison in the pot when it stood outside the Head's room. You see, Twirt didn't like things hot. He liked them tepid. He'd put in heaps of sugar, stir round and then gulp the lot noisily. He was gross in drinking as in everything else. Then the chemistry master—young Grey—said there was a flaw. Twirt—as a science man—might detect a strange smell or taste from sheer habit."

"But you weren't serious about all this!" said Wharton, horrified.

"Of course we weren't," said Castle amusedly. "It was something for the mind to gloat over. It was consoling to think of Twirt as dead, it didn't matter a damn how."

Travers at last let out a breath. "My God! what a hole to work in! It's a miracle you weren't all driven insane."

"We did have a breakdown or two," said Castle. "And I'll give you my word that more than once I've seen the world spinning a bit dizzily myself."

"But about that poison suggestion," said Wharton. "You say it wasn't serious. And yet someone carried it through after planning it out—only the other poor devil got it." He shook his head. "And were the mistresses of the same mind as the men? How many of them are there, by the way?"

"Eight—including the drill-mistress and Miss Gedge. Tennant christened them the Eight Step-Sisters—which is also a joke. Except for Miss Gedge, they were even more furious with Twirt than we were. He used to bully them unmercifully." He paused. "You'll find them a repressed, neurotic collection—especially after the grind of a term like this."

Wharton raised a cunning eyebrow. "Nervy, eh? Just the type to drop the poison in the sugar." He saw the quick frown. "I mean it's the sort of thing a woman might do if she were driven into a corner, or bullied, as you said."

Castle shook his head. "If you don't mind I'd rather not discuss it. I'm here to give you all the help in my power, not to incriminate any particular person."

"Of course, of course!" said Wharton placatingly. "But they knew about the poison suggestion?—the women. I mean."

"Why not? Men and women naturally met a lot, and there was only one vital topic. That shows what a maddening obsession Twirt had become."

"It was a dirty, slinking trick—slipping in that poison with the sugar," said Quick. "A woman did it. A man wouldn't."

"How many men are there?" asked Wharton.

"Twelve, including myself and the drill-sergeant."

Wharton pursed his lips. "Well, we'll wipe out Tennant altogether. His death was an accident. What we have to find is the two who murdered Twirt twice—which is what it amounts to. And the poisoning side of it shouldn't be too hard. We know the poison was slipped in just after a quarter past three. Can you test the alibis of the staff for that time?"

"With absolute ease," said Castle. "But there'll also be the alibis of Flint and his wife and—if her father will pardon me—of Miss Quick."

"Could a stranger have got in?"

"Possibly, of course," said Castle. "But I take it a stranger isn't the kind of person who'd want to murder Twirt. Besides, there's a plain notice—as you may have seen—at the foot of the stairs that all visitors must ring the bell and wait. The caretaker—or Miss Quick, whichever was handier—would then find out their business."

"One last question, then," said Wharton. "Twirt was killed in that shrubbery. Mightn't something suspicious have been seen from one of the class-room windows that overlook the drive?"

Castle smiled. "I admit that six rooms—seven to twelve in-
clusive—do overlook the drive. But pupils don't look out of windows. All the time from three to four they'd be hard at work at
their desks. Also the windows are so high that only the older
pupils could look through, and I doubt if they'd see much more
than the top of the wall—the boundary wall by the road."

"And what about their teachers?"

Castle smiled again. "If you remember, the teachers would
be up to their eyes correcting examination papers and register-
ing the marks. If they'd finished that—and I know few of them
who have—then there'd be their form reports to get on with.
You've no idea what a rush it is. The school should break up next
Tuesday, and every pupil's report has to be signed for every subject, and by the form master or mistress and also by the headmaster, with assessments of character and conduct in the two
latter cases."

"I don't think there'd be much time for the staff to admire
the local scenery," smiled Travers.

"Well, then, what about the hall?" persisted Wharton. "If any
pupil or anybody was looking out of the windows there, he'd
have seen all sorts of things."

"There again it's impossible," said Castle. "In the first place,
the hall is closed to pupils except when it's wanted for commu-
nal things like prayers and powwows. I grant you that if it was
being used for gym—as it constantly is—then there'd have been
heaps of people there to see things. Only, if you remember, in
the summer term there's no gym indoors if the weather's good;
and to-day, as it's a Wednesday, the pupils who'd normally have
been taking gym were at the baths."

Wharton blew out a breath. "Well, that settles me. But as a
giver of help, Mr. Castle, you've certainly been a godsend."

But Castle was wiping his forehead with his handkerchief.
In spite of the dusk, it was close and clammy inside that room,
and all at once Castle's face seemed weary, and a haggard grey
came over it. It was strange how completely and in what deep,
malevolent way he had dominated the room for that long spell;
not as something evil himself, but as a senser of evil, who—even

in his deliberate assumptions of flippancy—could make others see something of the deadly hate that had hung over the daily, unavoidable lives of a handful of ordinary men and women, whom none had seen reason to pity since the outer world had been wholly unaware.

"You're not feeling well," said Travers concernedly. "Let me get you some water."

"I'm all right." He got to his feet. "Just played out, that's all. But if you want me any longer, I'll ring up our next-door neighbour and get him to let my landlady know."

Wharton looked concerned too. "Well, it's sort of life and death to us for you to stay on if you anyhow can. You see, we haven't an idea from minute to minute what might turn up."

"I know," said Castle. "I'll just have a word over the phone and then take it steady for a bit."

Just then Wharton's specialist arrived from the Yard. Castle had found nothing in that mysterious catalogue, and the new man set about an official examination; and for comfort and seclusion Wharton installed him in the masters' common room.

When the General got back he busied himself with an examination of the contents of the dead man's pockets. There was a letter which he read while Castle was phoning.

"He's got a sister, I see. She'd better be notified at once. Make a note of it, Quick, will you?"

Quick began to copy the address. He, too, had watched Castle and the haggard grey that had come to his face.

"You know, sir," he said, "you ought to be headmaster of this school. Everybody has been saying so—them that know—"

"Don't say that, please!" Castle's voice cut him curtly short, and a look that could only have been abhorrence was on his face.

"Well, it's true," persisted Quick, "and the truth never harmed no man."

"Maybe," said Castle, with a touch of his old irony; "but there's a time for truth as for everything else."

"These cigarettes he smokes," broke in Wharton, displaying Twirt's case. "Fragrants, I see they are. Pretty poor, scented rubbish for a headmaster to smoke, aren't they?"

"His tastes were common as hell," said Castle. "He came from the gutter, and he was at home in it."

Before Wharton could speak, the telephone went. In a moment he was across, and the receiver in his hand.

"Yes . . . speaking." There was a long wait, punctuated by grunts and nods. "Well, stick on the job till there's nothing left to find. . . . That's right. Then go home. . . . Yes, I shall be here—at least for a bit."

He took the room into his confidence.

"That address the Hindu gave is an accommodation one; just a tobacconist's where letters can be sent. The owner doesn't know Mela Ram from Old Nick, except that a Hindu of sorts did call for one letter on Monday. That'd be the one the headmaster sent, making this afternoon's appointment. Also, according to my men, the neighbourhood is full of Hindus."

"It would be," said Castle. "It's in the university district."

"How much do you know about Mela Ram?" asked Wharton.

"As much as you," said. Castle. "The entertaining was part of Twirt's publicity stunting. Mela Ram was probably told about this place by a friend who'd been here. Also, sometimes the university authorities asked if they might send research students in education here for a look round. That also was Twirt's idea."

"Ram was a student?"

"I gathered so from the few words I had with him. But he was an uncommunicative cuss. Still, if you like, I'll get out a list of university departments and colleges, then you can phone them in the morning."

Wharton beamed. "Didn't I say you were a godsend? You get on with it at once, Mr. Castle. And, Quick, make up a Press Bureau notice, to the effect that a Mr. Tennant, etc., etc., died suddenly from poisoning at so-and-so, and the police suspect a practical joke. Any hogwash like that will do. Get it off at once, and that message to Twirt's sister."

While Quick phoned, he resumed his examination of the ring of keys from Twirt's pocket. The smallest one seemed likely to open the safe that stood in the far corner, and he nodded across at Travers. First from the safe came a leather-bound book. It was a Staff Register—a scholastic record of the men and women who had worked in the school since the day of its far-distant opening. Wharton and Travers inspected it together. Castle had been there twenty years, and his age was forty-two—though he didn't look it. He had come up to Cambridge from a well-known school, and Travers wondered what curious chance had sent him for a living to a place like Woodgate Hill instead of to a public school. There was also one Oxford man on the staff, a lot of London people, and a few of the youngest universities. Wharton lingered for a moment at the pages devoted to Gladys Gedge—B.A., University of Wales; age, fifty-two.

"Likely to be useful!" whispered Wharton, and laid the book aside.

Next came a cheque-book or two, relating to various school accounts, and then the account-books themselves. Then a clip of tradesmen's bills; and the firm:

THOS. J. SANDYMAN & SON,
ITALIAN WAREHOUSEMEN,
GROCERS, ETC.

"Hallo!" said Wharton. "That man Sandyman, Mr. Castle, seems to be a grocer of sorts."

Castle looked up from his job. "Yes, he has an oil-shop and groceries as well—or rather the son has. The old man's taken over a branch he's just opened."

"How on earth can a man like that be the governor of a school?" asked Travers.

Castle's lips took on a cynical droop. "You mustn't think of governors in the terms of your own school. A lot of these fellows are rag-and-bobtail; make-weights appointed by their pals on the local council, and out for a little cheap publicity."

But he seemed surprised to see the bills there. Lists of brooms, they were, and brushes; cleaning materials, oil and groceries, and totalling to a goodish amount. And then Quick, who had finished with the phone, said he would get his daughter, and promptly did so. Castle conducted the phone conversation. Miss Quick, as Castle had known, kept such bills in her room. These, however, had been asked for by the Head some days previously. Miss Quick thought he was trying to work out an economy scheme, as his tail had been twisted for overspending. Also, Mr. Castle would see in the room the last consignment from Sandyman, which the Head had had sent in.

A large, roped box was certainly standing in the corner, with the Sandyman label plain to see. Incongruous enough it looked, even for that untidy room. But Castle was smiling cynically.

"I think I know now why the Head wanted to see our grocer friend at four o'clock to-day. He'd been making an inquiry into the quality of the stuff Sandyman supplied. That case has been opened, as you can see. You remember what Vincent told you, about the Head poking his nose into every conceivable corner?"

"But if Sandyman's a governor, how on earth is he allowed to supply goods to the school?" asked Travers.

Castle smiled. "My dear Mr. Travers! you of all people should be an authority on parochial politics and graft. Why did Sandyman turn his business over to his son, and open a branch for himself? Simply so that the son, who isn't a governor—yet—can go on raking in the local contracts."

"Blast all politics!" said Wharton. "Half those fellows ought to be locked up for keeps. But what on earth's this?"

It was an unmounted photograph; the school staff in their gowns and hoods, and Twirt, full of smug importance, in the midst. But from the body of a man and the body of a woman, the heads remained only as blanks; and the cutting out had been a neat job.

Castle's eyes narrowed. Amazing though the riddle was, it was plain that he was making sense—and then he shook his head.

"Curious, isn't it? I wonder why he cut out those two heads."

"Who are they?"

"We can soon see." On the wall was a mounted photograph, and he brought it across. "An annual stunt, this. The whole school used to be done too." He peered with just a little too much earnestness at the cut copy. "Yes, I see who they are now.

The woman's a Miss Holl—geography; the man's Godman—junior language master, and I've mentioned him before."

"Why the mutilations?"

Castle shrugged his shoulders. "Perhaps he wanted them in a locket!"

"Godman," said Wharton reflectively. ".He was the gentleman who first suggested putting poison in the Head's teapot, wasn't he?"

"The very one," said Castle. Another shrug of the shoulders, which asked plainly enough what the hell it mattered, and he resumed his job.

Wharton had a quick look at the records of the mutilated two—then the bell shrilled again.

"Who?" said Wharton. "Who? . . . Oh, I see! . . . You don't say so! . . . Fancy that, now! . . . Very good indeed! . . . Excellent! . . . Yes. Good-bye."

A broad smile was on his face as he hung up.

"Well, we weren't so far out? Mrs. Flint is now at a house at Highfield Park. Your man, Quick, had the gumption to ask next door for Mr. Flint. They said he was the next house. A Henry Flint. What's our man's name?"

"Sam," said Castle. "I remember now he *has* a brother at Highfield Park."

"Capital!" He rubbed his hands. "For all we know this case may be over and done with by morning." He took the list Castle was holding out, and once more he noticed the tired look. "We're most grateful to you, Mr. Castle. And I think we might manage now. When did you last have a meal, by the way?"

"At one o'clock lunch," said Castle. "And if you don't mind, I think I will make a move now. I'd like a spot of brandy at the local pub before closing time."

"I'll go along too, if I may," Travers told him.

"I can have some food for all of you across in ten minutes," said Quick.

"Not for me," said Travers. "I'll have some sandwiches at the pub."

Castle held out his hand to Wharton. "Well good night. What time in the morning?"

"As early as you can," Wharton told him. "As soon as it's light we're going over every inch of those shrubberies."

There was a tap at the door and in came Wharton's man with the catalogue. The General's face brightened.

"Found anything?"

The man shook his head. "What I really came in about, sir, was to make a suggestion. Why not phone the firm first thing in the morning and get a duplicate of this catalogue? They'll have it in their files. Then we can make detailed comparisons."

Wharton thought for a minute. "Very well then. You be responsible for all arrangements." Another thought came and he turned to Castle. "You take the catalogue home to-night and have another peep. Would you mind? Then we can get it to the Yard in the morning in time for the duplicate—if you haven't discovered anything meanwhile."

"As you wish," said Castle. "Anything to-help." He picked the huge volume up. "I'll get my bag then. I left it in the common room."

But for the detective sergeant the room was empty. Wharton was wandering round, opening locked drawers.

"A rare nice gentleman, that Mr. Castle don't you think, sir?" the sergeant suddenly said.

"Very nice indeed," said Wharton. "Not a bad day's work for him either."

"How do you mean, sir?"

Wharton pursed his lips. "Well, if he gets the job of headmaster here himself, it won't be a bad day's work, will it?" He opened the main drawer of the desk. "Have a go at the top papers, though I doubt whether anybody's had a chance to do any tampering."

Then Wharton remembered his pipe and pulled it out. He knew, somehow, that all the things he was doing were matters of routine with no particular heart to them. But his mind was on Castle for a moment as he filled the pipe. On his own admission the senior master had been absent from his room that afternoon. And as Wharton lighted the pipe, the match burned to his very fingers as he remembered that false trail Castle might have laid, when he said so airily that the time of Twirt's death was between ten past four and a quarter past.

And yet, somehow, Castle was no murderer. Of that Wharton was as sure as Travers had been. He was not the type. He could hate to the last scarifying moment, but he was no killer. And Wharton even smiled as he thought of Castle. He, too, had come under the spell of the man's voice and personality. Wharton knew a gentleman when he saw one. A fine fellow, Castle; and above all a veritable godsend to any inquiry.

Then Wharton shook his head. No. Flint it was who had done that murder. And he'd done it doubly, so that there should be no mistake. He had been listening in that store and had heard Godman's remarks. He'd tried the poison first, and when that failed—the hammer. And he'd bolted, losing his nerve as weak men do when they've had a temporary strength.

And then Wharton smiled, remembering that he had told Castle that that night he would not be home. Maybe the case would be over in an hour or two—though, in the words of the song, he wouldn't be home till morning.

CHAPTER V
DEAD MAN'S STORY

THERE WAS a cosy corner with tables and chairs in the private bar-room of the Running Stag, and thither Travers took his drink and his plate of sandwiches.

"I think I'd have something to eat with that brandy of yours," he said to Castle. "When one's as played-out as you are, drinking on an empty stomach is none too good."

So Castle had a sandwich and they went on talking. Mention of schools had been avoided with stilted caution, and they resumed their original theme of book-collecting, which was Castle's hobby.

The talk matters little; it was what emerged from it that was ultimately to count. Travers had delightful manners. He was the perfect listener, and supremely well informed. For all his disregard of die-hard convention and his occasional quaint mannerisms, one knew one's self assuredly in the company of a man of breeding; who had a rare sympathy and insight; with whom confidences would be implicitly safe, and to whom sharp practice would be an abominable thing. Travers himself, often puzzled why people made him the depository of their secrets, was wholly unaware of the qualities that invited them. Once more he was to be surprised when Castle hinted at a confession that had to be made.

"There's something I'd rather like to tell you." He hesitated again. "I've had it on my mind this last hour or so. You see, I didn't want it to be public property; but if I tell it to you, you can tell it to Superintendent Wharton."

"I will," said Travers. "That is, if you wish it."

"I'd like to get it off my mind before I go home," went on Castle. "It's about Charles Tennant."

Travers nodded.

"I'm going to do something damnably dirty. You probably guessed what Charles and I thought of each other. I hate social snobbery, but I do claim that you'll see for yourself that our men are a mixed lot. In other words, he and I had things we were disinclined to share with others. It's important to remember that, or you won't understand what follows. For instance, I told you—or I implied it that every one on Twirt's staff would have murdered him without compunction."

"I believe you did."

"Well, I was wrong. I made Miss Gedge a possible exception, but I should have made another—*Charles Tennant himself.*"

He smiled. "I see you can hardly believe that. You wonder why a man of Tennant's sensibility and breeding could have arrived at any attitude of compromise with an emetic like Twirt. That's why I'm telling you all this. It's a mystery to me. Other people didn't notice things because they weren't close to his mind, as I was. The mystery was this.

"Tennant was always a cynical sort of cuss, and in the early days he regarded Twirt as a Stoic philosopher might regard a louse. But he also got furiously angry sometimes, though he never ranted or uttered wild threats like some of the staff. He kept a sense of proportion, thanks to that ironic outlook. All the same he felt things deeply, as I know well.

"That was up to about four years ago. Then suddenly he changed. Instead of a man with a private stake and a grievance, he became a humorous contemplator of events. Whereas at staff meetings he had been accustomed to enliven the proceedings and infuriate Twirt with a series of apt but disconcerting interruptions, now he would sit out one of those hellishly windy affairs with nothing on his face but an ironical sort of smile. And listen to this. He was in charge of history, and Twirt—a science man himself—regarded history as his personal hobby. He was always infuriating Charles with suggestions and schemes. But four years ago, Twirt made some maddening alterations in the methods of teaching history, and what do you think Charles did? He didn't give a damn for Twirt. He disregarded the instructions entirely, and went on his own sweet way!"

"And what did the Head do?"

"Damn-all," said Castle. "He shut his eyes. He never joined issue with him. But of course it was bound to be commented on by the staff, and when the men said something to Charles about it, he only laughed. 'You fellows haven't been handling Twirt properly. You want tact!' That's what he'd say. But if you really want to understand Charles's dramatic change of attitude towards Twirt—and Twirt's towards him—recall that matter of the tea-tray. No other man would have dared to interfere with the Head's tea; and no other man would have been so humorously indifferent about being found out."

Travers was polishing his glasses. "A blunt question, and you'll forgive me for it. Could Tennant have been blackmailing Twirt?"

Castle shook his head. "I doubt it. It was so foreign to his nature. But listen to some more evidence. After his dramatic change, Charles never indulged in common room recriminations. He was the only really cheerful person on the staff—and perhaps that's why everyone liked him. Then one day he told me he was trying for a headship. and was going to get Twirt to throw all his influence behind him. I asked him why on earth Twirt should do that. Then he laughed—and I know why. It was to cover up what he'd let slip. He said Twirt would support him over a headship so as to get rid of him. Charles meant he had once been such a thorn in Twirt's flesh that Twirt'd praise him to the skies and tell any God's-amount of lies to have him out of the school. And apparently that's what happened. Charles did get a headship—this very term. It took him and Twirt two years to manage it, though I admit there were painfully few vacancies."

"And what was Twirt's public attitude towards him?"

"Perfectly natural," said Castle. "Twirt showed no hostility. On the contrary he was always affable. I admit Charles no longer went out of his way to be an irritant."

"And any other manifestations of the mystery?"

"Yes," said Castle. "I haven't come to the real mystery yet. But you see, don't you, that whereas Charles might bamboozle the rest of the men by all that fluff about handling the Head with tact, he couldn't deceive me. I kept badgering him to know the real reason. I badgered him so much that finally—one day at the end of last term it was—I got a clue. I happened to say, 'I suppose Twirt will really leave this damn school one day?' and then he looked at me in the most peculiar way. 'I'll tell you when he'll leave.' I said, 'You mean when he's dead?' Then he hesitated, and what he said was, *'Well, if the police came in it might help!'* And that's every word he'd say."

"A prophecy!"

"It was," said Castle. "This afternoon Twirt sent for a policeman to come at four o'clock, and when I saw him that remark of Charles's flashed into my mind. Also, you people came in later, and the prophecy came true. Twirt left the school—feet first!"

Travers gave a Whartonian grunt.

"There's something else," went on Castle. "I still kept on at Charles, especially these last few days since he got that headship. You see, he was not entitled to a headship, either by seniority or special qualifications. We all know those things are shamefully wangled, but there must have been some barefaced manipulation in his case—not that he wouldn't have made a first-class Head. Still, as I was saying, I kept plugging away at him, and at last my importunity wearied him. *He promised me on his word of honour that he'd tell me the secret the day he left the school.* In other words, next Tuesday. Then he shut right up, and I couldn't get another word out of him."

Travers's face was extraordinarily serious. "Therefore the secret lies in that book he was lugging across the floor."

"You're right," said Castle. "Melodramatic as it sounds, I believe now that there's some message for me in that book. And now something else comes back to me. One day this term the men were playing that game of golf, and one of them accidentally kicked over that book. Charles called out, with far too forced a humour, 'Hi! don't hurt that book. I wouldn't change it for any other in the building.' Or words to that effect, as you policemen say."

"Let me see," said Travers. "You have the book here in your bag, haven't you?"

"Yes," said Castle, and suddenly seemed to freeze up.

"May I have just a quick peep?"

Then the hesitation became something more. In that one moment the Case of the Dead Shepherd might have been solved. Travers did find it strange that Castle should delay in producing the bag where the book was. His excuse was even more peculiar.

"I don't think I'll get it out again now. You'll be able to see it in the morning. Besides, it must be near kicking-out time here."

He got at once to his feet. Something had scared him, and at all costs he had to be away—though it still lacked ten minutes of closing time.

And away he went, with a nod and a smile that had something forced in them. Travers, from the inn door, watched him turn up his collar again against the rain, and mount a bus; then he hurried back to the school himself to break the news to Wharton.

The General had finished a scratch meal and was watching the sergeant busy puffing powder and comparing finger-prints.

"Anything happened since I was away?" Travers asked.

"Nothing much," said Wharton, "except that a woman has been examining the papers in the drawer of this desk. She must have been in the very hell of a hurry, because somehow she busted her necklace, and didn't have time to pick up all the beads."

Greenish wooden ones they were.

"That ought to be easy," said Travers. "Miss Quick should know whoever wore a necklace like that."

"She's in bed with a racking headache," said Wharton. "However, her father's just gone along home to see if he can get any information from her. He ought to be back in a couple of shakes."

Then Travers's eyes suddenly opened. "But how on earth could a woman get the keys? She couldn't have taken them out of Twirt's pockets when he was dead, and put them back again?"

"You never know," said Wharton. "Still, there's nothing gained by hurry. We'll know all about it in the morning—if we're here so long."

"I suppose we shall," said Travers, a shade less philosophically. "But just listen to this, George. Castle told me it in the Running Stag, over a drink and a sandwich."

Half-way through Travers's story, Wharton began making notes in his book. Then he seemed to tire, and by the time the tale had ended, he was almost bored.

"What do you make of it?" Travers asked him anxiously.

"I'll ask you one first," said Wharton. "What's the use of it? We've washed out Tennant entirely. He couldn't by any conceivable variety of circumstances have used that hammer—"

"Why not?"

"A score of reasons," said Wharton contemptuously. "Also, Menzies just rang up, and when I asked him, he said Twirt was killed round about four o'clock, and certainly when Tennant was dying." "All right then," said Travers. "I accept that. But why else isn't Castle's tale important?"

"Haven't I just told you?" said Wharton grimly. "We've washed out Tennant entirely. We don't want to know anything about him. It was Twirt who should have been poisoned, and therefore for the purposes of this case, Twirt *was* poisoned."

"All the same," persisted Travers, "how do you explain Castle's story?"

"It's child's play," said Wharton. "Tennant had some hold over him. Something happened four years ago, and nobody but Twirt and Tennant knew it. If this were a different sort of case, I'd say that if the worse came to the worst—which it won't—we might have to do a bit of digging into the past to find out just what it was that happened."

But Travers was loth to leave the subject. "I admire your large optimisms, George, but there's something you've missed. I trust Castle. I trust his knowledge of Tennant. Castle assured me Tennant wasn't the kind of man to resort to blackmail. Indeed, he apologized profusely for being such a blackguard as to tell me the story at all."

"Life's full of surprises," said Wharton, in one of his most irritating, sententious moods. "If every man ran true to public form, Scotland Yard might close its doors to-morrow."

"As you say," said Travers. "But listen to this. I asked Castle—in the Running Stag—to let me have just one more peep at that book which you'd asked him to take home and examine again, you remember? Do you know, that simple request scared him dizzy. He wouldn't open his bag. He simply grabbed it and bolted for the bus."

Wharton made a face. "Well, I don't deny that there's something in the book. Probably it's something trivial that has no bearing on the case. I'd say that Castle's already discovered what it is. Perhaps he wants to erase it—and if he does, we'll know what it is when we compare the book with the copy we get from the firm to-morrow. Maybe he's trying to shield Tennant's reputation in some way. Doing the quixotic, and so on."

There was a quick tap at the door, and the plainclothes man came in.

"Flint's just coming, sir. I left him at the cottage with his wife."

"Flint coming!" Something like panic was making a tingle along Wharton's spine. The optimistic bubble was near to bursting. The case was not to be so easy after all.

"He and her left that house, sir, and took a tram. I couldn't get near to hear what they were saying, but they was both as bold as brass."

"Right!" said Wharton. "Get outside now and stand by handy."

And in less than a minute there was another tap at the door. In came a total stranger—a thin, cadaverous man in working clothes, with as furtive a pair of eyes as Wharton had ever looked into.

"Yes? Who are you?"

"Flint, sir. The caretaker, sir. They told me you wanted to see me."

"Yes," said Wharton, running his eyes over him as if hunting for clues. "That's quite correct, Flint. And where've you been all this time? To Monte Carlo?"

Flint refused to see the joke. "At my brother's. My nephew brought a sudden message just before four o'clock that he wasn't well and I was wanted, so I slipped off at once, sir. I knew it didn't make no difference about the work—not in the summer. I could always get up early and do it."

"Of course," said Wharton. "And how did you find your brother?"

"Better than I expected to, sir. It was his heart, sir. A very weak heart."

"But why didn't you leave word with your wife?"

"Well, sir, I was so flustered, sir, and in such a hurry, I didn't know if I was on my head or my heels. Besides, I knew it wouldn't make no difference to her, sir."

"And why'd you come back?"

"Why, to do the work, sir."

"Yes, but did anybody fetch you?"

"Only the wife, sir. She sort of had an idea where I'd gone."

"Did she give you any news?"

A lugubrious expression came over Flint's face. He would have made a fine professional mourner.

"Only about the poor headmaster being dead, sir."

"*Only* is good," said Wharton. "But when did you last see the Head alive?"

"Not since this morning, sir."

"He wasn't in his room when you brought his tea?"

"No, sir. That's why I set it down outside."

"And what did you do after that?"

"I went right down the corridor and out the girls' stairs, sir, and to the cottage where I read the paper."

"Yes. Go on."

"Then, sir, just before four I happened to be coming round the boys' way when I see Mr. Sandyman—one of the governors, he is, sir—and he asked me if the Head was in. I told him no, sir, and just then I see my nephew—and that's all, sir."

Wharton rubbed his chin. "All right, Flint. We shan't need you any more to-night. Oh, by the way. You went out by the boys' entrance, and neither you nor your nephew saw a sign of the Head?"

"No, sir. We never see him."

Wharton nodded "Very well, Flint. You can go. But you're not to mention to a living soul that Mr. Twirt is dead. You understand that?" His anger was slowly rising, as it always did in the presence of a liar. "And remind your wife that I told her the same thing. I gave her an order, and she disobeyed it. And tell her her memory's not all it should be. Oh, and, Flint! You might let me have a pot of tea and a plate of bread and butter as soon as you're up in the morning. Bring the bill with them. I'm sleeping here all night."

He waited till the steps had died away.

"Sergeant, find that man of yours and tell him to nip back and make inquiries about the brother. That sort of person doesn't go to bed much before midnight. And see Flint's house is watched all night."

The door closed on the sergeant. Wharton was still fuming.

"Went out the boys' way, did he? With his nephew. A pack of lies from beginning to end. And his wife knew perfectly well where he was. The thing is, why did she fetch him home as soon as she knew Twirt was dead?"

"Because she didn't suspect her husband of killing him," said Travers.

"Then why did he come back if he knew he'd killed him?"

"Because he'd wormed out of her that we didn't suspect him."

Wharton shook his head. "That's too easy. Besides, she couldn't have known that. We'd questioned her about him." He shook his head, and the last of the optimisms went with the shake. "Ten minutes ago I'd have sworn he was the one we were looking for. Now I'm just as certain that he isn't."

Travers smiled. "Now perhaps, George, you'll be prepared to admit that there was something in that story Castle told me about Tennant."

Wharton grunted, then cocked his ear. "This sounds like Quick."

Quick it was. He reported that his daughter had a blinding, sick headache, and he had asked only the minimum of questions. But Daisy had definitely identified the beads as from a necklace worn by Miss Holl.

Wharton's eyes popped open. "Why, she's the other one who had her head cut out in the photograph!"

"About the keys, sir," said Quick; "she thinks she knows how Miss Holl got them, but she'll tell you in the morning. The poor girl was fair blinded with pain."

"Right," said Wharton. "Now begin a main covering letter about Mela Ram. And make a note that first thing when school opens, I'm to see the boy who took the tray back to the kitchen. Which reminds me. Wasn't there a school time-table of sorts lying over there, Mr. Travers?"

Travers found it. It gave the work being done at any particular lesson by any form, and the name of the teacher in charge.

"I'd like to have a squint at one of those rooms that overlook the front," said Wharton. "Room 9 wouldn't be a bad one. It's apparently the one where Mr. Castle spent his time from three to four."

There was a light on the landing. Wharton and Travers turned sharp right. On the first door to their right was the figure 4. Wharton walked in, turning on the switch, and at once the room was well lighted.

Travers sniffed. "Same old smell of ink. Sends me years back; doesn't it you, George?"

But the room was very different from the one in which Travers had spent his youthful days. It was lofty, for one thing. In it there were thirty-five separate, lock-up desks, so arranged that the light from the window fell across a pupil's left shoulder. There was no board and easel. The whole of the wall behind the teacher's platformed desk was one immense blackboard.

As for the windows, they were as Castle had described, and began so high from the floor that no mischievous pupil could ever risk falling out. And there was something ingenious about the construction of those windows. The main parts could be lowered and raised with cords and weights like any other window. But below those main parts were subsidiary windows, that fell inwards by loosening a catch, so that it would be easy to ventilate the room without moving the immensely more heavy windows that were above them.

"Too dark to see outside," said Wharton. "Tell you what. We'll make some excuse to-morrow for Mr. Castle to let you be in here when a class is on, then you can find out just what a pupil could see if he looked out, and also if Mr. Castle could see anything when he stood up to stretch his legs on this platform—which he'd be sure to do after a long spell of sitting."

They returned to their headquarters again. Travers, sensing that for some time he would be more of a hindrance than a help, made his excuses and prepared to leave for town. He would be along in the morning bright and early, he said.

Wharton smiled as he said good night. He had considerable affection for Ludovic Travers, and considerable difficulty in consistently disguising it. Then the smile turned to an ironic one.

"Be along early, will you? In search of romance? But surely not! Now if you were coming to a theatre, or a pub—"

But Travers smiled feebly and fled.

CHAPTER VI
SCHOOL ON PARADE

WELL BEFORE eight o'clock the following morning, Travers drew his car in under the shade of an elm that overhung the road by the school wall. Wharton was standing there contemplatively.

"What's the problem, George?" was Travers's morning greeting.

"Just turn this way and have a look," Wharton old him.

So they turned their backs on the space of rough parkland and Travers followed Wharton's pointing finger. It was the tall laburnum at the foot of which Twirt had been found dead that was interesting him. The tall trunk canted so badly to the right hat of all the trees in the long line of double shrubbery, it was the only one that attracted the eye.

"Here's my point," said Wharton, "and this is low Twirt might have been killed. Say he's coming this way towards the entrance there. He may be alone and then meets somebody, or that somebody may be with him. What strikes the eye of both of them? Why, that tree. A remark is made, and Twirt—anxious to air his knowledge or show his grip of the situation—takes his companion to point out just what's happened to the tree. When they're inside the shrubbery, the hammer catches the eye of the other man and he contrives to manipulate the circumstances so as to land a wallop—by picking up the hammer and admiring its strength, and so on. Am I right or am I wrong?"

"Damn it, George, don't be so trenchant!" protested Travers. "I've hardly got the sleep out of my eyes yet. Still, I'd say you were wrong."

"Wrong," said Wharton, afraid to trust his ears. "Why wrong?"

"Well, is there room to swing a hammer?"

"Heaps," said Wharton. "I've just tested it."

"Then who've you cast for the village blacksmith rôle?"

"Nobody in particular," said Wharton, "unless it's that slippery Hindu."

"But what's he done?" protested Travers again. "Hadn't he the right to slip off home yesterday afternoon?"

"That's just it," said Wharton. "A man wouldn't have slipped off. A man would have insisted on being allowed to go. And why did he give that accommodation address? Why did he make his original proposition to visit the school, not by letter, but over the phone?"

"I don't know," said Travers. "But you'll admit that only Vincent's prints were found on the hammer. A man couldn't very well ask Twirt to wait a moment while he first of all obtained some gloves, and then put them on."

"Wasn't Mela Ram wearing gloves?" countered Wharton. "What did he want with gloves on a day like yesterday, hot enough to scorch the hide off you?" He nodded grimly. "Mr. Ram and I'll be having a little chat before this day's out—or my name's not what it is."

They went through the main gate and Travers's eye rose to the barrack of a building. He shook his head.

"On a glorious morning like this, George, you'd think that building would look a bit cheerful. But I don't know. The sun seems to me to make it more damnable than it was in the rain."

"Yes," said Wharton. "I thought so myself. It's the sort of place that'd get a man gradually down. There's that groundsman coming. Wonder what he wants?"

Vincent had come from the boys' entrance. He flicked his forelock at Wharton.

"Morning, sir. You *are* the police, sir?"

"Some of them," said Wharton jocularly.

Vincent's face remained straight. "Then there's been a burglary at my shed, sir. Someone broke in during the night."

Wharton looked at him. "What's been stolen?"

"I don't know, sir. I haven't had time to look."

The three went across the field to inspect the site, Wharton with the air of a man who takes a holiday. The shed lay by the fence on the boys' side, and Wharton remembered it from his evening squint from the lavatory window. Just short of it he halted. His finger indicated the line of footprints that led from the shed to a gate in the fence.

"Looks as if someone come along that fence and broke in to see what he could get," said Vincent.

"If so, he flew," said Wharton. "The steps go *from* the shed. Where're the ones that brought him to it?"

"He probably came some other way, as across the grass there," suggested Travers. "After all, we shouldn't have seen these if it hadn't been that the grass was bare."

"Maybe," said Wharton. His eye ran to the gate. "That's the back lane you spoke about, Vincent, isn't it?"

"That's it, sir."

"Hm!" said Wharton. "Well, it's as much like a woman's print as anything else, except in the heel. It might be one of the boys, playing a trick on you. But let's see the damage."

The shed door had been fastened with staple and padlock, but all that was left was a wrenched staple. The padlock had gone altogether. Then Vincent made a discovery.

"Blowed if he ain't emptied all my water, sir!"

There was certainly a considerable puddle still on the floor, and Wharton had taken it for a leakage after the rain.

"What water's that?"

Vincent explained. There were some young plants he had to keep watered and so he kept a pail of water in the shed so that the chill should be taken off.

"And nothing else gone?" asked Wharton sardonically. "Sure he hasn't pocketed half a dozen lawn-mowers?"

The fine edge had gone from the General's morning humour. He was growling as they moved off.

"Worrying you and me with that! What's he think we're here for? I'll lay a fiver it's some boy he's offended, who's been getting his own back."

But by the boys' entrance they ran into Quick, and Wharton gave him the details. When he had gone again, Travers suddenly remembered the shrubbery search.

"Find anything in those shrubberies this morning, George?"

"Not a thing," said Wharton. "That clay soil must have been hard as iron before the rain came. An elephant wouldn't have made a mark in it."

"Any more news about Flint?"

"Not yet," said Wharton. "Our man's still on the job."

They were mounting the porch steps and Wharton's eye had naturally turned towards that shrubbery that lay between it and the girls' entrance, when suddenly he halted. Between the shrubbery and the building was a two-foot strip of gravel that made a space when the groundsman did weeding. On it Wharton's eye had caught the stub of a cigarette, and he was kneeling by it when Travers joined him.

"A Fragrant! Bit of luck, that—finding the right end."

Travers smiled. "Why so excited, George? Surely it's only a stub that Twirt threw away as he entered the school one day? Even he couldn't smoke inside there."

"Call that a stub?" said Wharton. "It's more like half a cigarette. What's more, he didn't throw it. He was here and dropped it deliberately. Look at those marks on the gravel where he trod round it in putting it out."

He got out his note-book and made a quick drawing, then put the stub in his case. Up on the porch again he was about to make some remark when another voice came in first.

"Good morning!"

It was Daisy Quick, looking fresh and dainty as a daffodil.

"And how are we this morning?" said Wharton paternally.

"Absolutely all right, thanks. Going to be a lovely day, isn't it?"

"Yes," said Wharton, and then archly, "But business before pleasure, you know." His voice lowered. "*How did she get those keys?*"

"Miss Holl, you mean?" Her own voice lowered. "She came in my room about half-past three. People are always doing that, you know, because I have to give them any books or stores they want. Well, she sat down on the spare table and began gossiping, and I remember I'd laid my keys there. Then she went out, and in five minutes she was back again."

"Did she know the Head was out?"

"She asked me and I told her. If not, she'd have tried the encyclopedia trick."

Wharton nodded. "And what's she like personally?"

She frowned. "She's a cat—and the laughing-stock of the school. She's all affectation and talks in a refained voice, and makes eyes. She thinks she's beautiful, and she's always talking about the holidays she has abroad. Hallo! Here's Mr. Castle."

A quick smile and she was gone through the door. The two turned to meet Castle, who was carrying the bag in which was doubtless the mysterious catalogue. Travers gave him a pleasant nod, but Wharton thrust out a hand.

"And how are we this morning?"

They chatted away up the stairs, and Castle laughed when his steps turned instinctively towards the masters' common room. He smiled more cynically as he hung his hat on the peg in the Head's room. Then he handed over the catalogue.

"Nothing in this that I could find. I think Mr. Travers wanted to have a go at it."

"I think he does," said Wharton. "But first of all I want from you the best method of tracing the Head's movements after he left here yesterday afternoon."

"That's easy," said Castle. "I'll ask the drill people whether he really went to the baths."

"Splendid!" said Wharton. "Then there're the staff alibis and their finger-prints."

"Easier still," said Castle. "The whole school will assemble as usual in the hall for prayers. I shall ask the head boy and girl in each form—captains, they're called—to stay behind, when I shall state that while a master or mistress was *absent* from a room, something terrible occurred. They'll think I mean that the pupils did something in the absence of the teacher, and so they'll tell me—in their own defence, since they're supposed to keep order when the teacher is absent—which teacher *was* absent, and when. After that I shall call the staff together, while the school go out to the playing-field, and hand each member a sheet, on which—strictly confidentially—each will make a statement. Those, checked against the statements of the form captains, give the alibis. You'll also have the staff finger-prints."

"Very brainy," said Wharton. "You ought to join us at the Yard, Mr. Castle. And now I'm going to Twirt's house to see his housekeeper. Any chance of Mr. Travers being allowed to wander round and look at things generally?"

"Of course," said Castle. Then he smiled. "I'll allow him to disguise himself as an inspector."

"Splendid!" said Wharton, and moved towards the door. "I'll be back long before you're ready, but you might send me, after prayers, that boy who took the tray away yesterday."

Travers took up his position in the masters' common room in a corner seat by the window; his head well behind the morning paper. At twenty minutes to nine the first man entered. His entry was typical of the humorous sequence, for he took Travers for one of his colleagues, and began to talk as he hooked one of the gowns from its peg and slipped it across his shoulders.

"One more bloody day, then?"

And then he saw that Travers was a stranger. His face flushed.

"Oh, I'm sorry. . . . You're waiting to see the Head?"

"I'm afraid not," smiled Travers. "Mr. Castle turned me in here. I'm a sort of friend of his."

"That's all right, then." He smiled with what might have been relief. "My name's Godman, by the way."

Travers remembered. The junior language master, who had suggested the poison, and whose head had been cut from the photograph. He was an alert young fellow, with a round, plump face; quite well-dressed and spoken, and in age about thirty. But before the conversation could develop, the next man appeared, and the humorous sequence continued. Each man who was to enter took Travers as granted, till a hush warned him of the presence of the unusual.

There was no need to ask who the newcomer was. His cheek-bones were high, he had a back like a ram-rod, and his moustache had waxed ends. And he took no gown from its peg.

"You're early, Pete?" said Godman.

"Yes," said Pete. "I got here to give young Furrow the tip. The Old Man caught him out yesterday afternoon. The crafty old bastard came—"

Godman coughed loudly. "Oh, Pete; this is—I didn't catch your name?"

"Travers."

"This is Sergeant-Major Tangent, Mr. Travers. Mr. Travers is a friend of Castle's, Pete—so that's all right."

Travers solemnly shook hands. Then the drill-sergeant scraped his pipe out in the empty fireplace, and when he next spoke it was with the guile of the old soldier.

"You mustn't pay no attention to the way we speak of our headmaster here."

"That's all right," said Travers meaningly. "I've heard a thing or two."

That lowered the barriers. Tangent turned to Godman. "You haven't seen Furrow?"

"You know he isn't coming to-day, Pete. Don't you remember the Head gave him leave to go to his sister's wedding?"

"Blast it! so he did." He laughed. "Yesterday afternoon he fixed up with me to slip off, and if the Head came, I was to say he had a sick headache and had gone to the chemist's for something to cure it. That's what I told Twirt when he come."

"He didn't believe it?"

"Believe it, hell! You ought to have seen his crafty little old face when he stamped off."

In came a greying, disillusioned, lean man, to whom the secrets of education were bunk and ballyhoo. He growled out a good morning and hitched on a ragged gown.

"Bloody fool I was not to back that tip you gave me, Pete. Both ways, I mean. Did you see it came in second at a hundred to six?"

A ponderous silence announced the presence of Travers. Then a mild young man entered. He seemed to be a joke, and blinked through his pince-nez.

"Finished all your papers yet, Grey?"

"He's always the last!" Godman whispered in Travers's ear.

"Not yet," said Grey, and blinked a bit more.

Then the door opened and bumped into him. It was a tubby little man with a northern accent, and he must have heard the conversation.

"Those who want my papers will damn well have to wait. Other folk don't bother themselves, so why should I?"

It was Tennant's death that the room was itching to discuss. And since none knew of the poisoned sugar, there was no harking back to the suggestion which Godman had once made in that same room. The death of Tennant seemed indeed inexplicable, though some hinted at a skeleton in the cupboard. Everybody had liked him, if some spoke enviously of his good spirits. Then at five to nine the bell went for prayers. Outside by the playing-field the prefects were marshalling the school into lines, and soon the tramp of feet was heard as the pupils filed below. The common room got reluctantly to its feet.

"Where's Castle?" someone said.

"In the Head's room," said someone else. "I saw him go in."

"Oh, my God!" said the disillusioned man. "That's the damn limit."

Godman whispered an explanation to Travers. "Sometimes the Head stops in his room jawing, and we have to wait down there a quarter of an hour!"

Travers sat tight for a bit, then by way of the boys' staircase made his exit to the playing-field. Vincent was at work trimming the edges of a tennis-court, and then all at once there was a babel of voices, and but from their respective entrances came a stream of boys and girls.

"Bit noisy, aren't they?" said Travers.

"I don't call that noisy," said Vincent. "What I was thinking was that Mr. Castle had told them about Mr. Tennant—and so on, and that'd sobered them down."

Travers stood watching them, and to him their spirits seemed high enough. The unexpected break in the day's routine, perhaps. The girls looked smart in their gym dresses, and they made no bones about keeping to their own side of the field. The youngest scholars seemed about twelve; and the oldest, young people of eighteen or so—grave, dignified prefects who moved like reverend storks among bevies of sparrows. And then, as Travers turned to watch Vincent again, he heard the sound of Castle's name. Two boys had come up to within a few yards of him.

"Did you hear about old Castle?"

"What about him?"

"About him and the second fourth. They didn't half have a lark!"

"Not with Castle, they didn't."

"I tell you they did, then. Yesterday afternoon they was doing *Midsummer Night's Dream*—you know, acting the play like we did last term—and Castle said they might dress up. Coo! you ought have seen them! Tubby Miller told me. They weren't half a scream! And old Castle got wild. He nearly pulled Tubby's ear off."

"He didn't."

"All right, then. You ask Tubby yourself. His father's coming to see the Head this morning about it. Look! There *is* old Tubby. Come on! Let's go and get him to . . ."

The words trailed off. Travers watched them chasing the apparently elusive Tubby, then lost them in the crowd.

"Who are the second fourth in this school, Vincent?"

The groundsman looked up from his trimming. "Well, sir, the first of a form—like the fourth form, say—is them what have all the brains. The seconds are the duds, and then there's thirds of all the forms, and they're the regular duds."

"What are the second fourths like—in themselves, that is?"

"Them, sir? A lot of louts—and the girls are bad as the boys. A damn good hiding'd do the lot of 'em good, if you ask me."

Travers moved off back to the school. Voices lowered in the groups by which he passed. Eyes followed him, and more than once he caught the word *inspector*. The common room was empty when he passed it, and the staff had apparently assembled in some handy room to await the coming of Castle. But sitting on one of the chairs outside the Head's door was a fierce-looking man with a bowler held on his knees. He rose at the sight of Travers.

"Can you tell me if the headmaster is engaged, sir?"

"I'm afraid I can't," said Travers.

But at that moment feet were heard on the stairs, and Castle—gown flying behind him—came into view. He gave Travers a quick glance and then looked down at the man.

"You want to see the Head?"

"Yes, and you too. You're Mr. Castle, aren't you?"

"I am," said Castle, and waited.

"My name's Miller. You laid a hand on my boy yesterday afternoon. You got him by the ear—"

"One moment," said Castle. "Your son is Fred Miller? Tubby, they call him?"

"And what if they do?"

"Nothing," said Castle. "Only that I have much pleasure in informing you, Mr. Miller, that in all probability you will be asked to remove your boy from this school at the end of this term."

"Oh?" He glared. "You're not the headmaster—"

"Oh, yes, I am!" said Castle. "If you don't believe me, inquire at the police station." He brushed the man aside and entered the room.

Travers was hot and cold all over—and looked it.

"I shouldn't worry about him," said Castle. "He's been here before. Twirt used to toady to him and parents of his kind." He gathered up the pile of papers evidently prepared for the staff alibis, then had a look outside. "He's gone now. If he comes back while I'm away, send for Flint to order him out."

Within a minute Wharton was entering the room. He said he had questioned Twirt's housekeeper about anything strange that happened four years previously, and she knew of nothing.

Travers couldn't help laughing. "In this very room, only a few hours ago, George, you told me that Castle's story about Tennant wasn't of the slightest consequence. Now you're using it as a clue."

Wharton refused to be disconcerted. "When you throw a net you mustn't mind how far you throw it." He pulled a bundle of letters out of his pocket. "I told her it was my duty to look through these. We'll have a squint and then seal them up again for the benefit of his heirs and assigns."

But as he looked at one of those letters, his eyes bulged.

> *Re* yours of the 19th. We have given the matter careful consideration and are inclined to agree that the method of recovery hitherto suggested by us might involve the loss of the sum due.
>
> We therefore agree to the terms offered by yourself; the sum of £30 (thirty pounds) to be paid on the first of each month until the whole amount of £552 (five hundred and fifty-two) is cleared off. This, as you will note, includes interest at five per cent.
>
> If these terms are not carried out by you, we shall have no compunction in acting as per our previous communications.

Travers whistled. "That's the devil of a lot of money to owe! What's he been doing? Playing the market?"

"That's it," said Wharton. "Know the firm?"

Travers had a look, then shook his head. "Looks rather like an outside firm of the bucket-shop type."

"I'll get the Yard and have a good man sent round." He took off the receiver and gave his number. "What was Twirt's salary, by the way?"

"Eight-fifty," said Travers. "Castle told me so last night. Of course he didn't get that when he first came here."

While Wharton was phoning a tap came at the door. Travers opened it and admitted two boys. One was about fifteen, and the other had an incipient moustache and a dignity beyond his eighteen years. Wharton hung up and then surveyed them.

"Well, what's your trouble?"

"Mr. Castle told me you wanted to see this boy," said the elder. "And he said you might want me this morning, sir, to wait outside in case you wanted anything done. I'm the senior prefect, sir."

"Splendid!" said Wharton. "You go and sit outside and read a book till we want you. Got a book?"

"Plenty, sir," the head prefect reproved him severely.

The door closed and Wharton smiled paternally at the other.

"So you're the one who took a tea-tray from the masters' common room yesterday afternoon. Who told you to take it?"

"Mr. Tennant, sir. I was going past the door, sir, and he called me."

"Where were you going?"

A slight pause. "To be excused, sir."

"Hm!" went Wharton, gathering the purport. "And what time was it?"

"Five-and-twenty past three, sir."

"Really?" Wharton raised his eyebrows. "Why are you so sure?"

"I saw it by the clock on the mantelpiece, sir."

"He's wearing a Scouts' badge," put in Travers beamingly. "No wonder he keeps his eyes open."

"Well," said Wharton when he had gone, "that's that. It was a sweltering day, and as soon as he got the tray in here, Tennant filled that big cup, put in heaps of sugar, and lots of milk—the jug was emptied, you remember—and then gulped the lot down at a go. If he tasted anything nasty, he probably spat it out in the lavatory and thought someone was playing a trick on him."

Then in came Menzies.

"Anything new?" Wharton asked him.

"I don't know that there is," said Menzies, "unless it's something about the way the hammer hit him."

He explained. The angle of the hammer fitted the angle of the broken skull, for the wound was triangular, and the hammer had not fallen full-faced. But the wound was deeper towards the front than towards the back of the skull.

"What I think is that he moved, but didn't move fast enough when he saw the hammer falling."

"That might be it," said Wharton.

"Or why couldn't he have been looking backwards?" said Travers.

Wharton smote the table. "The very thing! The striker told Twirt to look upwards—say, at the top of that tree. That would make him lean backwards, and so the hammer fell more towards his forehead."

"That may be it," said Menzies. "And now what about finding out where the poison came from?"

"You can buy it openly enough," Wharton reminded him. "It's used a lot for cleaning."

"You wouldn't necessarily buy the stuff that was put in that sugar," said Menzies. "That was pure crystalline stuff, resembling granulated sugar. Which proves very careful working-out." He shook his head. "No need to buy oxalic acid when this place is a hot-bed of poisons."

"You mean the chemical laboratory?" asked Travers.

"What else? They've a poison cupboard down, there, and they've a dozen poisons in open use. I imagine any member of the staff could walk in and help himself."

Wharton made a note in his book. "We'll interview that chemistry master good and early. I suppose you didn't gather anything from Twirt's hat?"

"Except that he was wearing it at the time," said Menzies dryly.

Travers left them discussing the inquest, and made his way out to the porch for another minute's sunlight. But something seemed different about the drive, and then he saw what it was. Drawn in close to the shrubbery and almost at the girls' entrance, was the great-grandfather of all cars. Travers smiled. One hearty sneeze and the landscape would be littered with wheels. That ancient car seemed, however, to have been a feature of the local landscape, for there were faint ruts in the gravel and some spots of black that meant leaking oil.

Then the bell went, heralding the reassembly of school. Travers turned to see Menzies disappearing out of the main gate. And as he went up the stairs he suddenly saw Castle pass above him, a sheaf of papers in his hand. Alibis—and possibly romance! Travers began taking the stairs two at a time, then slowed decorously at the sight of the senior prefect, whose head was buried in a book. But he moved back his legs for Travers to pass to the Head's room.

Travers smiled. "You found a book then. Interesting, is it?"

"Quite interesting, sir," said the prefect gravely, and exhibited a page. It was a highly advanced treatise on organic chemistry.

"Yes, isn't it?" said Travers, wholly abashed, and one hand was fumbling at his glasses as the other turned the knob of the door.

CHAPTER VII
PARADE CONTINUES

"I've got Twirt's movements for you," Castle was saying. "If he left here at twenty past three, then he went straight to the bath where the girls were because the mistress in charge says it was half-past when he got there. He stayed about five minutes and then went to the boys' baths, and that'd take five minutes more. Tangent, the drill-sergeant, says he was with him only a couple of minutes, and then went off in a flaring rage because a master named Furrow had left the baths on the plea of being unwell. That would mean he left at about eighteen minutes to four. If he hurried he could have been back here by ten minutes to four."

"My own idea exactly," said Wharton. "I think he was killed at about five to four."

"That's not for me to say," said Castle. "There is one thing, however, I did think of doing while all the school was present. I asked if anybody had seen the Head on their way home. You see, people leave here for all points of the compass, and yet no one saw him."

"Therefore for once he was in time for an appointment," said Travers gently.

"Yes," said Castle. "I'll certainly admit I was wrong there. But about the lists. I've checked the staff statements against those of the form captains. Furrow, whose name you'll see, you won't be able to interview till to-morrow. He got permission from the Head to attend his sister's wedding."

"I heard about Furrow in the common room," said Travers, and repeated the conversation.

"Why did he want to slip away early yesterday afternoon?" asked Wharton.

"My idea's this," said Castle. "No doubt he'll own up frankly when you see him. He's an extraordinarily nice chap, but I'd say he wanted to catch an early train for wherever it was his sister's wedding was." He smiled meaningly. "After all, if he had a headache, he'd a right to get away."

Travers looked over Wharton's shoulder at the list.

Miss Gedge
Miss Holl
Mr. Godman
Mr. Furrow (Not available till Friday)
Mr. Castle
Miss Quick

"Vincent's alibi is all right," Castle told them. "The senior prefect was with him all the time, sitting by the tennis-courts doing private study. Flint says he was at his cottage, so we can't test his. Mrs. Flint was in the kitchen and we can't test hers—except that no one saw her out of it. Miss Quick I've put down because she was in her room and her statement helps that of Miss Holl—though she hasn't any alibi herself. Of the rest, only Miss Holl had a pukka free period."

"You mean that Miss Gedge and Mr. Godman weren't supposed to be out of their rooms?"

"Hardly that," said Castle. "You haven't the right to leave your form and go on a gossiping tour, but everybody's the right to go and relieve nature, or go to the common rooms for necessary papers or books. As a matter of fact, if the staff hadn't been so busy over examination papers yesterday, you'd have found far more names on that list."

"Pardon me," said Travers, "but how can people correct papers and work with their forms at the same time?"

"They don't," said Castle. "They give the forms private work to do. Take my own case yesterday afternoon. I had a very restless lot—the second fourth. When I had them the day before I told them that the next time I took them, provided they worked quietly for a half-hour, I'd spend the last half-hour with them doing Shakespeare, which they always like."

"And did you?" Travers felt himself blushing. "I mean I was thinking of Tubby Miller."

"We didn't," said Castle. "We were going to do some acting, but one or two clever ones had got ready beforehand to take a rise out of me. All they got for their pains was that I cancelled the Shakespeare, and I made them go on working. Then just before four o'clock I finished my batch of papers and thought I'd get some more from the common room, so I went down. But just as I opened the door I realized I shouldn't have time to begin them properly, so I merely squinted into the room and went back to the form again. You'll find that on my own paper." He smiled dryly at Wharton. "That, by the way, is all I can give you about my alibi."

Wharton waved a deprecating hand. "We're not worrying about you, Mr. Castle—and we didn't want any statement."

"You'll pardon me," said Castle, "but I insist on someone checking up my alibi with the form." He smiled. "Don't you see that it will help me no end in handling the staff, if I can tell them I've placed myself unreservedly in the hands of the police?"

"Do you know I think you're right," said Wharton. "But I shan't check it myself. Perhaps Mr. Travers will."

"The second fourth it is," said Castle. "Room 9. But before Mr. Travers goes, there's something I want to say. It seems pretty bad taste for the school to go on normally after what's happened. As soon, therefore, as Mr. Travers has finished with that form, I propose to let the pupils go home for the rest of the day. The staff can stay here and get quietly on with their work."

"You're absolutely right," said Wharton. "You carry on then, Mr. Travers, since Mr. Castle insists on it, and we'll wait till you get back."

So Travers went along to Room 9, tapped at the door and entered. At the desk on the platform, the tubby master with the northern accent sat correcting papers. He smiled genially as Travers came in.

"I shan't disturb you," whispered Travers. "I just want to have a look."

The tubby man nodded, and Travers glanced round the room. He also glanced out of the windows. The girls in their neat gym dresses gave colour to the room, and every soul in it seemed hard at work writing, though one or two ran an eye over the stranger. On the black wall were the two tasks about which the form was busy:

1. Geometry. P. 83. Theorem 18.
2. Geometry. P. 84. Exercises 5, 8, 11 and 15.

Travers, thinking it all out from his new position by the window, was suddenly puzzled. He approached the tubby master again, and whispered hoarsely.

"Will you tell me something? If they're all busy writing, aren't things getting worse and worse for you? I mean, every paper you correct here, they're writing two over there!"

The tubby man whispered even more hoarsely—and he winked. "When they've finished what I've written on the board I shall collect the papers—*and then burn* 'em." He winked again. "Though they don't know that!"

"Oh," said Travers, and then smiled. Indeed, as an example of the economics of labour, he was beginning to find it hilarious. Then he stooped and whispered again. "Mind if I have a word with the form—officially?"

"Carry on," said the tubby man. "You won't disturb me."

"Just a moment," Travers called to the form. He was feeling an overwhelming urge to polish his glasses. "I have a question or two to ask you."

Eyes stared at him and then at each other. Then at the back of the form Travers saw the boy who had carried that tea-tray to the kitchen, and he pointed to him.

"You tell me, will you, what happened yesterday afternoon when Mr. Castle was out of the room?"

The boy looked surprised. "Nothing happened, sir—not then."

Travers smiled. "Very well. When did it happen?"

"It happened before, sir." He grinned, and the room grinned with him.

"Well, we'll get at it another way," said Travers cheerfully. "What was the time when Mr. Castle left the room?"

"About five to four, sir."

"How do you know?"

"Looked at my watch, sir."

"Why?"

"Because I thought it was time to go home, sir." He grinned again, and again the form grinned with him.

"An admirable reason," remarked Travers—and then had another thought. "Did Mr. Castle at any time have his back to the form? I mean, so that he couldn't see what you all were doing?"

"Oh, yes, sir; when he was at the window."

"Why was he at the window."

There was a brief hesitation. "I suppose he wanted some fresh air, sir."

"This bottom window was open?"

"All the bottom windows were open, sir. It was hot, sir, on account of the storm."

"Exactly!" smiled Travers. "And when was Mr. Castle at the window?"

"Just before he left the room, sir."

"At about five to four?"

"Yes, sir."

Travers smiled his thanks. But he stood there for a moment or two till the form resumed its arid labours, then with a genial nod to the tubby master he made his way out.

In the Head's room the sergeant had apparently been busy over the prints on the staff papers. Castle was waiting to ring the bell, and as soon as Travers appeared he went out.

"About five to four he left," said Travers to Wharton. "Also no pupil could have seen the spot where Twirt died. When I stood upright on the platform, I could only just see it myself. I admit Castle might have seen it from the window, but a shorter person couldn't. Also, Castle was definitely looking out of that window just before he left the room." He fumbled at his glasses. "You see what that might mean? He may have seen Twirt killed, and he may be shielding the man who did it."

Wharton shot a look at him. "You're rushing to extremes. Why shouldn't he have had a perfectly normal look from the window, just for a change of scenery? And why should he have noticed that one tiny spot?"

But he made a note in his book, then gave him Miss Holl's statement. On it was written:

Free period. In common room all the time.

ELISE HOLL.

P.S.—Also got something from stores about 3.30.

E.H.

"Now look at Godman's," said Wharton.

With form all period except—

1 Saw Miss Holl in corridor for a minute at about 3.35.

2. Started my car at exactly 3.50.

3. Slipped down again to see if it was still running at 3.58.

H. M. GODMAN.

"Miss Holl has missed something out," said Travers.

"Yes," said Wharton. "And in the Staff Register her name appears as Elsie—not Elise. I don't think it would be at all a bad idea to have Godman in first, instead of that chemistry master. Then we'll have her in next."

"The prints on those drawer papers are hers all right, sir," said the sergeant.

Wharton didn't even trouble to look. "All right, sergeant. Just stand by." He remembered something. "And ask that old gentleman of a prefect to get Miss Quick to come here, will you?"

"Are all the addresses in the Staff Register up to date?" was what he wanted to ask her.

"Oh. yes," she told him. "I do those myself."

"Then they certainly are up to date," said Wharton. "And about your friend, Miss Holl—"

"She's no friend of mine." Her lip curled. "And there's something I ought to tell you. She came to me just now, after the staff meeting, and reminded me she got some paper from the stores yesterday afternoon. I said she hadn't any right to without telling me, and she said she knew I wouldn't mind." A vicious nod. "She didn't take any paper. All she took was my keys."

"Well, keep it to yourself," said Wharton. He rubbed his chin. "Anxious at all, was she?"

"Not she! All silly baby-talk, that's what she was. All Milne-ish. She makes me sick."

Wharton smiled. "Well, don't be ill this morning—it's far too fine. But tell me. Why does she sign herself as Élise when her name is apparently Elsie?"

"Oh, that!" She sniffed. "That was some Frenchman she was supposed to have had an affair with on one of her holidays. She christened herself Elise after that."

No sooner had the door closed on Daisy Quick than Wharton turned to the sergeant.

"Sergeant, I may be going to waste your time and my own, but I never believe in trusting to chance. Here's the address of that Mr. Furrow—who hasn't an alibi for yesterday afternoon. Go down to his rooms and find out what you can."

As soon as he had gone, the telephone bell rang.

"Yes," said Wharton, and immediately shifted uneasily with his feet. There was a longish wait. 'Oh, he did, did he? Well, listen to this. You go to Pullingers and make inquiries. Do it tactfully. . . . Certainly I'll tell them you're coming! . . . And get permission for John Tennant to come here his afternoon.'

"Quick—ringing up about John Tennant," he explained. "Last night after he left here, he went straight to Charles Tennant's rooms and asked permission from his landlady to take away some books and things he said were his. She knew him and gave him the run of the place. Wonder what the game was?" He sat down again, glancing at Pullingers' number which Travers had had the foresight to look up. "And while I'm phoning, find out what daily paper Twirt took, will you?"

But Travers made no move till Wharton had hung up again.

"He takes the *Telegraph*, George. At least, here's to-day's copy which Flint left, and yesterday saw an old one in the waste-paper basket." His hand went to his glasses. "Why do you want to know what paper he took?"

"I don't know that I can tell yet." said Wharton, chary as ever of having his coups anticipated. And at that moment a tap came at the door, and a plainclothes man entered.

Wharton clicked his tongue. "No peace for the wicked! And what do you want?"

"The caretaker, Flint, sir. I had him under observation as instructed, and he's just got back after spending a quarter of an hour in the shop of a grocer named Sandyman. They were talking confidentially, sir."

"You couldn't hear what they said?"

"I tried, sir, but it was too risky."

"Never mind," said Wharton. "And is he still under observation? If so, you'd better report back."

"I'm supposed to be lending a hand now with that burglary in the groundsman's hut, sir."

"Good," said Wharton. "Run along and enjoy yourself."

"And that's how public money's wasted" he remarked to Travers. "Casts of footprints and Gawd-knows-what for the sake of a bust padlock! And all done by some skylarking young devils in the school. Which reminds me. What was that private joke you and Castle had about someone named Miller?"

Travers told him. Then Castle came in, and Wharton let out about Flint's visit to Sandyman. Castle made no comment, and yet Travers could have sworn the news had started him on some unusual train of thought. But the matter was left where it was. Everything was ready for the staff interviews, and Wharton himself was pawing the ground.

Mr. Godman

"Anything to tell us about him before we have him in?" asked Wharton. "Any special grievance against the Head, for instance?"

"Well"—Castle made a face—"his special grievance was about his car—if you can call it a car. He was the only one of us to bring a car to school, and Twirt objected to his parking it in the drive and spoiling the front of his lovely school. Godman stood up to him, and Twirt knew he was wrong because he for once gave way. All the same, he didn't forgive Godman. When Twirt got his knife into anybody, he was absolutely unscrupulous in making that person's life hell. He was trying in every conceivable way to catch Godman out."

Godman was quite self-possessed as he came in. Travers had liked the look of him in the common room, and he was finding it even harder now to think of him as the furtive poisoner. Wharton began his usual preliminary palaver about helping the police, and easy consciences and minds at rest. Then he peered over the tops of his antiquated glasses at Godman's statement.

"I take it you weren't more than a minute in the corridor with Miss Holl?"

"It might have been two or three," said Godman. "I admit we were only talking about examination papers; still, we were both together if it comes to an alibi."

Wharton was shocked. "Come now. Who's talking about alibis? We're not trying to catch you out. We want information—that's all. For instance, did you see any strangers about?"

"I didn't."

"And about starting up your car. Just explain that, will you?"

"I wanted to get away at four o'clock to the dot," said God-man. "If Mr. Castle will permit me to use his name, I'll say that I gave him a hint about it beforehand. You see, the old bus has been giving a lot of trouble lately and I wanted to be dead sure she'd go. She conked out on me twice that morning, and as I had some hilly country to be going over, I knew she'd never do it if she weren't red-hot."

"And this is the first time you've done it?"

"Oh, no," said Godman calmly. "I've often done it—when I had good reason, and the Head was out."

"The encyclopedia trick?" Wharton gave a smile of genial archness.

Godman flushed slightly, glanced at Castle, and then grinned.

"You were popular with the Head?" went on Wharton.

Godman's eyes narrowed. "There was nobody he hated more. He'd have gone to any lengths to get rid of me."

"Yet you took the risk of starting up that car!"

"He couldn't have given me the sack for that," said Godman. "In any case it was my wits against his. There's no one so easy to fool as the one who knows himself clever."

"I wonder," said Wharton, and grunted. "And what about yourself? You liked your headmaster?"

"I hated the sight and the sound of him," said Godman. "I despised him and loathed him. He was the filthiest little squirt I ever ran across."

"Well, that's plain speaking," said Wharton, with simulated regret. "And did you see anything strange while you were crank-ing up your car?"

"Not then," said Godman. "But when I slipped down by the girls' stairs just before four to see if she was still running, I saw Sandyman—one of the governors—and Flint, having a chat by the boys' gate. Then I dodged back by the same way. I didn't trust Flint."

"Between ourselves," said Wharton, "we knew about Flint. But here's where you can help. Did the meeting seem by design or accident?"

"From what I could see, it was by accident," Godman told him. "Flint came round the boys' way and Sandyman called to him."

"That's all right then," said Wharton. "Any more questions for Mr. Godman? No? Then you may go, Mr. Godman, thank you." He peered at him over the glasses. "Everything strictly confidential, mind. Not a word to a soul—even Miss Holl."

He avoided Godman's start of surprise, but opened the door for him.

"Ask Miss Holl to step this way," he said to the prefect. "She may have to wait a moment though."

"Well, that stops all collusion," he remarked to the room. "But a remarkably frank young fellow—that Godman? He made no bones about admitting going down to see to his car."

"What's principally needed in our job is a sense of proportion," said Castle dryly. "That's what Twirt hadn't got. The educational fabric of England won't dissolve because a man starts up his engine in school hours. That's why I didn't see any reason to mention actual names when I hinted last night that I knew a man who'd done all the things Godman has just owned up to."

Wharton looked at him. "Mr. Castle, I'm beginning to be of the mind of Inspector Quick. You'd make a fine headmaster— and of this school."

Castle's jaws clamped together. "And I'll tell you what I told him. I'd rather not hear it. Even if I were offered the job—which I shan't be—I'd never be headmaster of this school."

Miss Holl

"Hm!" went Wharton, just the least bit disconcerted. "I suppose we'd better see Miss Holl, if she's waiting." His voice lowered. "She suffered that decapitation in the photograph the same as Godman did, and they had a pleasant chat in the corridor yesterday afternoon. Anything you can tell us before we have her in?"

"I can't stand the woman," said Castle. "She's got an exaggerated idea of her own importance. She thinks she's a gipsy melody, if you know what I mean, and all she is, is a tune on a cracked record." He hesitated for a moment. "She's what the novelists call sex-starved. By the way, at the beginning of this term she was talking in the mistresses' common room about the best ways of committing suicide. Pure pose. She'll do anything to call attention to herself."

"Right," said Wharton. "Let's have a look at her."

Elsie Holl was just above the average height. Her figure was good, though running to seed. Her hair was a mousy brown, and the pose of passivity she assumed merely gave her face a sulkiness. Her skin was coarse and her complexion muddy, but there was something of sex somewhere in her, though nothing could have been more primly gracious than the way she smiled during Wharton's preliminary patter.

"You'll probably find some of my questions silly," Wharton said, "but you mustn't mind that."

"Oh, that's quaite all raite," she told him, and Travers felt Castle wince.

"For instance, did you see any strangers about when you were talking to Mr. Godman in the corridor?"

"Oh, no."

"And did you see anything peculiar when you were in here yesterday afternoon?"

"In here? . . . But I wasn't in here. I mean I hadn't any reason to come in here. Besides, Mr. Twirt was out. Miss Quick told me so."

"Then you didn't come in here?"

She smiled patiently. "How could I come in when the door was locked?"

"Angels have wings," said Wharton. "And, while you're here now, allow me to give you these. I'm sure you'd like to have them back." He held out his hand, palm upwards. "We hunted the drawer through thoroughly but these were all we could find."

He poured the beads into her hand. Her face was scarlet, and she licked her lips as she hunted for words.

"Why have secrets when you're among friends?" went on Wharton. He leaned towards her and peered whimsically over the tops of his spectacles. "Tell us—in strict confidence—why you borrowed certain keys, came in here, examined the drawers, *and then went at once and reported your success, or lack of it, to Mr. Godman.*"

She bit her lip and for a moment he thought she was going to cry. Then she stared defiantly.

"Mr. Godman hadn't anything to do with it. It was examination papers I spoke to him about."

"Then why didn't you put it on your statement?"

"Well . . . because I forgot."

"Pardon me a moment," cut in Castle, "but just what was the substance of your conversation with Mr. Godman?"

"About the marks. I wanted to know if he had my form's papers marked because I wanted to get on with my reports."

"But surely you didn't need to call him out to the corridor to do that?"

She bit her lip again. "Perhaps I didn't—but I did. I didn't want to disturb his form."

Wharton resumed. "Just what was it you came in here to find?" he asked in his best paternal manner. "It must have been something very important, young lady, for you to have run such a risk as you did?"

"It was the dossier."

"The dossier?" He looked questioningly at Castle.

"Mr. Twirt once tried to put pressure on his staff by threatening to keep a secret dossier," said Castle. "It was either pure bluff or else he was too lazy to carry on with it, because I know it never was begun."

"Then you didn't find a dossier, Miss Holl?"

She shook her head.

"And why did you think there'd be anything damning about you in it?"

"Because he was always down on me." She glared defiantly again. "He was always sneaking into my rooms and trying to catch me out. He hated me."

"And you hated him?"

"Yes. He was the dirtiest little rat." She shook her head fiercely. "He was disgusting. . . . A dirty little beast!"

Wharton nodded sympathetically. "I see. Still, that doesn't get us any forrader. Your knowledge of chemistry might help us, however. For instance, what do you know about oxalic acid?"

She stared, thinking he was joking. "Oxalic acid? . . . Well, I know people use it sometimes for cleaning clothes."

"And do you?"

"Oh, no. I always use ammonia."

"Everyone to his taste," smiled Wharton. "And one last question. Everything said here is in the strictest confidence. We're here to help. Tell me, then—as my own daughters might tell me—was there anything"—he waved his hand about as if hunting for words—"anything between you and Mr. Godman?"

She flared up rather too indignantly. "Of course there wasn't! Mr. Godman is no more to me than . . . than you are!"

"I see," said Wharton, with rather less aplomb. "But you'll pardon me asking."

"That's quaite all raite," she told him, and accompanied the forgiveness with a little bow.

"Any more questions for Miss Holl?" asked Wharton. "No? Then thank you very much, Miss Holl. No word to a soul, mind you."

Her exit was a relieved scramble. Wharton gave a grunt as he closed the door on her.

"She's in thick with that chap Godman."

"It's one-sided then," said Castle. "I've heard Godman say some pretty shattering things about her. Also everybody knows he's in love with Miss Quick."

"Really!" Wharton beamed. Then he peered ironically at Travers. "A regular hot-bed of romance, this place is. And does Miss Quick look acceptably on him?"

"It's not my business," said Castle. "I do know that they had a row this term and haven't been on speaking terms since. That's merely common room gossip."

"Abolish gossip and I'd be out of a job," said Wharton unctuously. He picked up the list. "I'm not ready for a moment, but what about having Miss Gedge in next? She'll be rather annoyed, won't she, at not having been called in first?"

Castle smiled. "Let her wait. She's made me wait often enough."

"There was that chemistry master," said Travers.

"Right," said Wharton. "Ask the old gentleman outside to fetch him nice and handy."

And while he waited, he found a special page in his notebook, and wrote carefully, and in ink:

1. Liaison between Holl and Godman. Twirt knew it and they knew he knew. She for poison and he for hammer.

2. Daisy Quick?

3. Flint and Sandyman? Hammer business?

N.B.—Don't lose sight of the Tennants.

CHAPTER VIII
PARADE STILL CONTINUES

DAISY QUICK tapped at the door and put her head inside.

"Come in," said Wharton. "And what's amusing you?"

"There's two men downstairs from the Press. They've been taking pictures of the school, and now they want to come inside. Flint's keeping them out."

Wharton grabbed a piece of paper. "We'll soon put a stop to that."

"They wanted to take me too!" There the giggles refused to be suppressed.

"Why not?" said Wharton, still scribbling. "The papers need a bit more brightening."

"And they wanted to take Flint."

"Let them," said Wharton, handing over the note. "Murder cases can always do with what Mr. Travers calls comic relief. Perhaps they'd like to take Mr. Sandyman with him."

She stared, and he knew he had said too much.

"You run along and give them that." He patted her shoulder paternally, and as soon as the door closed, went over to the window for a look. But the fake porch of the upper storey and its continuance to the roof hid everything within the far edge of the drive. Something occurred to him.

"If there'd been houses across the road there instead of that bit of open country, we shouldn't be sitting here. Nobody would have done funny tricks with a hammer with people looking out of bedroom windows."

Travers was having a look too. "Funny that the headmaster could overlook only the boys' entrance, and Miss Gedge only the girls'." He chuckled. "I can see now, too, why Godman always parked his car at the girls' end of the drive."

Wharton grunted, and went back to his seat again as if ashamed of such trifling.

"See if the Professor has fetched Mr. Grey."

Mr. Grey

Though Travers was prepared for the appearance of Grey, he could not keep back a smile. No wonder Grey was a common room joke. His face was long and pallid; he wore pince-nez and an expression of desperate earnestness. He was young, and he was plainly stored to the tonsils with information—and only too ready to impart it.

"Now, Mr. Grey," said Wharton, after the usual preliminaries, "I suppose you'd be surprised to hear that your colleague— Mr. Tennant—was poisoned with oxalic acid?"

The balloon failed to go up. Mr. Grey remained calm.

"We all had the idea he *had* been poisoned."

"Exactly," said Wharton. "Now—still regarding the conversation as most confidential—am I right in saying that oxalic acid was accessible, in your laboratory, to any member of the staff?"

"Well, yes." He nodded. "But, you see, oxalic acid is obtainable at any chemist's. It's very commonly used for—"

"Pardon me," said Wharton, "but that's not the point. Don't think for a moment that I'm accusing any of your colleagues of being thieves first and poisoners afterwards."

Grey smiled in sympathy with the other's smile of deprecation.

"I'd have given anybody anything if they asked for it," he said. "Only last week I gave Miss Gedge some."

Wharton with difficulty restrained a start. "Did you now! And what for?"

"She'd sat down in some ink," said Grey, with never a smile. "I told her she ought to use sodium hyposulphite, but she would have the oxalic, so made her a ten per cent. solution of some I had put by."

Each listener saw the mental picture—Miss Gedge, bossing and fussing, and Grey only too anxious to oblige.

"Did the crystals bear any resemblance to ordinary sugar?"

Grey frowned heavily. "Yes, perhaps they did. But they'd be much more like magnesium sulphate. There have been cases, you know, where people have died through mistaking them for ordinary liver salts. I remember—"

"That's very interesting," broke in Wharton, who knew all that himself. "And have you missed any from the laboratory?"

"I don't think I have."

"Given any more away?"

"Oh, no!" He made the position perfectly clear. "I shouldn't have given Miss Gedge any, if the accident hadn't happened in school. I wouldn't give away school property. I haven't the right to."

"Of course you wouldn't," said Wharton, and peered round. "Any more questions for Mr. Grey? No? That's all then, Mr. Grey, and thank you."

The door closed.

"It looks to me," said Travers gently, "as if you ought to ask your friend the Professor to bring along Miss Gedge."

Miss Gedge

"One point I must have made clear first," said Wharton. "Would you call her a kind of headmistress?"

"You certainly wouldn't!" said Castle. "In a school like this, certain matters of health and so on arise with the girls, and a woman must see to them. As she, therefore, has to interview parents sometimes, she has a room of her own. As a matter of fact, the reason why she's so unpopular with the staff is that she tries to assume the powers of a headmistress, and interferes with the women of the staff."

"Unpopular, is she?"

"Five minutes of her company and you'll know all," said Travers. "She's a champion thruster. She got her present rank by shameless wangling, and she's kept it by toadying. She's treacherous. She'd grovel to Twirt to his face and laugh at him behind his back."

"Would she have dropped in that poison?"

"That's not a fair question. You'd better see her first."

Interested eyes surveyed Miss Gedge. Her hair was greying, and the most striking thing about her was the thin line of a mouth. Her face seemed moulded of multitudinous curves, with the tiny oval of chin stuck on as an afterthought. Her eyes were a hard grey.

She was annoyed—there was no doubt about that. The angry spot glowed on her cheek, and she flounced into the chair. Her thin lips were set as Wharton ran through his preliminaries, then she spoke her own mind.

"It's no use asking me. I know nothing about anything. I've been left absolutely in the dark."

Travers stole a look at Castle, who sat with chin on chest and eyes on the floor. But Wharton had handled women who were fifty times as difficult as Gladys Gedge. He smiled with an infinite comprehension.

"That's because *we're* all in the dark, Miss Gedge. We didn't wish to trouble a lady as busy as you—and, if I may say so—as important as you, till we had something really worth the while.

We've just learned, for instance, that Mr. Tennant was poisoned with oxalic acid!"

"Really!" Her eyes opened wide. "Not the oxalic acid you clean things with?"

"The very stuff," said Wharton.

"Why, I was using some only last week!"

She told them about it. It had been a scorching day, and so she was wearing a cotton frock. She had been talking to Mr. Twirt in his room, and when he got up to go, he noticed marks of ink on the frock. They had talked over various things to remove the marks, and then she had gone straight to Mr. Grey, who gave her some oxalic acid. After that she got Miss Quick to lend a hand, and they had got out the stains. But they had made none too good a job of it.

Wharton went off at a complete tangent. He consulted Miss Gedge's statement.

"You were out of your room for five minutes yesterday afternoon—for an excellent reason, I'm sure. From ten past three till a quarter past."

She gave a titter. Of all the devastating sights this world affords, that of the flirtatious schoolmarm is surely the most distressing.

"It was silly of me. We women are silly sometimes, don't you think? But I've been thinking over what I wrote down, and I believe I was just a teeny little bit longer than five minutes."

Wharton shrugged his shoulders. "Of no consequence, I assure you. But did you see anything suspicious at any time?"

She frowned. "I did see something suspicious after I left it." Her expression became severely condemnatory. "As I opened my door I saw Mr Tennant disappearing in the corridor as if he were carrying something he'd fetched from this very room." She leaned forward. "The peculiar thing was that the Head was out. The room was locked—for I tried it. I'd heard the Head go downstairs a moment or two before."

"He was taking the Head's tea-tray," said Castle calmly.

"But why?"

"To drink the tea," Castle told her.

Her mouth clamped shut again. "Well, I could have believed a good many things about Mr. Tennant, but hardly that."

"About twenty past three that would be?" asked Wharton gently.

She thought that was so, and for a moment Wharton appeared to be gravelled for lack of matter. Then he too leaned forward.

"In the strictest confidence, Miss Gedge; can you think of anybody who would have been glad to see the Head dead?"

Her little eyes narrowed. There was something she knew, but a considerable deal of persuasion would have to be expended before she parted with the knowledge. In her own opinion Miss Gedge was no common bearer of tales.

"All sorts of things have been going on in this school that ought never to have been allowed," was her guarded answer.

"I imagine so," said Wharton. "And of what—and whom—are you specially thinking?"

Miss Gedge drew herself up. "I'm not going to mention any names, but Mr. Twirt had warned two people that they mightn't be here much longer."

Then Wharton proceeded to coax, and the story came out. When two members of the staff—a man and a woman—come back from the Easter holiday and let out that they've been abroad, and their faces are burnt to the same degree of blackness, then it is not unreasonable to assume that they've spent the three weeks in the sunny south of France—and, therefore, why not in each other's company?

"If the staff don't look after their own morals, you can imagine what would happen in a school like this," she said.

"You're talking about Miss Holl and Mr. Godman?" Castle challenged her bluntly.

She sniffed. "Well, of course, Mr. Castle—if you want to let everybody know?"

Castle gave the faintest groan, and his chin went to his chest again.

"You yourself were on excellent terms with the late headmaster?" asked Wharton.

"Of course!" she snapped at him. Then she smiled, remembering that she was no longer having a passage at arms with Castle. "I think he'll be very much missed." A shrewd glance round at unresponsive faces. "Not that he was the ideal headmaster."

"Is there an ideal headmaster?" asked Wharton wistfully.

"Oh, I think so." She stole a sudden look at Castle, then, and for some days to come, in the seat of the Dead Shepherd. "As a matter of fact—I don't know that I'm really supposed to say it—the whole staff have got up a round-robin to send to the governors, asking that Mr. Castle should have prior consideration, and giving our opinion of him."

Castle sprang to his feet. He was desperately indignant. "Miss Gedge, I can't allow that. I can't possibly permit the staff to do such a thing."

"But it's been done already," she told him, with an assumption of innocence. "While we were waiting for you we talked it over and as soon as the meeting was finished, we drew it up and we posted it in case any of the staff changed their minds—not that they wanted to."

The stress of defence had brought her to her feet. Wharton cut in manfully.

"We're most grateful to you, Miss Gedge. More than grateful, in fact. Whenever we want to make use of your valuable experience I'm sure you'll allow us . . ."

The voice was lost in the outer passage. When he came back he blew out a deep breath.

"When heaven deprived that woman of a husband," said Travers, "it also left vacant a suicide's grave."

Wharton gave a grunt or two and then turned to the silent Castle. "You knew about that Holl and Godman scandal last night, didn't you?—when you saw the cut photograph."

"I did," said Castle. "But I don't believe in pawing over muck—if it is muck."

"I quite agree," said Wharton hypocritically. "All the same, if it's anything that concerns the good of the school?"

"It doesn't," said Castle. "What's it matter to the school if two members of the staff take a holiday together a thousand miles away from it?"

"None whatever—to you and me," said Wharton placatingly. "But Twirt didn't see it like that." He whipped round on Travers. "Give me that copy of the *Telegraph*, will you?"

He took off the receiver and asked for the Yard. As he waited, he ran his eye over the advertisements and found what he wanted on page one.

"Hallo! Superintendent Wharton speaking. Is Chief Inspector Norris in? . . . Well, who is then? . . . Right, put me through to him."

He folded the paper carefully and held it handy for reading. Travers could see the advertisement was one that concerned private detective agencies.

"Hallo I . . . That's right. Take this, will you? Get all details where you are. Inquire from all detective agencies—beginning with the two I'm now going to give you—whether they had inquiries about a job from a Mr. Leslie Twirt. . . . Yes, that's the one. One of the dead men in this case."

Travers tackled him as soon as the call was over. Wharton owned up at once.

"Why did he cut out the two heads if it wasn't for identification purposes? Miss Gedge probably went to him with the first tales and he saw a means of getting rid of two undesirables—people, in other words, who stood up to him too much." He glanced at the clock. "What about adjourning till after lunch? I've several things to do. The staff will be here this afternoon, Mr. Castle?"

"They'll have to be," said Castle. "They've got heaven's own amount of work to get through before school can break up next Tuesday."

"A bit of lunch and a drink is what I have in mind," said Travers. "If Mr. Castle will allow me the favour of his company, I'll be host at his special tavern."

"That'll suit me down to the ground," said Castle. "But before we go, I'd like Mr. Wharton to tell me if Miss Gedge is a candidate for the poisoning."

"Answer me one question first," said Wharton. "What did she stand to gain by poisoning Twirt?"

"Nothing at all," said Castle. "She was well enough off, even if he didn't always see eye to eye with her."

"There's your answer then," Wharton told him. "In my own mind I'm pretty sure she had nothing to do with it."

He already had his note-book ready and was making an entry. It was an extra to the three already occupying the page.

4. Daisy Quick knew all about the o/acid.

Before he could put the book away, the telephone bell went. Quick was ringing from town to say John Tennant had a perfect alibi. Pullingers moreover gave him an excellent character, and he had been with them since the age of sixteen. John Tennant would be at the school by two o'clock.

While that was going on, the sergeant came in. "Sorry to be so long, sir, but that landlady of Mr. Furrow's was out. I pitched her the tale when she did come, and she says he didn't come back there after lunch yesterday. It was all right about the wedding and she gave me the name of the place. I said we wanted to see him some time, but not so badly as to disturb him at the wedding. To-morrow would do."

But the look he gave Wharton was obviously one of inquiry as to whether the General was of the same mind.

"And where is this wedding?" Wharton asked.

"Place called Stonecroft — near Chelmsford, sir."

And because Wharton was cluttered up with work, and in a hurry at that very moment—and not because as he afterwards brazenly claimed, that he had a hunch—he sent the sergeant off to Liverpool Street station to catch the first available train for Stonecroft.

Rarely had Travers felt himself so drawn towards anyone as he was towards Maitland Castle. Outside the walls of that damnable school, the senior master lost his cynicism and showed himself as he really was. And that was wholly unlike a schoolmaster. He gave his views with a modest reticence, and there were sides to his character that Travers could never have suspected. As for classing Castle among the killers of Leslie Twirt, the idea was grotesque—whatever furtive thoughts George Wharton might harbour to the contrary.

It was not till the two were near the school again that Travers ventured to refer to the case.

"Who's your favourite so far?"

Castle frowned. "Well, I wouldn't like to think we had on the staff a woman who'd get so low as to put the poison in the sugar—unless it was a sudden, mad impulse and was done and then couldn't be undone. In that case, strictly between ourselves, I'd have Miss Holl in mind."

"And the hammer?"

"If I knew who wielded the hammer," said Castle, "I'd have no less respect for him than I have now. Sometimes I've hardly kept my own hands off him."

As they entered the main gate, they saw Wharton waiting on the porch for them.

"There's a very agitated gentleman—a Colonel Mawberry—who calls himself the Chairman of the Governors, waiting upstairs to see you," he told Castle. "You go and talk to him while I stretch my legs."

He took Travers's arm and led him towards the boys' entrance, and so to the playing-field.

"Miss Quick's been crying," he said suddenly. "I spotted it when she spoke to me just now."

Travers raised his eyebrows.

"I hardly know how to carry on in her case," went on Wharton. "She has no alibi for the vital time of three-fifteen to three-twenty, when the poison was slipped in."

"You're not suspecting her of that?" asked Travers in amazement.

"I suspect everybody," said Wharton magisterially. "She saw the oxalic acid—"

"But not in crystalline form."

"She knew it was crystalline before the solution was made, didn't she? Miss Gedge would have told her all that. And something else. Her father, *as a detective inspector*, would have books on toxicology in the house, wouldn't he? Couldn't she have looked it all up?"

Travers shook his head.

"And a woman in love would do anything," went on Wharton.

"Who says she's in love?" challenged Travers.

Wharton smiled enigmatically. "Didn't I say she'd been crying? And to get down to facts. Didn't Castle tell us she was supposed to be in love with Godman?"

"So he did," said Travers, and quoted—"He was her man but he done her wrong!"

"Exactly!" said Wharton. "Can't you see a picture now? She quarrelled with him because of that scandal about the Holl woman, and that's why she hates her. She knew about the acid and she could have filled in any gaps from her father's books. If Godman got the sack, she lost her man. She also hated Twirt for many reasons. Therefore she tried to poison him and save her man at the same time. No wonder she was taken ill when she knew Tennant got the poison instead!"

And straight away Wharton got out his note-book. He ripped out a certain page, and sitting down on a barrow by Vincent's shed, began the composition of another.

Poison, 1. D. Quick.
2. Holl.
Hammer, 1. Godman.
2. Flint.
3. Mela Ram.

N.B.—Must get exact time of Twirt's death. And keep eye on Tennants.

By the time he had finished, Castle was seen coming across.

"The Chairman of the Governors has just gone," he said, "and he agrees with me that the school ought to be closed till virtually the end of term. When are the inquests?"

"Saturday morning," said Wharton. "Purely formal, but we shall want you there."

"Then if you don't disagree, this will have to be the procedure. The school will have to assemble to-morrow morning for the simple reason that there's no way of stopping them. I shall have to pronounce an oration, and collect for a couple of wreaths. Then I shall dismiss the school, keeping back the staff in case you want them. When are the funerals?"

"Monday," said Wharton. "While you were at lunch I slipped round to Twirt's rooms and saw his sister, who'd come up."

Castle nodded. "That's all right then. On the Tuesday, the school will assemble finally, to receive their reports and get any books they need for the seven-week holiday."

"The staff go on Tuesday too?" asked Wharton.

"Undoubtedly, if the reports are finished," said Castle. "They've earned a holiday, and most of them made their arrangements long ago. They'll give you their holiday addresses if you want them. Was that why you asked?"

"Well—yes," temporized Wharton. "Also, if we've got to find the two people who killed Twirt, there's none too much time between now and Tuesday."

"But you'll do it?"

Wharton hesitated. Then he saw a quick vision of himself and Daisy Quick—a fatherly talk—tears —confession.

"Oh, we'll do it all right," he said. "Some of it's almost done already."

CHAPTER IX
PARADE CONCLUDES

QUICK WAS WAITING outside the Head's room with John Tennant. Castle had disappeared somewhere, but Wharton had the two in straight away. It was quite an informal affair—a sitting around and a chat. But John Tennant spiked all Wharton's guns in the first minute, for he apologized for his display of the previous night. He had been very distressed, he said, and over-wrought.

"We quite understood that at the time," Wharton told him. "But why were you so anxious to see Mr. Twirt?"

The answer came pat. Both Wharton and Travers could not get away from the idea that John Tennant had every conceivable move worked out. Throughout that interview he was to have no hesitations except those that were designed and artistic.

"You see," he said, "I got into my head the notion that Charles had committed suicide, and if that was so, then I wanted a word with the man who'd driven him to it."

"Quite so," said Wharton, and went on to give an account of the change, dating from four years previously, that had come over his dead cousin.

"I think I can explain that too," said John Tennant. He paused to nod to Castle who had just come in. "I quite agree that four years ago he used to get into furious rages—not in the actual school here, for Charles, though I say it, was a gentleman and knew how to keep himself under control. But sometimes he'd ring me up and say, 'Let's go out somewhere to-night. That perishing Shepherd has been up to his tricks again.' I don't mind telling you that those evenings used to be most unpleasant ones for me. That's why I tried to make him see differently. I told him to laugh at Twirt instead of getting angry."

"To cultivate a philosophy, in other words," suggested Travers.

"Exactly," said Tennant. "As I told him, if he didn't, he'd end up in a lunatic asylum. Don't you agree, Mr. Castle?"

"There's a lot in what you say," said Castle shrewdly.

"Well, I think that clears the air," said Wharton. Then he gave an account of the last seconds of Charles's life, with a further reference to the catalogue. "I know you've heard some of this before, but would you mind having a look at the catalogue, to see if you can make rhyme or reason."

But as soon as Tennant picked up the book and tested its weight, he appeared to find the story too highly coloured. All he could suggest was that the dying man had been delirious and had thought he was about to play that game of golf!

"Look through it," said Wharton. "Just to please us."

So John Tennant turned the pages over. And though it was with a hopelessness that amounted almost to indifference, the very casualness of the act showed an interest whose origins lay far deeper than the wish to help. His eyes pretended not to look— and yet they sought!

Wharton saw him courteously to the foot of the stairs. His face was much less kindly when he came back to the room.

"What's he keeping back?" he demanded of the room. "I'll bet everything I've got that he knew just what it was we wanted to know. And Mr. Travers knows it too. You think he was lying, Mr. Castle, don't you?"

"He was wrong in saying he made Charles adopt a philosophy as a defence against Twirt," said Castle. "No man could dismiss Twirt from his mind that way. He was far too real a menace. Also, why did Charles tell me that when the police came here, Twirt would go out?"

"Exactly!" Wharton smote the table. "I'll add another proof that he was a liar. Didn't you tell us that unobtrusively Charles did as he liked? And that Twirt refused to join issue with him?"

"I did."

"And suppose any other member of the staff— Godman, for instance—had tried the same procedure; what would have been the result?"

"He'd have been sacked—and serve him damn well right."

Wharton beamed round. "There we are, then. John Tennant is a liar, and Charles had some hold over Twirt. What's more"— he smote the table again—"as sure as my name's George Wharton, the answer to it all is in that book—or in John Tennant's mind, which is the same thing! Which reminds me. That book must go to the Yard straightaway."

"Why not give him a gruelling at the inquest, sir?" suggested Quick.

Wharton shook his head. "No, we'll give him plenty of rope. Besides, the inquest will be too formal."

Castle had been the least bit restless. Now he broke in. "Pardon me, but in five minutes or so I have to see Flint—and I'd like you to be present. It's a domestic matter."

"To do with the case?"

"That'll be for you to say. Miss Quick really discovered it. This morning, you remember, you were laughing at her about it. Flint and Sandyman having their photographs taken together. That set her thinking—and me too." He smiled. "I'd much rather you did the job, but you don't know all the ins and outs as I do."

"Carry on," said Wharton, with a renunciatory wave of the hand. "If it kills two birds with one stone——"

There was a tap at the door. Flint's head appeared—and was about to disappear.

"Come in, Flint!" called Castle.

"Miss Quick said you wanted that box removed, sir." He indicated the one with the Sandyman label.

Castle closed the door behind him. "So I do—in a minute. Sit down there. We want to talk to you."

"Talk to me, sir?"

"Yes," said Castle curtly. "You know who all these gentlemen are? They're the police, Flint."

Flint moistened his lips. "The police, sir?"

"Yes, the police. And don't keep repeating my words like a parrot. Mr. Twirt sent for the police, Flint, yesterday at four o'clock—and you know why. Sandyman knows why."

Flint shook his head. "I don't know a thing, sir. On my honour I don't."

"You haven't got any honour," said Castle contemptuously. "And keep your mouth shut till we ask you to open it. Which is now! We know what happened, but we want the story from you. If not, Inspector Quick will take you away in charge. If you do own up, we may be able to wriggle you clear."

Flint licked his lips again. He shuffled in his chair. Eight inscrutable eyes seemed boring into him. Fright seized him and kept him from speaking. Then he relaxed. The game was up and he knew it.

"All right, sir. I'll tell you. But you won't do anything to me?"

"Didn't I give my word?" Castle told him angrily.

Flint said he had known old Sandyman all his life. The plea that he had been Sandyman's tool was to be expected, but the main body of his tale rang true. When the grocer was elected on the local council, and transferred his main business to his son's name, it was because he wished to retain certain valuable contracts, among which that of Woodgate Hill County School was the most valuable, consisting as it did of supplying all cleaning materials and oil, all domestic articles and things needed for cookery and housework classes, and articles of food required for the daily lunch provided for such pupils whose homes were at a distance.

Then Sandyman over-reached himself. He and Flint put their heads together and arranged that bills should state so much, and actual deliveries be considerably less—profits to be divided fifty-fifty. The laziness of Twirt was their safeguard. And yet Twirt must have discovered something by chance. Intrigues were the breath of his nostrils, and a public scandal would mean publicity for him. Unfortunately he dropped a hint. When therefore Flint saw Sandyman coming in at the gate, he had a word with him and feared the worst. Then he caught sight of the policeman and learned from him that he was to be present too. And then, of course, Flint lost his head and bolted, having first left a note for his wife.

Castle took out his watch. "Mr. Sandyman is due here in five minutes."

Wharton took the hint. "Well, Flint, you heard what Mr. Castle said to you. Now listen to me. You told me barefaced lies and imagined you'd got away with it." He wagged a finger under his very chin. "Get this into your head. Let me even suspect that you're telling another lie; or keeping something back, and I'll have you under lock and key in a jiffy. . . . Now then. Did you see anything of Mr. Twirt yesterday afternoon?"

Flint grovelled. It was by mere chance he had seen Sandyman even.

"And did he see anything of Mr. Twirt?"

"He couldn't have done, sir. He asked me if I'd seen him. Then he came straight up here."

Wharton nodded at Quick. "Take him away somewhere. Bring him in to confront Sandyman when we give you the tip."

The door closed and he turned to Castle. "Well, you did that job better than I could—though it's my bread-and-butter. But why did you promise him immunity?"

Castle smiled ironically. "Because we can't prove a thing. You know Twirt by this time. If he did any testing, he was too lazy to leave any record."

Wharton grunted, then looked up. "Flint's a first-class suspect for the hammer business now."

"He's the very man," said Travers. "He's the one who fits your theory of someone meeting Twirt and pointing out that tree. He told tales, and Twirt would have thought it was just another tale. Twirt would have followed him like a sheep inside that shrubbery."

Feet sounded on the stairs, and the telephone bell shrilled at the same moment. Wharton grabbed the receiver with one hand, and with the other made signs for the door to be kept closed.

The message seemed to be something startling. Wharton was raising a hand for silence, and his exclamations were those of real surprise. It was a good three minutes before he hung up.

"That was the sergeant," he said. "Your Mr. Furrow is the son of a doctor, isn't he?"

"He is," said Castle.

"And he's also a good liar," said Wharton. "He's got a sister, but the village of Stonecroft doesn't even know she's engaged. The sergeant had a look over the garden fence, and there was your Mr. Furrow reading a book in the shade of the family lawn, and his sister with him. What do you make of that?"

Castle was very perturbed. "I can't understand it. On the face of it, it looks as if he'd simply told a barefaced lie so as to sneak a holiday. People do that kind of thing, you know." He shook his head. "I didn't think Furrow was that sort."

"The facts speak for themselves," said Wharton with a shrug of the shoulders.

Castle shook his head again. "It's incomprehensible. He was one of the men who didn't need to worry a cuss about Twirt. You see, he was leaving at the end of this term. Giving up teaching altogether, and going in for poultry-farming—with a brother, I believe."

"Giving up teaching?"

"Yes," said Castle. "Twirt sickened him."

"The sergeant's bringing him along here?" asked Travers.

"Certainly not!" said Wharton indignantly. "The last thing we want to do is to alarm him. Not a word, Mr. Castle, please. We'll see him in the morning as arranged."

"But you can't suspect—"

"I suspect everything and everybody," said Wharton. "And his father's a doctor, isn't he? He could have consulted books on toxicology, couldn't he? And if he didn't use the oxalic acid himself, he might—as the son of a doctor—have been approached by the one who did."

"You're wrong," said Castle. "I know you're wrong—just as I knew Charles Tennant didn't commit suicide. Besides, no man did that poison trick. If anybody did it, it was a woman."

"That remains to be seen," said Wharton, but with just a touch of the placatory. "Now what about admitting that governor of yours?"

"Governor!" said Castle, and his lip drooped. "As far as I'm concerned he's Sandyman the grocer. Governors—my God! The only time in the year we ever see most of them is when they wash their necks and spread themselves all over the platform on Speech Day; and move resolutions and pass votes of thanks—and Flint sweeps up the aitches next morning."

Sandyman was part mourner and part man-of-the-world. As a governor, he deplored an untimely death. As a man he was prepared to help his fellow-men, and to recognize their status and authority so long as they gave him his due.

"A terrible business, gentlemen," he said. "Whoever should want to lay hands on Mr. Twirt, I don't know."

"Yes," said Wharton, in the tone of a bankrupt undertaker. "But we must pull ourselves together, Mr. Sandyman. The world must still run on—and there's work to do. Alibis have to be tested."

"Alibis?" Wharton had put the word into his mouth.

"Yes; finding out where people were when the murder was committed. For instance—yourself; only, in your case we'll take it purely as an example of how we work. Where were you yesterday afternoon from three-thirty till four o'clock?"

Sandyman knew there was a catch; yet in the presence of Wharton and his geniality he was forced to follow the line of least resistance.

"Where was I, sir? In my son's shop, from three o'clock onwards; going into the books with my daughter-in-law. Then, 'Alice,' I said, 'what's the time?—because I have to see Mr. Twirt at four o'clock,' and when she said it was nearly ten to, you could have knocked me down with a feather. Still, I did it. Then I saw Mr. Flint and he told me he hadn't seen the Head yet, so I came straight on up here."

Wharton touched him playfully in the ribs. "Before this case is over, I'll bet heaps of people will wish they had an alibi as good as yours. But I may tell you that an appeal will be made at to-morrow's inquest for anybody who saw Mr. Twirt to come forward." He rose with a friendly nod to Castle. "Now pleasure ends and business begins."

A quarter of an hour later Sandyman had gone, breathing out threatenings and slaughter. Flint and he had hurled threats and abuse at each other. Not only had the grocer denied everything, but he had informed the room that he was off at once to see his lawyers about bringing an action for criminal libel. But though Wharton had leaned back in his chair and let thieves fall out, and though Castle had preserved a cynical aloofness, yet the honest men of the law got little that looked likely to help the case.

"You needn't worry about Sandyman," said Wharton, watching from the window the grocer making his infuriated way past the boys' entrance. "He'll consult no lawyers. And you take my advice, Mr. Castle. Turn him over to Quick. He'll take the matter off your hands."

"He'll he done for in this district by the time I've finished with him," said Quick.

The telephone went again. It seemed to be a call from the Yard, and the longish talk ended with Wharton's remark that he would be along. But he snapped the receiver back rather viciously.

"Not a word about that Mela Ram—or whatever his damn name is. He isn't on the register of any branch of the University—or the hospital schools."

"The University's a pretty tall order," said Castle consolingly. "There are all sorts of out-of-the-way branches they might have missed."

"Well, I've got to go up to town at once," said Wharton. "Inspector Quick will hold the fort here. And I don't know what your opinion is, gentlemen, but my views about Flint and his pal haven't changed a bit. They're still suspects for the main business."

"If you ask me, sir," said Quick, "I reckon we've got a stronger case against them than ever—especially Sandyman. You bet he'd have done anything to prevent being shown up locally."

"You go and get hold of Flint again and try him while the iron's hot," Wharton told him. "I'll be here a good few minutes yet."

Castle followed Quick out, and Wharton at once smote Travers on the back.

"Well, what about that little hunch of mine?"

Travers winced. "Which one?"

"The private detective agency. The very first one I read from that advertisement!"

"That was what they were calling you up for?"

"It was," said Wharton. "That and something else. Twirt wrote to the firm and suggested certain lines of inquiry, but when they gave him an estimate, he threw his hand in. That's one of the things I'm going up about now. The other's that firm of brokers, who sent that letter—which, by the way, I forgot to return to Twirt's sister." He took it from his pocket-book. "Hagger & Swift. Awkward people to handle, apparently. However, you run and stretch your legs for a bit. I've a job or two to do."

So Travers wandered out to the corridor. A peep in the masters' common room showed a blue haze of tobacco smoke and men brandishing blue pencils above piles of papers. A word of apology, and he made his way along the corridor. A hum of voices told him the mistresses were also at work, and on a sudden impulse he made his way to the kitchen. The rows of electric cookers told nothing, and he turned back again. Room 7 was open, and he entered it, wondering if by chance one could see from its windows the spot where Twirt had been killed.

It was as he emerged from that room that all at once he saw a something that made him snap his eyes and step back again. A flush had run across his cheek and he was fumbling at his glasses. But a second peep showed him the corridor all clear, and when he got back to headquarters, Wharton was just finishing a telephone conversation. And the news seemed to be good.

"What do you think! They've got Mela Ram! He's just turned up at the Yard, and says he wants to explain."

"What did he have to say for himself?" asked Travers.

"From what I can gather," said Wharton, "he said he's never done a thing. Only, he saw his name in the afternoon editions, and a friend advised him to report."

Travers smiled. "But when you come to think of it, George, he *hasn't* done a thing—that really matters."

"I'll tell him a thing or two he's done," said Wharton meaningly. "And what's on your mind?"

"Oh—nothing," said Travers. "Only that same thought which I had this morning when I was in Room 9. Whatever you think, George, we shall have to take notice of the fact that Castle was looking out of that room at near the time Twirt was killed. And as I told myself just now, when I was in Room 7, suppose Castle had seen the actual murder of Twirt and knew who did it, then there's no wonder he can regard it with a certain cynical indifference. He knows he didn't do it, but he knows the one who did!"

"Too easy," said Wharton. "I'll lay you a hundred to one that Castle saw nothing."

"And I won't take you," said Travers. "But there was something I actually saw just now in the corridor." His face took on a benevolent fatuousness, as of an elongated Buddha. "It was Miss Quick and Godman. He'd just come out of her room. I think they were throwing kisses back at each other!"

Wharton glared, then slowly smiled. "Didn't I hint that when I saw her this lunch-time, the tears were tears of joy?" He leered across at Travers. "Throwing kisses, were they? Romance, eh? Now if this building had been a theatre or a pub, or—"

Travers flushed again as he grabbed his hat. "If you're going to rake all that up again, George, I think I'll go and start the engine of the car."

CHAPTER X
ANOTHER DAY

As LUDOVIC TRAVERS drove towards Woodgate Hill early the following morning, the general gloom of his thoughts on the Case of the Dead Shepherd was more than once enlivened with the remembrance of what had happened late the previous afternoon.

Wharton had been rubbing his hands as he entered his room at the Yard, and Travers himself, hard at his heels, had felt somewhat sorry for the unhappy Mela Ram. But at the sight of his suspect, Wharton's face had been a study in the dramatic. His eyes had popped open and his mouth had opened too. And no wonder. The gentleman who was at that moment regarding him with large, patient eyes, was six foot tall, thin as a lath, and with a tiny head on a neck inordinately long.

But his name was certainly Mela Ram. He answered, moreover, in excellent English, every question asked him. He had once been a student at King's College in the Strand; he knew no other Indian student of his name, and at the moment he was doing private research work in town. And after that, nothing had been more amusing to Travers than the effort with which Wharton composed himself, and the string of thanks with which he ushered Mela Ram out.

Among the depressions at the back of Travers's mind as he drew near Woodgate Hill that Friday morning was that if anything happened after midday, he himself—on account of a prior engagement —would not be there to witness it. But little, he consoled himself, could happen. The inquest would take up Wharton's time till the Saturday afternoon, and with the funeral on the Monday and the staff away, the case, too, must needs halt.

And another cause of Travers's feeling of depression was that infernal catalogue on which he had spent a good couple of hours the previous night. The Yard had spent some unavailing hours on it, and for the life of him he had been able to spot no secret mark or sign that could have acted as a connecting link between the dead Twirt and the dead Tennant, or between the dying Tennant and the living Castle. But the sight of George Wharton promenading over his morning pipe in the road before the school cheered him somewhat. The General's features seemed unclouded.

"No more Mela Rams?" asked Travers.

"Blast Mela Ram!" said Wharton.

"Maybe you will, George," Travers told him. "And here's that catalogue of yours back. You'll probably want to blast that too. Any news since I saw you last?"

"Nothing special," said Wharton. "Twirt did send those two heads to the detective people. He also knew Godman and Holl had both been at Cannes. The estimate he was given was forty pounds to cover the first week."

Travers whistled. "No wonder Twirt threw his hand in. And what about that firm of brokers?"

"Nothing much. Twirt first got himself in a hole about five years ago. He'd been playing the market for some time—now up, now down. Then he tried a short cut, and he did it when the slump was just starting. Then he tried to catch up—and so on, to the old, old story."

"You'll pardon my suggesting it," said Travers, "but all this business of Twirt's debts doesn't help very much, do you think? Imagine he was sued for the money. The revelation that he had been speculating on the Stock Exchange wouldn't, surely, be enough to lose him his post. Therefore if anybody found out his financial position, it wouldn't be any real hold."

"I know," said Wharton. "I took the precaution last night of consulting two people who're authorities. Both agreed that the matter wouldn't constitute a scandal of sufficient gravity for the governors of the school to ask Twirt for his resignation." He smiled wryly. "I didn't believe Castle when he told us that only earthquakes could shift headmasters. Now I do."

"And just one other thing, George." Travers had stopped, and his hand fell on Wharton's shoulder. "It's been worrying me no end. You're not going to manhandle Daisy Quick?"

Wharton pursed his lips.

"I wouldn't, George; honestly I wouldn't, if I were you. I'm dead sure you're wrong about her."

Wharton shook his head. "Prejudices mustn't count—either way. Perhaps I'll have a quiet word with her father first."

"That'd be worse still," said Travers. "Why stir till you're dead certain? Quick's a decent soul. You'd break his heart, George, if you insinuated his daughter had done what you think she's done."

Wharton grunted. "Well, don't blame me if we're held up. Still, I'll see Godman again first, then we can make up our minds."

Travers smiled. "That's good of you, George. I like that girl, you know. I'm sure she's not the type."

Wharton turned back at the porch. He had something to do, he said, and perhaps Travers would go on ahead. It was getting towards nine, and the pupils had long been straggling in. Up in the Head's room Travers found Castle and Miss Quick hard at it. Both gave him a friendly smile.

"Catching up Twirt's arrears," said Castle. "From what I can see of things, we'll be here all to-day, most of to-morrow, and all Sunday."

Travers read the paper till morning prayers began, then the wish came over him to see the school in one assembled mass, and he made his way down the girls' staircase to take the congregation in rear. At the far end of the hall was Castle, most dignified and impressive on the lonely platform; and at that unfamiliar aspect of the acting-headmaster, Travers remembered again the thought that had nagged at him. Had Castle seen from the window the actual killing of Twirt? And had Wharton dismissed for ever from his mind that first theory—that of all the staff Castle had suffered most from Twirt and stood to gain most from his death? And yet what could Castle gain? Headmasterships went by no seniority within a school itself. Castle would not automatically step into Twirt's shoes. The post would be up for competition—hence the round-robin which Gladys Gedge had so playfully mentioned.

The prayer ceased, and after a brief shuffling of feet, the hymn was announced. From his safe cover Travers observed the resolute thumping of Miss Gedge as she played over the tune. Along the wall where the girls stood in close ranks were the other seven of Tennant's Eight Step-Sisters—worthy, enthusiastic souls whose voices could be heard in the singing, and among whom Elsie Holl alone appeared to have much chance in the matrimonial market. Nervy and bullied, Castle had called them. And one had almost certainly dropped in that poison. And Elsie Holl was unique among them in one other thing—she alone had no perfect alibi.

Among the men there seemed no stranger who fitted in with Travers's idea of Furrow, and with the realization that to spy in the course of what was really a memorial service was neither nice nor necessary, he sidled out by the girls' entrance, and made his way towards the main porch. There he ran into Vincent and a stranger.

"This is Mr. Furrow, sir," the groundsman said. "We've just been seeing my shed, sir. Mr. Furrow is cricket master, and this is the first he's heard about it. And while I'm talking, sir, since I saw you and the other gentleman I've found out that the one who broke in pinched a towel of mine."

"Rather ridiculous, don't you think?" said Furrow. He was an attractive young fellow of under thirty, with laughing eyes and a dimpled chin.

"Yes," said Travers. "The burglar certainly needed a towel pretty badly—if that's all he took."

Vincent left them then. Travers, stealing a look at Furrow, saw his face take on a seriousness that seemed unnatural to it. "You're Mr. Travers, aren't you?"

Travers smiled. "How'd you know?"

"I've heard about you and everything since I got here this morning," said Furrow. "You want to ask me some questions, I believe."

"The usual formalities, I expect," Travers told him unblushingly. "We'll go and see if the really important person's here, shall we? I'm merely a decoration."

Wharton was there and he had Furrow's chair placed ready. As he shook hands he gave the young schoolmaster a roguish look.

"Headache quite gone?"

Furrow was off his balance for a moment—then he grinned. "Oh, rather!"

"And you had a good time at the wedding?"

But there something went wrong. That delightful old humbug, Wharton, had perhaps been a shade too affable, and beneath the affability Furrow had heard a something else. Or maybe Furrow had been thinking over the folly of prevarication, now that the grand inquisitor—Twirt—was dead.

"I'm afraid I've got a confession to make there," he said, and again he looked confused. "It's going to show me in rather a bad light. You see . . . there wasn't any wedding."

"No wedding!" Wharton peered at him over the top of his spectacles.

"It was like this," explained Furrow. "The Head had his knife into me because as soon as I knew I was leaving here and giving up teaching, I took the opportunity of telling him a few home-truths. Then I had to ask for a day off to do some urgent business connected with the poultry-farm my brother and I are taking over. He sat there, sir, where you are now, and I was here. I said, 'I've come to ask for a day off on urgent business.' No sooner did I say that much than he assumed that clever, sneering attitude of his. 'You've got every Saturday and Sunday, haven't you?' Well, I didn't want to argue that I gave up most Saturdays to school cricket. Then he went on. 'Unless it's most urgent, I'm afraid I can't grant it.' So I thought that if he were going to be clever, I'd be clever too, so I said, 'Would you consider your sister's wedding urgent?' That's how it happened. I didn't actually tell a lie, and yet I did. Then it was he who told the staff I was going to my sister's wedding. Then it became sort of understood that there *was* a wedding."

"Ah, well," said Wharton with humorous resignation. "I suppose there comes a time in every man's life when the truth isn't easy. But I'm not here to judge morals." Another look, full of arch inquiry. "And why did you make an excuse to get away from the baths, when in the normal course of events you'd have been away at four o'clock?"

"That was a protest," said Furrow, and his boyish face took on a scowl—the last thing that was suited to it. "Everybody knows it's utterly unnecessary for more than half of us to be at the baths. You see, he used to dodge all his own work and he naturally imagined everybody else was trying to dodge too. And there we all were, with stacks of examination papers and reports to do, and we had to sit at those baths like a lot of comic ushers and twiddle our fingers."

"You expected to get found out?"

"Of course! I hoped I'd get found out! When Twirt called me in here, I'd have had too good an excuse. I could have looked him clean in the eye. He'd have known I was lying, and he'd have known I knew that he knew—sorry about that!—and he couldn't have helped himself. I could have laughed in his face, as he's often done in mine."

"Whew!" went Wharton, and there was no need for acting. "I must say this school seems to have been a cheerful sort of place. But about this getting away from the baths. You didn't see a sign of your headmaster anywhere?"

"I didn't. In fact, I was taking good care he didn't see me."

"How?"

"By nipping over to the railway station and taking a train to town."

"I see." Wharton frowned prodigiously. "And you know now about all the happenings here? You can throw light on anything?"

He shook his head. "I'm sorry—but I can't. It's utterly inexplicable as far as I'm concerned." A faint smile. "I don't mean that people should have killed Twirt—but just who did it, and how."

Out went Furrow. Wharton grabbed the phone. It was Quick he wanted. The inspector was to come over at once; see his daughter and get from her a photograph of Furrow; rush some enlargements and make inquiries at the local station about the actual time when Furrow took the train.

"That young man was very cheerful," he said to Travers. "When we know exactly where he was from a quarter to four till four o'clock, we'll be cheerful too."

Castle came in then. "About the staff," he said. "Do you want them here, or may they take their work home?"

Wharton glanced at the clock. "Let them stay till ten. Then I'll have finished with the lot of them."

Castle nodded. "And how did you get on with Furrow?"

Wharton told him. Castle smiled faintly.

"What's amusing you?" asked Wharton, with a kind of mild reproof. "I thought that you, as a potential headmaster, would have been rather annoyed."

"So I am—officially," said Castle. "Unofficially, I think it rather funny. After all, Twirt asked for it. And as to my being a headmaster, if a staff of mine told me lies, I'd know the fault was mine— not theirs."

Travers coughed gently. "Wasn't it young Furrow who would have been prepared to carry out that highly dangerous affair of pretending, with Tennant, to catch Twirt and Miss Gedge *in flagrante delicto*?"

"He was the one," said Castle. "Why did you ask? Didn't he strike you as equal to it?"

Travers smiled. "Only too equal!"

"As the Professor doesn't seem to be here to-day, Mr. Castle," said Wharton, "would you mind asking Mr. Godman to step this way for a bit?"

"A very unpleasant business for me," he confided in Travers. "Quick will be out of the way in a few minutes if we do decide to speak to his daughter. But I don't like it somehow. I don't like it."

Then Godman's steps were heard. He took the chair Furrow had vacated, and somehow he looked less at ease than on his former visit as examinee. Wharton, too, assumed a look of the utmost gravity.

"I'm sorry to have to tell you, Mr. Godman, that in our opinion you're in a very awkward predicament."

Godman looked at him. "What do you mean, sir?"

"You should know," Wharton told him severely. "If ever a man wanted his headmaster out of the way, it was you."

"You mean, because he wanted to get rid of me?"

Wharton thrust out a finger. "Young man, don't prevaricate! I ask you to tell us in your own way things we know already." He leaned forward with a look of infinite awarement. "About that little holiday of yours with a certain lady—and what resulted from it. All in the strictest confidence, of course."

Godman looked away for a moment. His face flushed. "I couldn't do that. It'd be a low-down trick."

Wharton rose. "Very well, then. I must ask you to get your hat and come with us to Scotland Yard. There you'll be asked to make an official statement. If you won't do that, then I'll have you on the stand at to-morrow's inquest and expose you in public."

"All right," said Godman, "I'll tell. And a damn dirty trick you're making me do."

He had always wanted a spring holiday in the sun, he said. Winter work was very exhausting, and the urge had come over him to get out of England for that three weeks. Not knowing the ropes, he had consulted Elsie Holl; and he knew he was a fool, for she had been setting her cap at him for some time. However, she advised him of a spot, and an hotel, and there he went. Two days after his arrival, she turned up too, and it appeared that she had engaged a room there well beforehand.

There was only one thing to do—to make himself as agreeable as possible. This he did for a few days, and the two went bathing and on expeditions together. But her baby-talk, her tantrums and her advances wearied him, and finally he bolted elsewhere—pretending a recall to England. Then when the summer term began, she assumed a new relationship and began a persistent haunting inside school and out. Life was becoming unbearable, till at last he told her point-blank that he wanted nothing to do with her. Then, with the idea of forcing his hand, she announced to the mistresses' common room that she was thinking of committing suicide.

Her conduct generally was so tactless that Miss Gedge got to hear of it. People on the staff put two and two together and made the answer more than four. Then something happened to bring the couple together again, for Elsie Holl got wind of the fact that Twirt was aware of that compromising holiday. Twirt had hinted at something disastrous in store for her—summary dismissal, in short. Then Twirt hinted at the same thing to Godman himself, and the two forthwith made a new alliance. Hence Elsie Holl's attempt to search the drawers of Twirt's desk for incriminating evidence, and hence her report in the corridor to Godman that she had been unsuccessful.

"It's been nothing but worry and trouble all round," said Godman. "I know it was partly my fault, but I seem to have got most of the punishment. Even the girl I was as good as engaged to broke things off when the scandal got about, and she wouldn't even speak to me. And there was I going about in daily fear of getting the sack as well. If I'd enjoyed that holiday I wouldn't so much have minded—but that was pretty hellish too."

Wharton patted his arm with a fatherly smile. "But you and Miss Quick are on quite good terms again now."

Godman stared. "How'd you know that?"

Wharton smiled mysteriously. "Young man, if you knew just what we know about this school and the people in it, the hair would stand up on that head of yours. But now tell me one thing. I suppose, when you had that quarrel, you told Miss Quick you were threatened with the sack?"

"I did," said Godman. "One day when I was trying to make her see sense." He smiled sheepishly. "I said that one day when I'd got the sack she'd be sorry."

"I know," said Wharton. "And then she tossed her head in the air, and you didn't know which you'd rather kill—her or yourself. But one other thing. Why were you so anxious to be away early in your car?"

"I was playing in the semi-finals of a tennis tournament," said Godman. "I can give you all details if you like, but I had to change and be away in the country and on the court by five o'clock—or be ruled out."

"And you saw nothing but what you told us?"

"Not a thing. I went straight down in each case and came straight up again."

Travers had been looking at the time-table. "I see you were at work in Room 8 that afternoon."

"I was," said Godman, with quite a show of interest. "It was the next room to where Mr. Castle was. I know that—if it's of any help—because soon after the half-hour I heard the devil of an uproar; people laughing like mad. I thought there was nobody in the room, perhaps; and then before I could go and see, I heard Castle let out a holler, and I wondered how such a thing could have happened in one of his classes."

"Some amusing episode connected with the acting of a Shakespearean play, I believe."

His manner was so natural that Godman told tales without being aware of it.

"Yes, his form were going to act the last bit of *A Midsummer Night's Dream;* the play within the play—Bottom and his gang—you know. At least, that's what I was told. They'd been told to bring the necessary clothes and things beforehand—Thisbe's mantle, and all that, you know. But what they did was arrange to have a rag. Pretty risky thing to do with Mr. Castle, and they'd never have tried it if it hadn't been the very end of term." He smiled. "Even then, only a crowd like the second fourth would have had the nerve. And all I know is, the boy who was doing Moonshine brought along an acetylene lamp and had it going full blast; and the bloke who was doing Lion had got an ox-tail from a butcher's and had it sewn on the tail of his breeks."

Travers laughed. "And Mr. Castle twisted their own tails for them?"

"He did," said Godman meaningly. "Good and proper."

The door closed on Godman. Wharton picked up the paper-knife from the desk and toyed with it for a good minute. Then he grunted.

"Hm! He was her man, even if he done her wrong. Just a little stirring among the sugar, and he doesn't get the sack."

Travers was genuinely upset. He liked Daisy Quick and her pert competence. Anybody who could retain an honest humour in that school—as she and young Furrow had—must be pretty sound at heart.

"But you're not going to put her on the grill, George? She won't run away. If the worst happens, she'll still be here."

"Don't I know it?" said Wharton. "And do you think I want to have her tell me she did it? All the same, I don't know that since seeing Godman, I don't feel the least bit less certain."

Castle came in again. "Hope you didn't want me, but I took advantage of the opportunity to have a quick staff meeting to arrange about the funeral and things."

"Can you call them together again?" asked Wharton. "Then they can all go. There's a question or two I'd like to ask them."

In a couple of minutes Castle was taking him to Room 4. Wharton was quite an impressive figure as he surveyed the staff from the teacher's platform. The way he held and waggled his glasses would have done credit to a statesman.

First he touched on the tragedies. Suspicion must rest on somebody in the room, and that suspicion must be removed. The staff must keep eyes and ears open. They must be attentive to the chatter of their pupils when school assembled again for that short time on the Tuesday. Even the most insignificant remark should be reported to him.

And there was one other thing. He was afraid he could not go into details, but the authorities were more and more of the opinion that the deaths of Mr. Twirt and Mr. Tennant were bound up in some mysterious way with a something that had happened four years before. The point then was: could any member of the staff recall any event of any importance that took place at about that time—the event to be connected with either or both of the dead men, or merely with the school itself.

"Now then, ladies and gentlemen," said Wharton. "Someone tell me of such a vital event."

Miss Gedge wrinkled her forehead in thought and tried to look inscrutable. Some of the staff looked self-conscious, and the bespectacled Grey looked more earnest and egg-bound than ever. Then up spake the elderly, disillusioned man with the badger hair.

"Wasn't that when we had that big row and Twirt threatened us with the dossier?"

Wharton cut in at once. "What row was that?"

"Nothing you'd understand," said the disillusioned man bluntly. "Some of the staff coming late for school—according to him."

"Mr. Tennant wasn't concerned?"

"No more than the rest of us."

"Then I'm afraid that's hardly what we're looking for," said Wharton. "All the same, every suggestion is welcomed."

But there were no more suggestions. The company wriggled in their seats and wrestled in thought. Wharton was about to offer thanks and declare the meeting closed, when there came a gentle cough from Mr. Grey.

"I don't know if you consider it worth mentioning"—he tittered slightly—"I mean, if it's any importance. I mean, I know it isn't really important—only you said anything might be—"

"Get it out!" came a hoarse whisper from the back.

Mr. Grey, thrown out of his erratic stride, tittered again. "Well, perhaps I hadn't better mention it after all."

"Nonsense, Mr. Grey," Wharton told him. "I insist on you telling us."

"Well, sir"—for the life of him, Mr. Grey couldn't keep back another titter—"it was just four years ago that *I* first came to the school."

A moment's silence, a suppressed guffaw, and then came a general laugh. Grey beamed round as if fully aware that he had made a fool of himself, though in a good cause.

But the solemnity had gone from the meeting. In a couple of minutes the staff had loaded their cases and departed; and the connecting links between Charles Tennant, his friend Castle, the chemistry catalogue and the late Leslie Twirt were as far from discovery as before. Then, the staff gone and no further excitements in view, Ludovic Travers departed too. Alone in the Head's room, Wharton crossed out a page in his note-book and began all over again.

Poison. DAISY QUICK.
Holl.
Hammer. Play off Flint against Sandyman.
Mela Ram.

N.B.—Must know to within a minute when Tw. died. Watch Castle at inquest. He may have seen something, as Travers said.

CHAPTER XI
MELA RAM OWNS UP

TRAVERS WAS AT his sister's place in Sussex, celebrating her husband's birthday; which was the special engagement that had taken him out of town. For years he had been trying to shake himself free of the stigma of high-browism which even his relatives insisted on attaching to him, and on the Sunday he made his unobtrusive way to the house of the village vendor of newspapers and invested twopence in the journal with the lowest possible brow and the most lurid headlines. His confidence was justified and the money well invested.

Wharton's two inquests were reported at full length. Castle had very wisely been kept to pure evidence, and had given none of his opinions on the late Leslie Twirt. But as far as Travers was concerned, there was one surprise.

At the last moment a witness had been found to give information as to the movements of Twirt. The foreman of the gang of navvies who were making the new roads near the school said he had actually seen Twirt enter the main gate of the school at about eight minutes to four. Questioned by the coroner as to his certainty about the time, the witness swore his watch was never more than half a minute out either way. Twirt had passed quite close to him, had remarked that a storm was brewing, and then had gone on towards the school. The foreman, struck by his geniality, had asked who he was, and one of his men had told him. Thereupon the foreman had turned for a last look at the stranger and had consulted his watch at the same time.

Travers had a good memory for figures. On reading that new evidence, therefore, he got out pencil and paper and proceeded to find out just how that new evidence affected the case. If Godman were dead accurate in saying he had started up his engine at 3.50, and had then bolted upstairs again, it seemed clear that the foreman's watch must have been correct. For the time was right when Godman came down a second time to see if the engine was still running, for then the meeting of Flint and Sandyman confirmed it.

> Godman comes down 3.50
> Twirt enters gate 3.52
> Godman comes down again 3.58

Those were the undoubted times, and Twirt had therefore been murdered in those six minutes between 3.52 and 3.58.

Then Travers cast about in his mind for other evidence that might cross the same trail, and he found it in the movements of Castle. If the Scout's watch were correct, Castle left Room 9 at 3.55. And then Travers realized that like a fool he had not asked the boy when it was that Castle returned. But that did not so much matter. He must have been back when the boy fetched him to Tennant at about 3.58. So Travers made another set of figures and put them side by side with the first.

Godman at car 3.50
Twirt at gate 3.52
Godman returns 3.58
Castle leaves room 3.55
Castle fetched 3.58

And if those sets of figures proved anything, they proved two interdependable things.

(a) Castle could not possibly have killed Twirt, since the time would have been far too short. And Travers was glad of that irrefutable proof which bore out his own judgment of Castle.

(b) Twirt had entered the main gate at 3.52, which was at the very moment Godman disappeared again. Twirt must therefore have been stopped at once on some pretext by somebody, for if not he would have gone straight upstairs. And if he got upstairs as late even as 3.55, Castle must have seen him. Therefore Twirt was stopped and murdered between 3.52 and 3.55.

Godman therefore had a perfect alibi. So had Sandyman. But two people had not, and they were Flint and Mela Ram. Flint could have killed Twirt and still have been by the boys' entrance to catch sight of Sandyman. As for Mela Ram, Travers had a wholly new theory to work out. And, taking a leaf out of George Wharton's own book, he had no intention of submitting it for discussion till the moment was ripe beyond all question.

The school bore a singularly deserted appearance that Monday afternoon, and Travers's feet seemed to echo hollowly on the stone stairs and landing. But no sooner was he there than the door of the Head's room opened and Flint came out, with a growl from Wharton accompanying him. By the time Travers was in the room, the General was phoning, and he merely waved a free, welcoming hand.

"Mr. Sandyman senior—not junior. . . . Yes, I'll hang on." He clapped his hand over the phone "Any discoveries?"

Travers shook his head. "No—have you?"

"Just trying one," said Wharton. "Flint says that when he first caught sight of Sandyman he was coming *from the main gate towards the boys' entrance,* and not from the direction of his shop."

He broke off. "Ah, Mr. Sandyman, can you come round here at once? . . . No, just as you are. . . . Oh, dear no! . . . Nothing unpleasant this time. . . . Thank you very much."

Wharton hung up. "Flint swore it on the Twelve Apostles, and I think he was telling the truth. Alters the complexion of things; don't you think so?"

"You still think that fear of exposure was sufficient motive for Sandyman to commit murder?"

"You never know," said Wharton. "A fortuitous set of circumstances and a sudden blow, and then what about it?"

"Very well," said Travers. "Assume that Twirt came in the gate at the time stated by your witness on Saturday—3.52. Let him stand and contemplate that laburnum. Let him even go inside the shrubbery. Let Sandyman be hailed by him there. Let Sandyman manipulate the circumstances so as to land him that wallop. Then you're wrong."

"Why?"

"Because Sandyman wouldn't then have calmly strolled back towards the boys' entrance and turned again. He'd have lost his nerve and bolted. No one inside the school would have connected him with the murder."

"I don't know," said Wharton dubiously.

"And what about prints?" went on Travers. "Sandyman had no gloves on. Once admit the circumstances were fortuitous, and you rule out preparation."

"He might have wiped his prints off the hammer with his handkerchief?" challenged Wharton. Then he shook his head. "But he'd have wiped off Vincent's too."

"Well, we'll know more when we see him," said Travers. "But something more important—to me. You haven't tackled Daisy Quick yet?"

"I haven't," said Wharton, "and more fool I. But I give you my word that she and that Holl woman are going on the carpet to-morrow first thing, unless something extraordinary happens." He listened. "Here's our friend Sandyman. Perhaps he'll tell us just how he did it, and save argument."

There was nothing of the bumptious about Sandyman's latest appearance. He was slightly on his dignity, perhaps, as became a man who had been falsely accused; there was also an obvious desire to ingratiate. When Wharton asked him if he had come straight from his son's shop to the boys' entrance, he thought for a moment and then actually smiled.

"It's funny you should have asked me that," he said. "As a matter of fact I didn't—and I'll tell you just why. I didn't know how long I should be with Mr. Twirt, so—as I told my daughter-in-law— I thought I'd go on from here to see another man about a bit of business. And what I did, gentlemen, was to come away in rather a hurry—as I told you before—and when I got to the school I never intended to go in by the boys' way at all. Naturally I should have gone in the main way."

"As a governor of the school," suggested Travers.

"Exactly, sir. And now you'll see what I mean, gentlemen. I did go as far as the main gate; only, when I was just short of it, I suddenly remembered the papers I was to bring to do that other bit of business. I wondered if I'd forgotten them, so I began patting my pockets—like this—and while I was thinking and worrying, I went right past the main entrance; and then I thought to myself I'd better go home and fetch the papers—so I turned back. Well, gentlemen, I just got past the boys' entrance on my way back when it suddenly occurred to me that I was a fool to go running home then. I'd only be late for seeing Mr. Twirt. If I did have to go home, I might as well go *after* I'd seen him. So I turned back once more, and just as I got to the boys' entrance I saw Flint and called to him. Now do you see, gentlemen?"

"Perfectly, thanks," said Wharton. He always boasted that he could smell a liar a mile away. In this instance there was nothing to smell, for Sandyman's words and manner had been devoid of all artifice. And by a curious chance, Wharton chose to show Sandyman as much, for he smiled at him graciously, and said he wished there were more witnesses as clear in their statements. It was that unexpected beam of sun from the icy officialdom of the law that made Sandyman say something else.

"While I'm about it, gentlemen, there's something I think I ought to mention. I thought about it yesterday morning when I was reading the Sunday paper: only, when I said I ought to mention it, both my son and my daughter-in-law reckoned I'd better keep my mouth shut, and it wasn't no business of mine. It's about something I heard." He paused. "I tell you what, gentlemen. If you like to go right down to the spot, I could show you exactly. Of course you mayn't think it worth while. You see, it was only a queer sort of noise I heard."

Wharton was already up. "Come along, Mr. Sandyman, and show us."

In a minute the three were on the road before the school. Sandyman began his exhibition at the main gate, and then went a yard or two beyond it towards the girls' entrance.

"Here's where I'd got to, gentlemen, when I heard a noise. It was as if someone or something was in the bushes over the other side of the wall there. It was a kind of scuffling, and I wondered if it was a dog or something, or somebody working there. It was all in a flash—if you know what I mean. I was busy feeling for them papers what I'd forgotten, and I was half turning round again, but still I heard it. Then when I saw in yesterday's paper the spot marked with a cross where Mr. Twirt was killed, naturally it all come back to me, and I spoke to my son."

"And you didn't think of looking in?"

"Well, no, sir. Why should I? It wasn't as if I'd seen a strange man or anything loitering about the school premises. Besides, I had something else on my mind, as I told you."

"And what were you wearing at the time in the way of shoes?" asked Travers. "The ones you have on now?"

"As a matter of fact, I was, sir." He thought for a moment. "I see what you're getting at, sir. You meant, was they rubber soles? Well, I always wear rubber soles. My feet get bad with all the standing I have to do, and rubber soles seem to ease them."

"I expect they do," said Wharton sympathetically. "And now we're going to ask you to do something for us. We'd like to know the exact moment when you heard this noise, and as we can't get at it by timing you all the way from the shop, we'll do the job the other way—by working backwards from four o'clock. Will you start at the boys' entrance, then, and do just what you did on Wednesday afternoon, and we'll time you."

Perhaps it was because the road was so secluded that Sandyman did his job so well. There were no windows to overlook him, and there was no need to be self-conscious. Moreover, he was doing something that might put him well in with the police. Twice he did his little performance.

"Well," said Wharton, "how long do you think it was from the time you first passed the boys' entrance to the time you spoke to Flint?"

"Two or three minutes, perhaps," suggested Sandyman.

"One minute and a half," said Wharton. "Which shows how we can be deceived about the passage of time. And now think on from there— and think as if it meant liberty or jail. How long did that talk last between you and Flint?"

"Him?" The grocer's face darkened. "Not long, I wasn't. Not a minute. A half, more likely."

"And after that?"

"Well, after that I walked at my usual pace up to the Head's room. And just as I got there, the bell went for four o'clock."

"But it needn't have been right."

"You'll pardon me, gentlemen," said Sandyman, "but it *was* right. It was right by my watch, and I boast that that's always right."

That was all that was needed from Sandyman. Wharton gave him an affectionate shake of the hand, and sent him thus on his way rejoicing. And as soon as he had gone, he turned to Travers.

"Where'd Flint be? In his cottage?"

He happened to be coming towards the school as they went round the girls' way. Wharton seized him at once and tried to work out the duration of his conversation with Sandyman at the boys' gate that Wednesday afternoon. Ten minutes' argument left Flint still of the mind that it had taken a good two minutes.

"One minute's ample," said Wharton to Travers as they made their way towards the front door again. "He simply daren't have been seen in conversation as long as two minutes. They'd have spoken quickly and nervously." He stopped, then went on again. "We'll wait till we get upstairs and then work the times of everything out."

They mounted the porch steps, and Wharton was just about to enter the door, when his eyes turned towards the girls' entrance. Again he stopped— and his eyes bulged. Then he threw his arms dramatically upwards.

"My God! What a couple of fools we are! Don't you remember? Down there, look! Where I found that cigarette!"

Then Travers stared too.

Wharton hauled him by the arm back to the main gate. "Now listen to me as I talk, and watch what I do. I'm Twirt, entering this gate at 3.53 on the afternoon of Wednesday last. Here I go. I'm smoking a cigarette, and I smoke it to the very last second. Up the steps we go, then, and then my eye catches something which always displeases me. There's that damn car of Godman's, cluttering up the front again. And, look! it's shaking! I can hear the engine! Why, he must have slipped down during school hours and started it. My God! I'll catch the blighter out. I'll go down here behind these shrubs by the porch and wait for him in case he comes down again. Flint told me he did it, and now I've got the chance of a lifetime. But I must put out the cigarette in case he smells it or sees the smoke. But suppose he slips down the main stairs instead of by the girls' stairs as Flint said! He'd see me here! And Sandyman's coming in a minute or two, and Flint and that policeman. They'll be bound to see me as they come up the steps there. . . . But I remember. Vincent went into that other shrubbery with the hammer and the stake for the tree. That's where I'll hide. I can catch Godman just as well from there, and better, for if I happen to be seen, or if I have to tell Godman where I was, I shall have a perfectly good excuse for being there. I can say I went to see the best way to fasten up that tree!"

So saying, Wharton sprang round the end of the small shrubbery and made for the main gate. There he stopped. There was no need to carry the test further.

"Marvellous, George!" said Travers. "You're dead, plumb right. And don't you realize the implications?" Then his eyes bulged at the implications which he himself only then saw. He clutched Wharton's arm. "George, do you realize that when Twirt backed into this shrubbery to watch Godman, in all probability the man who murdered him was in there already!"

Wharton raised his hands again. "Don't set me thinking too far ahead. Let's hang on to what we've got. We'll go upstairs and work things out in peace."

So upstairs they went. But there was no need to argue about the times. They fitted too perfectly.

Twirt enters main gate 3.52
Twirt decides to watch for Godman 3.53
Twirt changes position to other shrubbery 3.54
Sandyman hears murderer 3.57
Sandyman and Flint seen by Godman 3.58
Sandyman leaves Flint 3.59
Bell goes 4.00

"In other words," said Wharton, "we've got the time of Twirt's murder as from 3.54 to 3.57. What's more, we know the murderer was in the shrubbery at 3.57, when Sandyman heard him."

"All the times being subject, of course, to at least half a minute's error either way."

"Exactly," said Wharton. "And now let's see where it's got us. Castle's definitely let out—if ever he was in, which he wasn't. Godman's got an alibi. Everything we're now doing rests on Sandyman's story, and so we've got to believe it. Therefore

Sandyman is out. All that's left is Flint—and Mela Ram. Flint hasn't an alibi. He could have been in the bushes when Sandyman heard the noise, and still have had time to nip out again and round by the boys' entrance in time to catch sight of Sandyman."

"Why should it necessarily be a man who wielded the hammer?" asked Travers quietly.

Wharton stared. "What could a woman have been doing in the shrubbery?" He smiled. "And what woman could have used the hammer?"

"Elsie Holl," said Travers. "She's a strapping wench. She had motive and everything—and no alibi for that particular time."

Wharton clicked his tongue. "Yes, but how the devil could she have got in the shrubbery?"

"Jealousy," said Travers. "She was watching Godman's car. She wondered where he was going, and who was going with him. It was into Elsie Holl that Twirt backed when he went into that shrubbery. No wonder she grabbed the hammer and struck!"

Wharton thought for a moment—then shook his head. "No. I'm not having it. It's against every conception. She doesn't fit."

And then the telephone bell cut in. Wharton leaned forward with elbows on the desk.

"Yes, Superintendent Wharton speaking. . . . Who! . . . I see. *Mr. Mela Ram!*"

A quick glance at Travers, and he was staring at the telephone again.

"You did, did you? . . . And may I ask just why? . . . I say, may I ask why? . . . Hallo! Hallo! . . . Are you there?"

But the line was dead. Mela Ram had gone.

In a second Wharton was getting Exchange and asking frantically for the supervisor; then patiently breathing out who he was, pleading that the tracing of the call was life and death. The words *Woodgate Hill Murder* no doubt helped, for inside three minutes he was hanging up again.

"Call-box at Piccadilly Circus," he told Travers— then grabbed the receiver again. It was the Yard he was calling. "Anybody asking you for me?"

"Funny you should say that, sir," said the voice, "but we've been trying to get you, and the line was engaged. Someone who reckoned he was the real Mela Ram called us up and wanted you. He refused to give us anything, so we told him where he could get you. We're tracing the number now."

"Don't bother," said Wharton, and hung up.

Then he sat frowning at the desk. He frowned, indeed, so prodigiously that Travers said no word, for fear of spoiling his train of thought. Then he gave that smile which always made Travers think of a Roman lion who has missed his grab at a particularly juicy Christian.

"Mela Ram, eh? Said he killed Twirt with the hammer. When I asked why, he hung up."

"It was the genuine article, George?"

"Yes," said Wharton. "All Lombard Street to a pinch of dung. I knew his voice. The funny little hisses. It was him all right."

He shook his head. When he looked up again, Travers was in the act of polishing his glasses.

"Well, George, that settles it. I was almost sure before—but now I know."

"Oh?" said Wharton. "Know what?"

"That—as such—Mela Ram has no existence. Mela Ram and Furrow are the same person!"

"Mela Ram and Furrow?"

He stared for a moment, then made a grab for his hat.

CHAPTER XII
WHARTON IS DETERMINED

"THIS LOOKS LIKE the road," said Travers. "Where'd you like the car left?"

"I'm not going," said Wharton. "You do the talking. Nobody'd take you for the police."

So Travers knocked at the door of Furrow's rooms. A decent-looking body opened it.

"Mr. Furrow in?"

"He isn't," she said. "Are you a friend of his?"

"Oh, yes," said Travers brightly, and the suspicion went.

"He's had a holiday from school," she told him. "On account of that murder, you know. I don't expect him back till lunch to-morrow."

"Will he go straight from Liverpool Street to the school?"

"Oh, yes," she said. "There's a train from Chelmsford that just gives him time."

Travers reported back to Wharton. In a minute the car was whipped round and they were tearing towards Liverpool Street. Travers thought he could catch the five o'clock train, which Wharton had remembered.

It was still ten minutes to the hour when they drew in at the station. There was a policeman handy, to whom Wharton gave instructions, and the two doubled across the bridge to the booking-office. But no sooner were they through the barrier than Wharton grabbed Travers's arm, with, "Hop in here, quick!"

It was the luggage van of the Chelmsford train into which they bolted, and the porters were still stowing away luggage.

"Hi! what do you reckon you're doing?" asked the foreman sarcastically.

"Fetch the guard," Wharton told him, taking a peep through the crack of the door.

But the guard had already observed the unlawful entry. Wharton showed him his credentials and explained. The guard unhooked the grille and led the way to a first-class compartment. Inside two minutes an "Engaged" label was being pasted on the window.

"Furrow was on the platform?" asked Travers.

"That's right," said Wharton. "He came up to town to do that telephoning, and now he's going back. Draw that curtain in case he saunters by."

Soon the train got under way. The last of the tunnels was passed and Travers became errand-boy as usual. Half-way along the train he spotted Furrow in an empty third-class compartment. But even Travers's guilelessness could not allay the quick suspicion that came to the schoolmaster's mind.

"Don't sit here alone," Travers told him heartily. "Come along to my carriage and have a chat."

It was an invitation impossible to refuse. Furrow went first along the swaying corridor till they reached the door. He glanced back as if surprised to find the compartment with another occupant. But he entered, and behind him Travers snapped the door to and took a seat by it. The newspaper fell from the face of that other occupant and there was George Wharton, his amiable old eyes beaming with pleasure at the sight of Furrow. He grinned hugely. He laid aside the paper and rose with outstretched hand.

"Well, well, well! If this isn't a surprise. My old friend—the elusive Mela Ram!"

Furrow dropped back in the seat. The staring look became one of fear and caution. He licked his lips.

"I don't know what you mean."

"Of course you don't," said Wharton. "But what's a little joke among friends?" His tone changed to one of courteous inquiry. "What was town like? Plenty of people in Piccadilly Circus?"

Furrow shot another look at him. Then he looked at Travers, who was polishing vigorously the horn-rims and holding them against the light.

"All right," said Furrow, and there was a faint touch of the rebellious in his tone, "I'll tell you. I suppose that's what you got me in here for."

Wharton ignored him. At all costs he always had to play a comedy out.

"Do you think we'd better stop the train, Mr. Travers, and ask Mr. Furrow to step along with us to Scotland Yard and make a statement there?"

"I don't know," said Travers reflectively. "I expect Mr. Furrow will come clean—as they say in the best crime circles."

"Perhaps he will," said Wharton. "Perhaps he'll make sure he leaves nothing out."

"At least I haven't got anything to be ashamed of," broke in Furrow. "You can't do anything to a man for a joke." The very words seemed to give an ease of mind. He smiled, but it was to Travers he spoke. "How'd you get on to me?"

Travers blushed at the honour. "Well, in all sorts of ways. But, you see, you had remarkably small feet."

"Small feet?" He was puzzled.

Then Wharton came in with his usual heavy irony. "Take your time, young man. We're in no hurry. I dare say the train will wait for us at Chelmsford."

"All right then," said Furrow, "and if you want me to tell you the lot, I'll begin with Charles Tennant. He and I thought it all out. Mr. Twirt—the headmaster, you know—"

"Call him just what you like," said Wharton affably.

That one friendly touch set Furrow at his ease. His manner expanded and his tale was embellished with little smiles and gestures. Sometimes he invited the company to laugh with him. The stern, stage-managed inquiry became a joyous chat.

"You know all about him, I see! Well, he was always having foreigners and people at that damn school. You ought to have seen him strutting about with the poor innocents, and showing off as if he was the President of the Board of Education—the humbugging bastard! It used to make everybody sick. Then I was leaving and I didn't give a damn for him, and Charles didn't either, and so we thought the whole show out. When I was at King's I knew a bloke called Mela Ram—"

"A tall, hop-pole of a chap?"

"That's the one," said Furrow. "Why? Do you know him?"

Wharton frowned. "Young man, if you knew how much we know, you'd be less comfortable than you are at this moment."

But it would have taken more than that to put Furrow out of his stride.

"Well, sir, I don't know about that. But I was telling you about Mela Ram. I sort of used his name, and we got the clothes and cheek-pads and spectacles and things, and had a rehearsal at Charles's house. Then I got hold of Twirt on the phone and he jumped to it. I took that fake address and he sent me a note that I was to come along for a preliminary interview. That's how it all was."

"That's how some of it is," said Wharton dryly. "Carry on, Mr. Furrow."

"Well," said Furrow, "it was arranged for a Wednesday because of the baths. Whereas I could get away from there, I couldn't have got away from the school. So at lunch I left my bag in the railway cloak-room. Then I had a headache at the baths, got away, picked up my bag and sprinted for a quiet little lavatory. You know the kind—no attendants, and put in your own penny. That's where I did my changing—two hundred yards away from the school. It was a bit of a rush, but I just got to the gate when the four o'clock bell went."

"And what were you going to get out of it all?" asked Travers.

"The most gorgeous exposure of Twirt," said Furrow. "There's one local paper that's rumbled him pretty well. I'd have exposed the whole thing in that. Showed up his laziness and damn carelessness, and made a general fool of him. He'd have been the laughing-stock of the district."

"I see," said Wharton. "And when you bolted from the common room you went to the groundsman's shed."

"You've got it," said Furrow. "I had my own key—as cricket master—so I had a clean-up in peace with Vincent's water and towel. Then I faked a burglary and slipped out the back way after I'd changed my clothes again."

Wharton pursed his lips beneath the huge moustache, cleared his throat and became more official.

"You didn't see a sign of Mr. Twirt?"

Furrow shook his head.

"You didn't see a sign of Flint?"

"No," said Furrow. "Why should I?"

"Never mind why," Wharton told him severely. "And now we've had our little joke, let's come down to earth. You've owned up to a burglarious entry and damaging property. You could be put under arrest this very minute; for that, and hindering the course of the law."

"How?"

"By ringing us up and making a false confession of murder. Why did you do that?"

"If I told you, you wouldn't believe me."

Wharton looked horrified. "My dear young man! You've got it wrong. Tell us lies and we certainly shan't believe you. But the truth's different. Truth and law go hand in hand."

"I'll own up then," said Furrow. "I did it to put you off the scent. I don't know who killed Twirt, but I guess he did it for a very good reason. The man was a public danger." He shook his head fiercely. "You don't know what he was like. He'd driven more than one of us to the edge of a breakdown. He was killing everybody—their nerve, their energy, their moral courage and everything. Look at me. Why have I been driven from teaching? He's ruined my life for all I know."

"Grant all that," said Wharton quietly, "and still you haven't quite answered the question."

"I wanted the staff left alone," said Furrow. "Whoever killed him did a public service. He'll have his punishment, whether he deserves it or not, without the law getting hold of him."

Wharton leaned forward. "Very fine—and chivalrous. But tell me. Would you have killed him yourself?"

"I?" He moistened his lips. "I don't know. I might. If there'd been a stand-up fight and he'd had a chance."

"But you didn't kill him?"

The eyes were boring relentlessly. But there was a hurt in Furrow's eyes as he shook his head.

"No. I didn't kill him. If every word I've told you isn't true, you can take me away and do what you like with me. Till I got to the school on the Friday morning I hadn't any idea Twirt was dead. I know it looks suspicious the way I had to tell lies, but Tennant was dead, and he was the only one who could have backed me up. And about the wedding, you see, don't you, that I had to be away from school on the Thursday once I'd arranged it so in order to be present as Mela Ram. It was Charles's death that put me off—not because I had any idea Twirt was dead."

"Well, then, we'll switch to Tennant. Any ideas who poisoned him?"

Furrow shook his head. "I didn't know what to do when I got to the school that afternoon and found he was dead. It was terrible."

Wharton leaned forward again. "You know as well as I do that it wasn't Tennant who should have been poisoned. It was Twirt. Now tell us. Who was trying to poison Twirt?"

"Who?" His eyes narrowed. "Miss Gedge. It's the sort of underhand trick she'd do." His face lighted. "Did you know she peeped through her keyhole? She can see everything that goes on round the Head's door. Charles and I suspected her of that and one day he caught her out. Someone was waiting outside the Head's door and she was in her room, so Charles slipped up quickly, gave a tap at her door and had the door open like lightning. It caught her full in the knees!" He smiled. "My God! we did laugh. That's why she had her knife in him."

"Pardon me," said Wharton, "but we're not making out a case for Miss Gedge killing Tennant."

"I know. I'm sure she didn't do that. She didn't know Charles often took the tea-tray." He in his turn leaned forward. "Did you ever know anybody who hated anybody else and managed to disguise it? I tell you, Miss Gedge hated Twirt like blazes. He wouldn't increase her authority. She wanted to be a kind of co-Head, and he wasn't having any. When she thought she could do it safely, she used to say some damnable things behind his back."

"Any other reason why she should be your choice?"

"Yes," said Furrow. "Look at the chances she had. She could peep through her keyhole and watch Flint put down the tray. Then she could slip out and drop in the poison and tap at the door at the same time. If the Head was out—well and good. If he was in, she could come on one of her usual visits. If the Head drank the tea, she would have blamed it on Flint or someone. If he tasted it and stopped, then he could never have blamed it on her. He was such an egomaniac that he thought all his staff admired him and took him for one of God's marvels. He'd probably have blamed that swine Flint too."

The train was drawing near Chelmsford. Wharton assumed his magisterial tone and uttered various warnings. Furrow was to wear his usual face next morning, and keep his mouth shut. On his conduct would depend the attitude of the law. And when Wharton put a last question—or an old one more fully—then

Furrow discarded with absolute horror the suggestion that there had been some hold that Tennant had held over Twirt. The solution of Tennant's easy time was that he had stood up to Twirt, who—like all cowards—had avoided conflict and taken the easier way. Also Tennant himself, for all the charm of his personality, was a dangerous one to tackle, and had more than one friend in high places.

Wharton and Travers waited on Chelmsford platform for the return train which was due in a quarter of an hour. Never had the General shown such self-control. He was furious with young Furrow and yet he was helpless. The law demanded the production of a murderer. He could never outrage its sense of proportion by providing it merely with a practical joker.

But in that unfamiliar scene, the General's wits began to work in an unusual way.

"I've been thinking," he said to Travers. "Why shouldn't there have been one of the more senior scholars who had a grudge against Twirt? Those boys and girls seem to be allowed to wander about the school as they like, on the plea of being excused."

"They couldn't have had the executive ability to carry out that poisoning," said Travers.

"Why not?" challenged Wharton. "They all do chemistry, don't they? And what about a chap like that senior prefect? What was he going to be?"

"A doctor, I believe," said Travers. "He'd just sat for his intermediate examination, and Castle said he'd pass easily."

"There you are then," said Wharton. "He had the executive ability, didn't he? For all we know, in a year or two's time he may be cutting us up and taking our livers out." He growled something. "I ought to begin at the other end. To-morrow I ought to find out every pupil who was out of the room between 3.15 and 3.20."

"Oh, no you oughtn't," smiled Travers. "You've had the word of the staff. And if you tried cross-examining children, the humane societies would raise such a storm that you'd never weather it."

Wharton said no more till he had taken his seat; then he nodded determinedly. "Well, nobody's going to stop me now. First thing in the morning I'm having Daisy Quick, and then Elsie Holl, on the carpet." He got out his note-book. "I was rather impressed with what young Furrow said about the Gedge woman. Yet I don't know. Castle said she'd stand to gain little by Twirt's death. I think I'll leave her for a bit and see what turns up. There's Mrs. Flint too. I haven't forgotten her though I've said nothing. She could have done it, easy as pie. She could have helped herself to the poison, and have had it mixed ready when her husband took the tray."

"She hadn't the brains," said Travers.

"Don't I know that?" Wharton almost shouted. "Isn't that why I've left her alone? Still, something's got to be done. Haven't you and I exceeded our strict duty in this case already, and what have we got? Damn-all!"

"Then concentrate on the other murder for a bit," Travers told him consolingly. "We've done pretty well there."

"How have we?" said Wharton. "We've got rid of Godman, and Mela Ram, and Sandyman. But what's left?"

"Flint is left."

"Very well then," said Wharton. "What do you propose? Keep him held on that other charge and hope to break his spirits? And what if he didn't do it after all?"

"Well, I'll suggest something else," said Travers, but most apologetically. "There's something I'd like to put up to you. I thought of it last night in bed. It's that we write down every mysterious occurrence in the case and try to find the logical connections."

Contempt was in Wharton's eye. He thought for a moment, but ideas of his own refused to come. The train was rushing on and time was getting short.

"Very well," he said. "You make your list and I'll make mine. Then we'll pool them."

Travers's ideas were all ready for he had them down in five minutes. Wharton took longer. But the completed symposium was as follows:

(*a*) Was there a hold which Tennant had over Twirt, or was it some trick of personality?

(*b*) Why was Castle so averse from the idea of being headmaster of Woodgate Hill County School?

(*c*) Exactly what did John Tennant know?

(*d*) What was the secret of the catalogue?

(*e*) Why, in the Running Stag, did Castle virtually refuse to take the catalogue from his bag?

"There is one sort of connecting link already," said Travers.

"Of course there is," said Wharton. "The catalogue itself's a link."

"Very well," Travers told him, with a kind of challenging defiance. "Tonight I don't stir from my chair until I've licked some sort of sense into those questions. And if you're not going over it again at the Yard, George, send round that cursed catalogue to my rooms. I'll have one more go at it, even if it unhinges me."

"Have it and be damned to it," said Wharton. "It's had me dizzy already."

The train was beginning to slow over the points at Liverpool Street, and he got to his feet for a leg-stretcher.

"Look through the book and good luck to you. But don't forget what I said. To-morrow morning Daisy Quick goes on the carpet—and no more sentimental shilly-shallying."

CHAPTER XIII
WHO KILLED TENNANT?

GEORGE WHARTON spent that night at home. By the time he had finished his meal and settled to thinking, it was well past nine, and as he consulted that list of questions, he told himself that he might as well be consulting an astrologer.

But there was one of those questions to which he found an immediately satisfying answer. It had been one of Travers's ideas, putting down as a mystery why Castle should not accept the head-ship of the school if offered it. And why, thought Wharton, should he wish to go on working in a place which had been nothing but a jail, and with a remarkably unpleasant head-warder?

And there Wharton's discoveries came to an end. Ten minutes more at the questions and he put them aside. There were notes on the day's doings to be written up, and when that was over he began a reading of those earlier notes he had made. And almost at once a wholly new mystery caught his eye.

Daisy Quick.—"They looked as if they'd been laughing at something, and the Head said to me, was there anything to sign? *I was surprised at that*, because he knew there wasn't. He was only showing off in front of Mr. Tennant."

So Daisy Quick had been surprised. And why should Twirt wish to show off in front of a man who knew him as well as he knew himself? But at the moment Wharton was in no mood for new mysteries. His brain was tired after five days of concentrated thought, and all that followed him to bed was a new mental restlessness.

But in the morning the old brain awoke alertly. At half-past seven, as Wharton swallowed the last of his tea, and began a meticulous folding of the napkin, that brain produced a definite logic out of the night's restlessness. Wharton went over to the phone, looked up Quick's private number, and asked for Daisy.

"And how are you?" he said. "Feeling fit and fine again? . . . That's right. . . . Well now, there's a question I want to ask you. Wasn't there some talk about a quarrel between Miss Gedge and Charles Tennant? . . . Yes, I know there *was* one. The point is, was it a desperate one? What I might call a notorious one? . . . Oh, it was! . . . Convulsed the whole school, did it? . . . And quite recently? . . . Capital! . . . Well, I'll be along with you shortly. Don't overwork. We've got to look after people like you, you know."

For a minute or two Wharton stood in thought. Then he became so engrossed that in another two minutes he found himself back in the dining-room. So startlingly were things fitting in, that he was almost afraid to think. Then came the final fitting—*that ink on a chair in Twirt's room, and the stains on the frock of Miss Gedge.*

Then Wharton turned and made for the telephone again. The number he called was that of Ludovic Travers.

It was half-past eight when Ludovic Travers settled down to thought on that Monday night. Half an hour's concentration and he was no nearer than before to a connecting link that should join the five problems he and Wharton had set down on paper.

So he turned once more to the catalogue. Over six hundred pages, there were; with illustrations and items that ranged from glass beakers at threepence a time, to intricate machinery and elaborate apparatus at scores of pounds—and in some cases, hundreds. And on each page Travers used a powerful glass, and he held the page to the heat of the electric fire in case there might be secret writing.

Half-past ten brought nothing—except the entry of his man Palmer. Palmer had valeted the colonel, his father. He had probably pushed the pram in which the infant Ludovic made his first appearance in public. He was of patriarchal appearance, and not unlike a bishop; and indeed, there were bishops who had in their noddles less knowledge of humanity than had Palmer.

"So you're still at that book, sir?" He spoke reprovingly.

"No, I'm not," said Travers, and laid it aside. "I'm going to turn in. I've reached years of sufficient discretion to know just when I'm beaten."

"And the morning, sir?"

"Seven," said Travers. "And the car at about half-past." He was about to add a good night when an idea came. "You've read up about this case, haven't you?"

Palmer bowed slightly. "I know as much, sir, as the public are allowed to know."

Travers smiled. "Well, pour me out the tiniest night-cap, and one for yourself, and draw up a chair. I'll tell you a few things the public don't know. And when you know them—which'll be just about as much as I know myself—I'd like you to take this book and see if you can make more sense out of it than I can."

So at seven o'clock on the Tuesday morning, Travers was duly roused. The sun shone, and the world seemed an optimistic place. Travers hummed to himself as he dressed, and he gave Palmer a quizzical look when the breakfast came in.

"Well, have any luck with that book?"

"I'm afraid not, sir," said Palmer. "I may have been helpful to you and Mr. Wharton on some occasions in the past, sir, but this time I'm quite at a loss, sir."

Travers shrugged his shoulders. "Well, we're all in the same boat. And you didn't see anything at all that struck you as being of interest?"

"I wouldn't go so far as that, sir. I was interested in a lot of things in it, sir."

"Such as what?"

"Well, sir, I don't know that they'd interest you—if you'll pardon me saying so. You see, sir, you've never been married, or engaged to be married."

"You should know," Travers told him blithely. "But why drag in matrimony?"

"Well, sir, I was thinking about my nephew; the one who got married last autumn, sir—if you remember. He and his wife had some argument. . ."

And no sooner did Travers know what that argument was, and why Palmer had remembered it from a sight of the book, than he got to his feet like a man who thinks desperately hard. He, too, saw a new coherence—*John Tennant, and most amusing of all, that funny little schoolmaster, Grey, blinking out that he might have been the mystery that changed two men.*

"Get me Mr. Wharton—at his private address." Palmer moved across to the phone, but its bell went first. He took off the receiver, listened, and spoke.

"It's Mr. Wharton himself, sir."

Travers's face was beaming as he took the receiver. When Wharton had finished the morning's inquiries or trivialities, it would be great to give him a shock.

"Morning, George. How are you?"

"Fine," said Wharton. "And I've some news for you. *I know who poisoned Charles Tennant.*"

Travers felt like a man who might hold in his hand a diamond of incalculable worth. When Wharton made that announcement, it was as if he had opened his fingers for another fond look, only to find that diamond gone—dissolved in air.

"And who did it?"

"Twirt did," said Wharton.

In a split second Travers was not grudging Wharton his discovery. In a way he was glad. And in his own palm a new diamond had appeared; not so superb as the one that Wharton had taken, but good enough.

"Good for you, George! And you'd better come here and let me drive you to Woodgate Hill, hadn't you? . . . That's right. Oh, by the way, I happen to have discovered something too. I suppose you don't know just why Twirt killed him?"

"Because Tennant had a hold over him."

"Yes, but what hold?"

"I don't know—yet." Travers heard the slight chuckle. "Do you?"

"Yes," said Travers, "I think I do. But I'm not telling you till we're both dead sure."

There was little traffic about at that hour of the morning, and Travers could listen to George Wharton and watch the road too. The General seemed to have his arguments in an order unassailably logical.

"Can we assume that Twirt knew Tennant was in the habit of taking away that tea-tray?"

"I think it's a certainty that he knew it," said Travers. "If a boy brought the tray back to the kitchen, he'd be almost sure to say, 'Mr. Tennant sent me here with this.' That'd set Flint and his wife thinking. Then everything's easy."

"I agree," said Wharton. "And do you also think Flint overheard Godman's remarks about the poison that day when it was first mooted in the common room, and that Flint mentioned it to Twirt?"

"There I'll say I think it's more than likely."

"Very well, then," said Wharton. "I'll say myself it's a certainty. If not, how did Twirt get the idea in his head?" He nodded to himself. "But that's not the snag. What's puzzling me is this. If Tennant had a headmastership, then he was going out of that school. If Twirt didn't kill him all the four years he was in it, why should he want to do so when he was at last going out of it?"

"Castle may throw some light on that," suggested Travers.

"Perhaps he may," said Wharton. "However, let's get on. Twirt decided he had to kill Tennant, and he saw at last a way to do it without bringing the least suspicion on himself. As a matter of fact, he could get Flint to bring evidence against Godman. And now I'll tell you some other peculiar way that cunning mind of Twirt's worked. I honestly believe now that he was going to expose Flint, and be in a position to have the man under his thumb. He wanted to be able to force Flint to say just what he wanted him to say. Am I right?"

"You are," said Travers, and dodged the car round on the blind side of a stationary tram.

"Very well, then," went on Wharton. "Twirt ran no risk. But he also had a second string to his bow. Miss Gedge had had a violent row with Tennant. Daisy Quick—a smart girl that!—tells me it shook even that school from stem to stem. So Twirt had Miss Gedge in one day and got her to sit on a chair where he'd put some ink. Then he called attention to the stains, and suggested she should go to young Grey and get some oxalic acid. After that, she would be first favourite for poisoning Tennant.

"All Twirt had to do then was to make his preparations. I'd say he chose a Wednesday because it gave him the chance to get out and leave the tray. He waited just long enough for Flint to bring it, pretended he was out, then doctored the sugar and actually went out, after having impressed on Tennant—in the presence of Daisy Quick—the fact that he *was* going out. He was a science man, you remember, and he'd know all about everything. And something else I've just thought of that clinches things. Didn't Castle say he was never in time for appointments?"

"He did."

"And yet he was in good time for this one!" said Wharton triumphantly. "He expected to find Tennant dead. And he'd have in the school two excellent people. One of the governors whom he also would have absolutely under his thumb, and a policeman whom he could tell just whatever he liked. All the vital, first evidence he'd have put in the constable's mouth."

"You're right," said Travers. "And all those people would have been a kind of fortifying audience. Instead of Twirt having to undergo a private questioning where his slips might be noticed, he'd be merely one of a crowd."

Wharton chuckled. "Never knew things so fit in. And now what about your own discovery? What's the secret of that book?"

"I don't know," said Travers frankly. "But I'll know one way or the other, George, before this morning's gone. It just depends on one or two things. What's happened, for instance, to the chemistry masters who were at the school before the arrival of Grey."

"You look into that," said Wharton, "and I'll have a quiet word with Castle, and tell him what we think, and find out that other matter we're puzzled over."

So when the school was reached, Wharton closeted himself with Castle in his room while Travers saw Daisy Quick. The sympathy he felt for her that morning she would never know. But for a stroke of amazing luck, Wharton would have been having her on the carpet, and the rest of her young life might have been embittered.

"I shall have to get the Staff Register," she told him. "You see, there were two changes before Mr. Grey came. One man was here a year and he couldn't stand it, and got another job."

But as soon as she had worked things out, Travers was alarmed. An old hand named Lustiford had been in the school up to five years previously. He had been followed by another man who, after a year, had got a job at Liverpool.

"Well," said Travers, "if the worst comes to the worst, I may be hurtling towards Liverpool some time to-day—though I can't tell you why. But where's that man Lustiford now?"

She showed him the entry—at Roybury Grammar School, which was a mere matter of thirty miles away. Travers thanked her, and went in search of Wharton. The General was already waiting on the landing. Travers took his arm and led him away down the stairs.

"A little trip to Roybury, George, if you can spare the time. Thirty miles."

"That means an hour," said Wharton.

"Not if I drive," Travers told him. "And what did Castle say about Twirt?"

Wharton lowered his voice. "He said that now perhaps we shouldn't worry our heads over who killed him, seeing that whoever used the hammer, spared the country the expenses of a trial and a hanging."

Travers smiled. "He's not far wrong, George. And about that other matter?"

"I don't see it very well myself," said Wharton, "but Castle seemed pretty sure. Twirt was making a bid for high honours in the council of metropolitan headmasters. He was evidently proposing to let the school look after itself for a bit, and devote his attentions to thrusting himself forward as President and so on. That'd have been personal publicity—and Castle says that with his gift of the gab, he'd probably have done it. But Tennant would stand in the way there. He'd be a headmaster himself. He'd put a spoke in Twirt's wheel. Castle didn't tell me this, but I shouldn't be surprised if Tennant told him that when he left the school he was going to hand over that secret to some other competent user of it. And that's why it was essential for Twirt to kill him before he left the school."

At half-past nine the car was entering the grounds of Roybury Grammar School. Mr. Lustiford was senior master, and there was no difficulty about seeing him, though he opened his eyes at the mention of strict confidence and police and Woodgate Hill. Wharton and Travers were lucky, he said. Roybury was also breaking up that morning, and a few hours later he was taking the train for a summer holiday in Ireland.

"I can't say I was sorry to hear about Twirt," he admitted. "If ever there was a poisonous swine, it was he. Between ourselves, I think he was damn lucky not to have been cracked on the skull years ago. I was sorry about Charles Tennant, though He was one of the best." He shook his head with a reminiscent sadness. "I haven't seen him for quite a long time. When was it now? About a year or so after I came here. He called up one Saturday morning, and we had a chat about old times."

Then somehow Travers knew his own hunch was right. "He didn't by any chance mention the chemical laboratory, did he? Or anything that was in it?"

"The chemical laboratory?" He thought for a moment, then his face altered queerly. "Now I come to think of it, he did!"

Travers took the attaché-case from Wharton's hand. He opened that monstrous chemical catalogue at a certain page and pointed at a certain object.

"Did he by any chance mention anything like that?"

"He did," said Lustiford. "That's the only thing to do with my sort of job that he did talk about!"

A quarter of an hour later Wharton came out of Roybury post office where he had been telephoning.

"I've fixed it up for an hour's time," he said. "Mr. Matthew Pullinger said he'd have everything ready for us, and there's a side door in Windbow Street where you can park the car. I warned him particularly against letting John Tennant know what was in the wind."

Travers got the car going clear of the town and Wharton prepared to extract information.

"Now then, young fellow, how'd you get wise to it all?"

"I didn't," Travers told him. "It was Palmer really. I gave him the book as a last resource and asked him to see what he could find. What struck him were the platinum beakers, especially when there was no price quoted on account of the fluctuating values of the metal. You see, his nephew got married not so long ago and the young couple had an argument about wedding-rings—gold or platinum. From that Palmer got on the things like platinum crucibles which might have been bought before the war when platinum was reasonable, and which might now be worth seven pounds ten or more an ounce. Then things began moving in my mind. I saw certain connecting links, George. John Tennant, working in a jeweller's, for instance; and funniest of all, the remark made by our comic friend Grey, that the only thing of importance that had happened at Woodgate Hill County School four years ago was his own arrival—which meant the departure of someone else."

"But why should Woodgate Hill County School have had a valuable crucible? You'd expect them to have merely the ordinary ones of about twenty-five grammes—not the more expensive ones like those others in the catalogue?"

"We shall see," said Travers. "Didn't Lustiford tell us that, as far as he knew, some wealthy old greengrocer or somebody gave an extra endowment when the school was built, with special reference to the laboratories? Besides, we're not expecting Twirt to have sold one that weighed five pounds, like those Lustiford said they had in use at South Kensington. It'll satisfy us if he sold one that weighed thirty ounces. Think of that, George, at over seven quid an ounce!"

"What I'm expecting to find is that he sold one that's illustrated in that damn catalogue," said Wharton. "That'd clear up the whole mystery."

"The fault with you young lads is that you're too impatient," said Travers. "And if you don't want to break both our necks, you'd better acquire the virtue till we get to town."

So Wharton asked no more questions for a bit. He always professed to be terrified of what he called Travers's hell-wagon, and Travers now had to drive really fast. After the business with Pullingers was finished, there might have to be a frantic message to Castle to keep back one or two of the staff.

Wharton was relieved when the car at last drew in at Old Bond Street and crept along it to the cul-de-sac by the side of Pullingers. Matthew Pullinger was waiting for them in his room.

"I think I've traced what you want," he said. "We were offered in the ordinary way of business a platinum crucible with lid, by a client of the name of Wicks. As we knew it to be chemical apparatus, we had to go warily. It might have been stolen, you see; so we asked guardedly for a reference. Wicks made no bones about that. He gave us the name of the headmaster of a London secondary school—"

"A man named Twirt?"

"Yes," said Pullinger, "that was the name. And this man Twirt gave us a full reference about Wicks, who was once a research student, just as he had told us. Well, of course, any sort of reference was good enough for us. We'd fallen in line with the technicalities, so to speak; so we bought the crucible. Here's the actual entry, and the date."

Wharton was reading it first. "Hm! Just over four years ago—and a hundred and thirty pounds!" He looked at Pullinger. "That's a pretty hefty sum to a man like me, but I suppose your firm think it a mere flea-bite."

"Well"—Pullinger smiled modestly—"I don't think it caused us any excitement. Recently during the high price of gold, we've more than once handled thousands a day. Still, I must say this crucible is a good example of shrewd investment for the man who sold it. It cost him originally a considerable deal less than that."

"And I'm sorry to have to tell you that it's going to cost you a good deal more now," said Wharton. "Since it's doubtless melted down, you can't hand it back, but you'll have to hand back its full value."

Pullinger looked at him. "Stolen property after all?"

Wharton explained most confidentially. And as for John Tennant, he was afraid Pullingers would have to promise immunity or his mouth would never be open. Travers threw his weight into the scale and Pullinger came round to their way of thinking —with certain hinted reservations.

"Well, have him in," said Wharton. "As far as I'm concerned— if he's done what we think—he can stew in his own juice. For all that, I bet he wriggles clear somehow—if I'm the judge I think I am."

John Tennant's eyes nearly bolted from his head when he saw the two callers. But when Matthew Pullinger had had a few words with him, he was badly scared.

"Well, you hear that," said Wharton. "Now tell us all you know."

"First of all," broke in Travers, "would you mind clearing up one certain point? I rather gather you knew what was in this catalogue, but would you mind finding the very crucible that Twirt sold—if it's here? The one, in other words, that your dying cousin was so anxious to show to his friend Castle?"

It was there all right. And John Tennant's story was easy enough to follow. By a curious coincidence, it had been himself who had handled the business with Wicks, *alias* Twirt. And he had spotted Twirt at once, since he had seen him at a School Sports which he attended in the company of his cousin Charles. But instead of mentioning his suspicions to the firm, he had spoken to Charles who had begged him to keep quiet. John Tennant, in fact, had placed in his cousin's hands the means to commit blackmail, and he had been well aware of what he was doing. He hated Twirt, if only from his cousin's reports, and he owned up frankly that he had jumped at the chance which had so miraculously presented itself. Charles had thereupon unearthed the whole secret. He could only guess that Twirt was hard pressed for money, but he knew that he had sold a crucible that was school property, and that he had sold it under conditions that could not possibly be explained away. That crucible, even then an object of very considerable value, had been handed over to Twirt by Lustiford when Twirt first came to the school. When Lustiford left, Twirt had no real reason to purloin it. But then, when he was desperately pushed for money, the inoffensive, credulous Grey came to the school. He knew nothing of the crucible—and Twirt was apparently safe.

So much for all that. Wharton gave out prodigious thanks, shook hands with Pullinger, and left John Tennant in his hands. Out in the side road again, Travers blinked a bit in the glare of the sun.

"Where now, George?"

"Somewhere where I can stand you a drink," said Wharton. "Then back to that damn school. And take it steady this time. Go sort of slow and stately —like a Roman triumph."

CHAPTER XIV
WHARTON FINDS HIS MAN

THE CAR was drawing near Woodgate Hill and the school when Wharton suddenly noticed something.

"Looks as if the school has only just broken up."

Travers cast a quick look round. Sauntering homewards were indeed the pupils of Woodgate Hill County School, wearing their unmistakable headgear of yellow with the purple badge. Some were even straggling through the exits as the car drew up outside the main entrance in the shade of a roadside elm. One or two of the staff were seen rushing round corridors with papers, and in the Head's room Castle and Daisy Quick were still busy over clerical work. But Daisy left for a breather when the two came in, and Wharton had a great time unfolding to Castle the secret of the catalogue.

"Now I remember something," said Castle, "and it fits in. Somewhere about four years ago, Twirt called me into his room and brought the talk round to valuable platinum pieces of apparatus and what the schools who had them ought to do with them. I wasn't interested, but I see now what he was trying to do. Before he sold that crucible he wanted to make dead sure that neither I nor any member of the staff knew of the existence of the one he had salted away." Then he shook his head. "All the same, I still find it hard to believe that Charles Tennant was a blackmailer."

Wharton shrugged his shoulders. "Well, I'm afraid you've got to believe it. For instance, John Tennant admitted that on some pretext he induced Twirt, *alias* Wicks, to sign a double receipt for that crucible money. One receipt went to the firm and the other went to Charles Tennant. And that, by the way, was the document John Tennant was after when he went round to Charles's rooms on the night he was poisoned."

"I see your point of view, Mr. Castle," put in Travers, "and I agree with it. I don't think Charles Tennant was a crude blackmailer. A blackmailer bleeds his victim white, and all Charles did was to make his own position less unhappy. All he probably did with that receipt was to throw out a hint. Then he challenged Twirt's position and Twirt refused to join issue. That was what I'd call artistic blackmail. Also Charles did promise to hand the flaming torch on to you when he left the school. Even when he was at his last kick he tried to redeem that promise. He hadn't the receipt on him, but he tried to show you the identical crucible in the catalogue."

"Mr. Castle's point of view is also this," said Wharton. "He wouldn't have done what Tennant did."

Castle's eyes narrowed. "My God, I wouldn't! If I'd known about that crucible business, I'd have had Twirt out of this school, even if it cost me my job. What's more, if things hadn't happened, and this very morning Charles had confided that secret to me, I'd at once have gone to the authorities. There's no such thing as compromise when you're dealing with Twirts."

"H'm!" went Wharton. "I admire your public spirit. However, you're a busy man this morning, Mr. Castle; and speaking of holidays, have you that list of addresses where the staff are spending their time?"

Castle had an extra copy ready for Wharton's own use. The General ran his eye over it.

"Going pretty far afield, aren't they?"

"Some are on their way already," said Castle, with the old cynical smile. "Can you wonder that they scamper from jail when the doors open? As for going far afield, they do as I do—go so far that for seven blissful weeks they can, by no conceivable circumstance, hear the name of Woodgate Hill mentioned."

Wharton grunted. There were still things in that damnable school that were only faintly felt, and their very dimness could give a horror.

"You're bound for Switzerland, I see," remarked Travers. "You like it there?"

"Yes," said Castle. "It's far enough away. I always go to the same spot. People know me, so to speak."

Travers smiled. "And even the chamois eat out of your hand."

Castle smiled too. "Well, not exactly." Then he remembered something. "By the way, here's the telephone number of my neighbour in case you should want me urgently before I go."

There was a tap at the door, and at Castle's holler in came Godman.

"I beg your pardon, Mr. Castle," he said, "but if you'll excuse me I'd like to ask Mr. Wharton if he could spare me a minute or two when he's finished with you."

"Why certainly," said Wharton. "No time like the present."

"I think Mr. Castle's likely to be busy in this room," put in Travers quietly. "Isn't there some other room?"

"The common room's free," said Godman.

"Capital!" said Wharton. "Then we'll leave Mr. Castle alone for a bit. And we'll come back and say an official good-bye before we finally go."

"And present the medals," added Travers.

"Exactly!" chuckled Wharton. "And present the medals."

The three gathered round the empty fireplace of the common room. The air was foul with the smoke of departed pipes, but the place was cool compared with the swelter outdoors.

"Now what's your trouble, Mr. Godman?" began Wharton, with an assumption of heartiness.

"As a matter of fact," said Godman, "I think you'll be very annoyed with me for bothering you, only, it's like this." He smiled sheepishly. "I don't mind owning up that you had me scared badly the last time you had me on the carpet, so I don't want it to happen again. I mean, I want to tell you anything that's on my mind before I go away for my holiday, so that I can go with an absolutely clear conscience, as it were."

"Well, that's a very sound principle," said Wharton. "Normandy, isn't it?"

"That's right," Godman told him, and blushed slightly. "But not till Friday."

"And just what was it you wanted us for?"

"Well, it was like this," said Godman. "That second time I came downstairs to see if my car was ticking over. There's just one little thing I forgot to mention. It didn't strike me as important at the time. All I did think important, if you remember, was that I saw Flint and Sandyman having a chat at the boys' entrance. Perhaps that wasn't any use to you after all."

"Everything's of use," said Wharton helpfully.

"Well, this other thing then. I'll go back, if I may, and describe just what happened. At about two minutes to four I nipped off down the girls' staircase. It wouldn't take me any time to do that, the rate I was going, but just as I got to the outside door that overlooks the playing-fields, I had some sort of a hunch, and I took a quick squint round in case anybody should be there. And lucky I did! There was Flint tearing round the corner as if Old Nick was after him. I shot my head back and didn't go round to the car till he was out of sight."

"I see," said Wharton. "And where was he coming from? His cottage?"

Godman smiled. "How could he? His cottage is in full view of that door, and it's across by the playing-field fence. No. He was coming from the girls' front entrance. Also, if you don't mind my pointing it out, there's the question of where he was going *to*. From what I saw in another few seconds, he was going to the boys' entrance, where he had that chat with Sandyman. If so, why did he go all the way round by the back of the school? If he was at the girls' entrance and wanted to go to the boys', why didn't he go either along the road or along the front? Why did he go three sides of a square to get one? And in such a hurry!"

Wharton's face was extraordinarily serious. "I see ... but just why did you think this information important?"

"Well"—he hesitated slightly—"we do read the papers. And God forbid I should get any man into trouble, and I wouldn't—if he weren't a dirty little swine like Flint. All the same, everybody knows that Twirt was killed in a certain place at a certain time. *If*

Flint did it, then he bolted round the back way when I saw him. Also I might reasonably suppose he was going like hell round to the boys' entrance to try to create some sort of alibi."

"Have you said a word of this to anybody else?"

"Not to a living soul," said Godman earnestly.

"Then don't!" Wharton told him, with almost a glare. "We're going to take you into our confidence to a certain extent. Not a word to a soul, mind you —male or female. Not a look or a sign; do you get that?"

"I get it all right," said Godman, who had stared fascinated at the wagging finger. "I'll do anything you want."

"Capital!" said Wharton, and got to his feet "Do you happen to know where Flint is?"

"Clearing up in the class-rooms," Godman told him.

"Right," said Wharton. "Perhaps you'll find him for us, Mr. Travers. And you go into that inner room, Mr. Godman, and stay quiet. Don't be surprised at anything Flint says or the way we handle him. All you've to do is check his tale against your own."

In a couple of minutes Travers was re-entering the room. Flint looked none too comfortable till the General put him at ease.

"A great morning this, Flint," he said. "And we're sorry to tear you from your work. Still, take a seat. There's something you can do to help us."

"To help you, sir?"

"Yes," said Wharton, and his tone took on the least official chill. "We want you to tell us something that happened. But no omissions, Flint—and no additions. You get that? Otherwise we may have to go back and rake up certain things we'd rather forget. So think hard, Flint; think hard. Think of last Wednesday afternoon. It's three o'clock. You got that? It's three o'clock on the afternoon when Mr. Twirt had his skull bashed in. Start from then, Flint, and tell us everything that you did, or saw or heard."

Flint fidgeted restlessly. "And it ain't going to get me into no trouble, sir?"

"Old scores are wiped out," Wharton told him. "Provided, of course, you tell the whole truth now."

"And it's three o'clock, sir?"

"Three o'clock," repeated Wharton gravely.

"Then it's funny you should say that, sir, because I was in my cottage, and just before three I looked up at the clock and I told myself I'd soon have to be going across to get the Head's tea, and so, after a bit, sir, I did go across and took his tea like I told you, and I come straight back to the cottage again." He hesitated for a moment. There was a furtive look and his eyes went away again. "I don't mind telling you, sir, I'd got that other business on my mind, because something told me he'd rumbled it, and he'd said I was to see him at four o'clock, and I knew he wanted to see Mr. Sandyman too, so I was in a bit of a sweat. Then about twenty past I heard the Head's voice, so I slipped out quick and heard him talking to Vincent about staking that tree—"

"To put it bluntly, you unashamedly heard all you could."

"Well, I did, sir," admitted Flint. "I was all in a sweat, as I told you. Then when they'd gone I went indoors again, and started worrying again, sir. What I wondered was if Sandyman had found out what the Head wanted him for, and if so, why he hadn't sent me word. Then about twenty to, sir, I tidied myself a bit, and when I'd done that I wondered if Sandyman was coming, so I slipped out to the boys' way and met him—like I told you before."

"Oh, dear no!" smiled Wharton. "Not like you told me before. Just what did you do before you went to the boys' entrance?"

Flint forced a smile. "Well, I didn't think you'd want to know that, sir. What I really did was to go to the girls' entrance first— that was nearest, see?—and I looked round the pillar and I did actually see Mr. Sandyman in sight—"

"How far off?"

"About a hundred yards from the school, sir."

"I see. Well, carry on."

"Then it suddenly come over me, sir, that if I slipped along to the boys' entrance I could catch him and have a word with him before he saw the Head, so I slipped round the back way and I caught him— as you know, sir."

Wharton nodded. "You say you slipped round the back way—which means that you hurried. Did you hurry?"

"Yes, sir. I had to catch him."

"I know. That's just what worries me. You wanted desperately to catch him, and yet, instead of simply going from where you were to where he was, you bolted off round the back of the school!"

Flint gave a tentative smile. "Ah, sir, that's what you don't see, not being used to the place as I am. Every minute I expected the Head back. He was due at four o'clock and it was almost four o'clock, as you know, sir. What'd the Head have thought, sir, if he'd seen me deliberately go and meet Mr. Sandyman? That'd have blown the whole gaff, sir. That's why I slipped round the back way to catch him—which I did—"

"Oh, no, you didn't!" said Wharton. "Let me remind you that but for an accident that made him retrace his steps, Mr. Sandyman would have been right inside the school building by the time you got to him."

Flint shook his head doggedly. "Well, I'm telling you the truth, sir. God's my witness!"

"Maybe," said Wharton curtly. "But with me— and in a court of law—it's only your own word. Who saw you looking from the girls' gate? Who passed by on the road?"

"Nobody, sir. Didn't I say I took good care nobody should see me?"

"So you did," said Wharton. The pointing finger went out, and he smiled. "Just look me clean in the eye, Flint, will you? And listen to a great secret, Flint, that mustn't be divulged to a living soul. Do you know what the police think? They think that someone who knew all about that laburnum tree went into that shrubbery with Mr. Twirt, for an examination—shall we say? It was someone the Head knew—someone like yourself, for instance. But that someone smashed the Head's skull with the hammer, holding it with a handkerchief round his hands, and at that very moment he heard something. *And what do you think it was?*"

Flint had been staring like one mesmerized. His eyes almost goggled. "I don't know, sir."

Wharton's voice became a ghostly hush. "He heard footsteps on the road beyond the wall. Sandyman's steps. So the murderer began moving away towards the girls' entrance through the shrubs and he stopped and listened, Flint, and the steps went back the way they came. Then the murderer stepped out of the shrubbery by the girls' entrance, and as he didn't want to be seen there, he bolted round by the back of the school." Wharton leaned back. "*Did you see anything of him, Flint?*"

Flint was moistening his lips. The sweat stood on his forehead. He gasped the words. "No, sir. . . . I didn't see anything, sir."

Wharton grunted. "That's funny. . . . Still, I must take your word." He pursed his lips. "Sandyman heard that murderer in the bushes. Sandyman doesn't like you very much, Flint?"

Flint moistened his lips again. "No, sir. . . . I don't think he does, sir."

Wharton gave a kind of snarl and got to his feet. "All right, Flint. That's the lot for the moment. Tell the truth and shame the devil. A good motto that, Flint—but not a paying one, eh?"

Flint licked his lips again. "I don't know, sir."

Wharton turned his back on him. The door closed on the caretaker and no sooner were his steps heard in the corridor than Wharton called.

"All right, Mr. Godman. Any discrepancies that you can point out?"

Godman shook his head. "To tell the truth, sir, I didn't know half he was talking about. That bit about Sandyman, for instance."

"You will do in time," Wharton told him. "However, that's all then, for the moment. And don't forget what I told you. No word or hint to a soul." He held out his hand. "And many thanks. If we need you again before Friday we can let you know."

A smile and a nod from Travers and out went Godman. Wharton stood for a moment contemplating the closed door. Travers cut in on his ruminations.

"So you've got your man then, George?"

"Yes," said Wharton, and smiled grimly. "It certainly begins to look like it." Then he gave a quick look. "But you didn't say it any too cheerfully?"

"Didn't I?" countered Travers, and fumbled at his glasses. "Perhaps I didn't. Somehow it didn't all seem right. Either Flint's a histrionic genius or else he was telling the truth."

"Truth be damned!" said Wharton. "He had everything worked out to the last second. All his reasons and everything. The truth!" He snorted, then allowed himself to smile. "We've been patient over this side of the case and now we're going to get our turn—and it's coming quickly." He lugged out his notebook. "There'll be all those times to check again. I'll have to get hold of Quick—and I'll have a preliminary word with old Sandyman. Tell you what you can do for me. You get Castle away outside for a talk on the plea you're going back to town, and I'll use the phone. In any case, don't you wait for me, because I may not get away from here for an hour or two. Later on I'll ring you up and say just how things are shaping."

Things worked out with amazing smoothness. Castle was alone in his room, and it was he who suggested a breather and leaving Wharton alone with the phone. He and Travers strolled out to the playing-field. Castle began commenting humorously enough on the ups and downs of fortune. For a brief moment he was still a Head; next term he would again be only a senior master. True, life in that school would be very different, now Twirt had gone.

"How'd you ever come to land in a hole like this?" asked Travers bluntly.

"How?" Castle smiled. "The old story. Father a country parson; large family; no money. Scholarships helped me through public school and Cambridge, then I took the first thing that offered, with the idea of helping out the old man with the rest of the family." He smiled less friendlily. "I thought it'd be for a year or two—then a change. Then the war came, and after it I came

back here. I got into a groove, and then it was too late to change.
. . . That's all."

Travers nodded. "Life's going to treat you less shabbily now.
And you and I are going to see more of each other in the near
future." He was stiffly awkward for a moment, then gave a humorous shrug of the shoulders. "Do you trust me?"

Castle stopped short in his tracks and gave a look at him. "Of
course I do. . . . Why?"

"Never mind why for the moment. You believe me when I tell
you that what we're going to talk about is wholly between ourselves? Not even to be confided to Superintendent Wharton?"

Castle smiled. "Certainly I do, if you tell me so. . . . But why
all the mystery?"

Travers smiled too. "Well, it's this. Mysteries I hate. They
nag at me like a forgotten name. Luckily I have the sort of brain
that can suggest reasons for mysterious results. But there are
two things I don't understand, and you're the one who can give
the answers. Mind then if I ask a couple of questions?"

"Ask away," said Castle.

"The first is this," began Travers, blinking away in the glare
while he polished his glasses. "That Wednesday when you came
down to the common room for some papers which you found
out after all you didn't want, you looked out of the window of
your room—for a breath of fresh air, I imagine—and at the very
time we imagine Twirt was killed, and with the very spot beneath your eyes."

"How do you know it?" cut in Castle.

Travers shook his head. "That's not in the bond. As George
Wharton would say, if you knew half we knew, each particular
hair on your head would stand on end." His face straightened
again. "But you looked out of that window. Possibly you saw
Twirt killed. If so, I know you have your own reasons for keeping your mouth shut. You may sympathize with the man who
did it—a situation with which I'm not entirely out of sympathy
myself." He hooked on his glasses again. "So tell me—between
ourselves. I don't ask what you saw or whom you saw. I ask only
this. *Did you see Twirt killed?*"

Castle's eyes had been on his own and now they turned away. He shook his head.

"As you say, I went to that window for a breath of air. That room was like the Black Hole of Calcutta. And I'll own up to something else. If I knew who killed Twirt I'd keep it to myself—and be damned to the law. But I *didn't* see him killed. I tell you that on my most solemn word of honour. I didn't even know he was dead till I saw him lying there. . . . You believe me?"

Travers smote him on the back. "My dear fellow, of course I believe you! Only, it just shows how one can run to false conclusions or take things for granted. A perfectly natural series of events could have been distorted to have a wrong meaning." His hand went to his glasses again, then fell. "The other question's more personal—and rather foolish. That night in the Running Stag. I wanted to have a peep at that catalogue which you had, you remember, in the bag at your feet. I got the idea you didn't want me to see it. . . . Why?"

Castle smiled. "Just because I actually *didn't* want you to see it. The whole of that afternoon and evening, and the ghastliness of everything, was getting on my nerves, and when you mentioned that book I'd just got to the stage when another word about Twirt or the school would have made me shriek. No wonder you noticed it. Why, as far as I remember, I simply got up and bolted!"

"You did," said Travers. "However, that's settled that." He glanced at his watch. "By Jove! it's getting late. I shall have to be flying. I can't give you a lift anywhere, I suppose?"

"Afraid not," said Castle. They were now at the main entrance and he nodded back at the school. "I'll be here the rest of the day. Oh, before I forget it. Don't think me inquisitive, but I'm interested in young Godman. He didn't want to see you because he'd got himself in any kind of mess?"

Travers smiled. "Lord, no! Something he told us about Flint. That's confidential, by the way."

"Flint? You're not suspecting him over that hammer business?"

Travers forced the smile. "In the words of George Wharton, we suspect everybody. Still"—in the best Whartonian manner he waved an airy hand—"that was nothing. Just a scrap of information. The law collects things, you know. It's an inquisitorial jackdaw."

"Yes," said Castle. "But Flint never wielded that hammer. He hadn't the pluck—or the brain."

"Of course he didn't," said Travers consolingly —and then suddenly stopped dead. "There's an example for you, of taking things for granted. I always thought May was the month for marbles."

Castle followed his look. Not twenty yards from the car, two urchins were engrossed in their game. One had red hair and ragged breeks, and the other looked a prosperous sheep who was being shorn. Travers was moving across to them. He hated a problem unsolved.

"Who's winning?" he asked.

"He is, sir," said the sheep morosely. "He always does."

"But why play marbles this time of year?" persisted Travers. "In my young days boys began to play marbles at the middle of April and went on till the end of May—and here are you two boys playing at the end of July!"

The problem was beyond them, and beyond Castle too. All the boys knew was that they were playing —and that was the end of it. The two men watched for a moment. It was the old game, where each put so many marbles in a ring, and each in turn dropped on them another marble from the height of his eye, all that were knocked out being his. When one boy had missed and the other was about to take his turn, Travers suddenly broke in.

"Mind if I had a go?"

Maybe the red-headed boy sensed a tip, for he didn't mind. Ludovic Travers, not giving a damn who saw him, held the marble to his eye, made a careful alignment, and dropped the projectile. It fell true—but too true.

"You don't want to hit 'em on the top," the redheaded boy told him. "If you do you don't knock 'em out. You want to hit 'em on the side, sir."

Travers smiled. "No more tries for me. You care to have a go, Castle?" Then he smiled again, but sheepishly. "Sorry. Perfectly preposterous of me, being childish like this."

He handed the marble back, hunted for a sixpence and found only a shilling. The urchins at once picked up their marbles and departed at full speed with the miraculous windfall.

Travers, strolling back to the car, watched them amusedly. Then he hoped again that Castle would not think he had been trying to make him ridiculous.

"Funny about those marbles," he said, as a kind of attempt to trail away the event in conversation. "It does show how you can take things for granted. Now if I read in a book about boys playing marbles in July, I'd think the author a very slovenly person."

Castle said nothing.

"Well, here we are then," said Travers, and took his seat. The starter whirred and the engine began its purring. Travers's foot pushed out the clutch. With his very best smiled he looked up at Castle and his hand went out.

"Well, good-bye for the moment."

Then he saw something on Castle's face. It was pale, and the hand was damp. In a flash Travers was all concern.

"My dear fellow . . . you're not feeling ill?"

Castle smiled. "Just a bit washed-out—that's all." He shook his head. "I've been rather overdoing it lately. . . . I had to . . . all those arrears of Twirt's —and things."

"I won't keep you," said Travers. "You go and have some lunch and a good drink—and damn the work."

The two smiled at each other, and with a little nod Travers slipped the car into gear. Fifty yards along the road he looked back, but Castle had already gone.

IT WAS LONG after his usual lunch-time when Travers arrived at his flat in St. Martin's Chambers. Palmer began hovering round as he always did, like a hen with a lone chick.

"If you'll pardon me saying so, sir, you ought to take a bit of a rest. Whenever you're engaged on anything with Mr. Wharton you're not your proper self."

Travers laughed. "What you mean is that I make myself a damn nuisance."

But Palmer was immensely pleased at what had eventuated from his investigation of the catalogue. And while Travers's congratulations were still being uttered, the telephone bell went. It was Wharton.

"Where are you speaking from?" asked Travers.

"Still at Woodgate Hill," said Wharton. "What's more, I look like being here an hour or two more. I suppose, by the way, you didn't ever hint to Castle that he might have seen something out of the window that afternoon?"

"I asked him point-blank," said Travers. "He didn't see a thing. What's more, I'm so sure that if you want to bet, I'm laying ten pounds to a box of matches"

"Gambling's a mug's game," came Wharton's voice. "Still, I've had the good luck to see the two people who were teaching in Rooms 10 and 8 that afternoon, and neither was looking out of the window —except when they heard Twirt's charming voice and Vincent's, at 3.20."

"I can save you the rest," Travers told him. "I went to Room 7, and you can take it from me that from that window you can't see a thing of the actual spot where Twirt was polished off. It's traversed by the whole line of bushes in the shrubbery, if you understand me."

"Good!" said Wharton. "That's lucky, because the one who was teaching in Room 7 is now on the road to Scarborough. You

172 | CHRISTOPHER BUSH

there? . . . Then I don't mind telling you I was just about to see Castle—only you've spared me the trouble."

"And how're things working out?"

"Can't grumble," said Wharton. "Everything's fitting in magnificently. By the way, there'll be a conference at the Yard later to-night, and I'd like you to do something for me. You listening?"

"With both ears," Travers told him.

"Well then, it's this. There's just one little vital step missing. We've got to lay some trap or other into which Flint will fall, or we've got to get evidence by hook or crook. We must have something in connection with the entering the shrubbery and from then till Godman saw him come tearing by the girls' door. You see that?"

"Yes," said Travers laconically.

"Well, you get your wits to work," went on Wharton. "You're infinitely more quick at the uptake than I am. Work out the case against Flint, and if you get what we want, send it round to the Yard. That all right?"

"A lot of it isn't," said Travers. "But if I do get anything, I'll most certainly let you know. But don't ring up here, George, because I shan't be in. Nothing else?"

And as soon as Wharton said that was all, Travers snapped back the receiver. The case was beginning to get on his nerves. Let Wharton do his own jackalling. Flint, eh? Romance there had been at that school, but there was neither romance nor decency in sending a snivelling little rat like Flint to the hangman's drop in the cold of an early autumn morning—and for having wiped out a specimen like Lionel Twirt. No. The case could get on very well without himself. Till the following morning at least, he would forget it. Everything in connection with Woodgate Hill should be wiped out.

But as Travers sat with a book before the open window, the roofs of the houses all at once began to remind him of the roofs of Woodgate Hill and the dense suburban mass that one could see from the windows of that school. And when to escape that, he took a bus and made his way to Hyde Park, the playing children and the grass itself brought back the playing-fields of that damnable school, and the urge towards the case which he had never really forgotten.

So Travers moved on to his club, had tea and browsed among the weeklies. Then the face of a certain man recalled that of Castle, and he thought of it again as he had last seen it—haggard and strained with the responsibilities of that same case, and the catching-up with the accumulated arrears that Twirt's slackness had left. And thereupon Travers decided that what he himself needed was some complete transportation, and he ran his eye over the early editions of the evening papers, for the list of shows on in town. But there was nothing that made an appeal.

Then his eye caught something. In Regent's Park that very evening was an open-air performance of *A Midsummer Night's Dream.* So there was no escaping that school—and Castle. That was the play that should have been performed while Twirt was being murdered. That was the play when the raggers of the second fourth had tried their luck with Castle. It almost seemed, indeed, as if fate were making a challenge. There was to be no escaping of the case. Very well then. He would accept the challenge and face up to things. He would go and see that play.

But as he made his way across the Park, there were more pleasurable thoughts. It would be jolly to see that play—of all Shakespeare's the most suitable— performed in the open air. And it was his favourite. He knew it almost by heart, and there was about its rustics and its preposterous fairies a gentle irony that always fitted his own humour. And, best of all, more years ago than he cared to remember, that same play had given him his only appearance on any stage; when, at his prep-school he had been Puck—a lanky boy with blinking, humorous, unbespectacled eyes.

His was a seat near the front row. It was a delicious evening of late July. The setting was perfect—no stage woods or backcloth of Athenian stalls, but open country, and a grove, and grass on which human feet could leave a real tread. Ten minutes, and Woodgate Hill had passed completely from Travers's mind. He chuckled at Bottom and his fellows as if he had never met them before. He felt the same faint irritation at the foolish squabbles of the fairy couple, and pitied the moon-struck lovers wandering distraught. To him it was as natural as evening itself that Bottom should be given an ass's head and make himself complacently at home in fairyland. He felt the magic of Puck's enchanted sleep, and his blood stirred at the merry horns that roused the lovers from their morning bed.

But the play was almost over. The woods were left and it was the nuptial eve. When Philostrate appeared with his list of plays from which Theseus would choose a something to pass an idle hour, Travers roused himself expectantly, and smiled when the one item came:

> A tedious, brief scene of young Pyramus
> And his love Thisbe; very tragical mirth.

A moment or two and Quince was coming in to manhandle his Prologue, and then with his troupe of actors to be introduced. There they all were: Pyramus brave in an ill-fitting armour; Thisbe in her mask and with down-hanging mantle; Moonshine with dog, lanthorn and bush of thorn; the grisly Lion with too obvious claws, and Wall with his rough-cast and a something he held in his hand. Then Quince went aside and Wall was left alone.

> *Wall.* In this same interlude it doth befall
> That I, one Snout by name, present a wall.

A bold, confident fellow he seemed to be, and no whit abashed by the company he was in.

> And such a wall, as I would have you think,
> As had in it a crannied hole or chink,
> Through which the lovers, Pyramus and Thisbe,
> Did whisper often very secretly.

This loam, this rough-cast, and this stone doth show
That I am that same wall; the truth is so.

Then, as Wall exhibited his garments and the something he was holding in his hand, a sudden blinding revelation came to Ludovic Travers. It was a revelation that so shocked and almost terrified, that without knowing it he rose and made his way through the protesting line of seats. Out in the open he stood for a minute or two, wondering if by chance he could be right. He moved on again, then again he halted; with a longer wondering wherein he could be wrong. And George Wharton wanted information. *Maybe he would have it.*

And forthwith Travers set his long legs moving again towards the road and the swirl of traffic. A minute later he was hailing a taxi and asking to be driven to Woodgate Hill.

The street lamps were alight as they drew near the suburb. Travers tapped at the window and directed the driver to a right-hand turn. The taxi passed those lines of new villas, then slowed where the road was up. A line of red lamps marked the way through the heaped earth, the slabs of paving stone, and the granite blocks that would make the entry ways to the garages of the new houses. Just short of them Travers tapped again.

He disappeared in the dusk. Woodgate Hill County School reared itself in the far background as a scarcely discernible blackness against the innumerable stars. Beyond it would be Flint's cottage, and Mrs. Flint no doubt sewing or reading the paper, and hopelessly unaware of the fact that in a few short weeks she might be a widow. But it was not with the school or the caretaker's cottage that Travers had business. Five minutes after leaving the taxi, he came back to it—much to the driver's relief.

"Now go to the police station," he said. "Back on the main road, about two hundred yards left."

Inspector Quick was up at the Yard, the station sergeant said. But he took Travers's word and gave the run of the phone.

It was Daisy Quick whom Travers wanted. Her mother said she was in—just back from the pictures. And she was sure she'd be glad to see Mr. Travers.

So out to the taxi again, with a constable there to show the way to Quick's house. Mrs. Quick showed Travers into the drawing-room, and in a moment or two Daisy came in.

"Absolutely unpardonable of me," Travers began, "but there's just one small piece of information I want from you. What's more, you must promise—finger wet, finger dry—to keep it a desperate secret."

She smiled. "For how long?"

Travers looked at her as if all the cares of the world were in his eyes. "The whole of your life perhaps. Can you manage that?"

"I think so," she told him.

"Then where does the boy live who's known as Tubby Miller?"

"Well"—she frowned—"his father's a butcher, you know. He has two shops in the High Street, and the biggest one's just past the police station, and that's the one where they live."

"Splendid!" said Travers. "And you couldn't make the information perfect by telling me if Tubby's still there? I mean, has he gone away for his holiday?"

"Oh, no," she told him. "I don't know if I'm supposed to tell you this, but Mr. Castle wrote that his father was to take him away from school at once, and his father wrote a most insulting letter and said he wouldn't have him in the school any longer on any account." She smiled. "He's going into the business. I saw him this morning myself, not long after we'd broken up, going an errand on one of the business bicycles."

Travers nodded. "Starting early, is he? Let's hope it does him good. But don't forget. It's a special secret between you and me."

She nodded. Travers moved off towards the door.

"Do apologize to your mother for my giving her all this trouble." At the very door he turned back. "Going away for your holidays soon?"

She flushed slightly. "Yes—on Friday."

"And where?"

The flush deepened. "To Normandy."

"You're a lucky soul then," said Travers. He smiled. "I seem to remember that another member of the staff is going that way too."

She was not displeased, for she was smiling too.

"And everything's all right now?"

"Yes—everything."

"Splendid!" said Travers—and meant it.

It was almost midnight when Travers reached home again.

"There's a message for you from Superintendent Wharton, sir," Palmer told him as soon as he got in. "Most confidential he said it was, sir."

"What time did it come?"

"Just an hour ago, sir."

Travers gave his glasses a quick polish and took the pad over to the light.

> Everything going splendidly. Quick brought F. along here and a statement was made. Much the same as you heard. No flaws but that doesn't particularly matter. A.C. and I seeing the D.P.P. first thing in the morning.
>
> *Urgent.* Will call you first thing to know if you've thought of anything to fill in that gap.

So Wharton had had his conference, and as a result Flint had been brought to the Yard and invited to make a statement. But Flint had incriminated himself no further. And yet the powers that were, considered the case sufficiently strong against him to have Wharton and the Assistant Commissioner put their views before the Director of Public Prosecutions. And, as Travers knew, Sir Claude was on a brief holiday near Dorking, and that was where the law would go to interview him. And if Sir Claude thought the case strong enough, no doubt Flint would be under arrest within twenty-four hours. Or maybe Wharton would go back on the promise Castle had given, and hold the caretaker on the less important charge. And for all his cocksureness, Wharton was none too sure; else why that second urgent appeal for extra evidence?

Maybe Wharton would get that extra evidence—but not when he wanted it. There was still a tale to be told and a link to find for the chain. And just how that tale should be told was the thing that required immediate thought.

That night Travers slept like a log. It was Palmer who roused him, but not with the usual cup of tea—it was still too early for that.

"Mr. Wharton on the phone, sir. He says it's urgent."

Travers rolled out of bed, blinked for a bit, hooked on his glasses, and went as he was to the phone.

"Morning, George—if it *is* morning yet."

"Morning!" said Wharton. "Why, the day's damn near gone. I'm just off to Dorking to see the D.P.P. as I said. You got that message all right?"

"Oh, yes."

"Thought of anything?"

"Lots," said Travers, and hesitated while he hunted for the right words. "You still there? . . . Well, promise me you'll come here and see me the very minute you get back, before you take any definite action. Will you do that?"

"You mean, you've found out something?"

"Almost," said Travers. "I can't go further than that. But you promise?"

"I say, look here," came Wharton's voice, "can't you tell me just what lines you're working on? You know what I mean. I'm about to put up our case, and every little might help."

"You know what lines I'm working on," said Travers. "Didn't you put a certain line of thought up to me? In any case, George, I can't tell you a thing—now. When you come back maybe. That'll be different."

There was a brief wait at Wharton's end of the line, then, "As you wish then. As soon as I get back to town I'm to drop in and see you."

"I'll be waiting," said Travers, and though Wharton had hung up, he still stood there with the receiver in his hand.

Palmer had tea ready and Travers set about his dressing. All the time he was teased in thought. Flint was on his mind and, try how he might, he could not thrust him out. Then at breakfast Travers began to see clearly the line he must take. Down went his napkin at once and he went over to the phone. It was that neighbour of Castle's that he called. A woman's voice spoke.

"Dreadfully sorry to trouble you at this unearthly hour of the morning," Travers began, "but it's frightfully important. Could you anyhow get Mr. Castle from next door and say that a Mr. Travers— *Travers*—must speak with him?"

He stood there for a good five minutes, and it was almost a shock when Castle's voice came in a tentative, "Hallo!"

"Good morning," said Travers. "Sorry to bother you so early, but I've got to report something desperately urgent to you. It's a matter of life and death."

"I'm afraid I don't get you." Castle's bewilderment was in his voice.

"It's Flint," Travers told him. "Last night he was taken to Scotland Yard and invited to make a statement. I may tell you he's in a very bad hole—"

"Just a minute. A bad hole about what? Not that hammer business?"

"That's it," said Travers. "Within a very few hours he'll be arrested for murder."

A wait—and Castle cleared his throat before he spoke. "What do you want me to do about it?"

"You may know something," Travers told him. "Flint's nothing to you. He's a bad egg—we all know that, but hanging's a different matter. Have you ever seen one?"

Castle mumbled something.

"I know you think I'm a bit hysterical," went on Travers. "You remember that marble game we saw on Tuesday morning, and how I dropped a marble? That's how Flint's going to drop, with a rope round his neck. Are you listening?"

"Yes."

"You've got to think, Castle There may be a flaw in the evidence that you alone know. Think it over. And let me know here. Don't telephone. You got that? Don't telephone. Write!"

There was a sound as of yet another clearing of the throat that showed Castle was still there, but Travers hung up at once. And he was shaking his head dolorously. Castle must have thought him suddenly mad. And if Wharton had been there to hear, he would have been certain of the same fact. Again Travers shook his head perplexedly as he went back to his meal. But appetite had gone and he lighted his pipe instead. A few minutes and he was telling Palmer to bring round the car.

It was about ten o'clock when Travers drove slowly along the High Street of Woodgate Hill, with an eye for a butcher's shop above which should be the name of Miller. In spite of his overnight puzzling, he had hit on no precise method of procedure, but his favourite plan, of all those he had toyed with, was to call boldly on the butcher, recall himself and the circumstances under which they had met, and to express sympathy for the ill-used son. For the purposes of all that, Travers had the highly impressive Palmer by his side. Palmer—and the Rolls—should be admirable guarantees of good faith.

But no sooner did Travers spot the shop than he spotted something else. A lad of decided plumpness, and in much better clothes than those of the ordinary errand-boy, was mounting a bicycle at the pavement edge, after having deposited in its carrier what looked like somebody's joint.

Travers turned into a handy side road, backed out again and moved the Rolls in pursuit. The lad on the bicycle was not wearing that cap of yellow with the purple blazonry—that hall-mark by which the county school of Woodgate Hill differentiated itself from its even gaudier neighbours. And he was whistling a tune which B.B.C. crooners had made familiar to the public—which was hardly what might have been expected from one who had imbibed learning at the feet of Maitland Castle. Yet Travers was sure the lad was Tubby Miller. The fat buttocks that wriggled on the bicycle seat fairly shouted it.

The High Street was left and the bicycle turned into a good-class residential district. Almost before Travers was ready to pull up, the bicycle was standing in the kerb and Tubby was off to the back door of a house with the basket that held the joint. When he returned, Travers managed with some artistry to collide with him just outside the gate. He apologized profusely, then gave a shrewd look.

"I think I know your face. I'm sure I've seen you somewhere?"

"It was at the school," said Tubby. He seemed a fat, inoffensive, mutton-headed youth.

"The school?"

"Yes, sir. You were the one who spoke to us one day about what happened when Mr. Castle was out of the room."

Travers smiled. "So I did! And what's your name?"

Tubby told him. He added that he had left the school, and to a further question, made no bones about admitting he was glad of it. Travers laid a fatherly hand on his shoulder.

"I wouldn't like you to think I'm interfering with your private business, but who do you think I am?"

"An inspector, sir," said Tubby. "Everybody knew you were an inspector."

Travers swallowed the implications. He nodded gravely. "It was curious I should happen to be at the school that morning when your father called round to see the headmaster. I think you had been unlawfully punished by one of the staff."

Tubby grinned. Obviously he now bore no malice. "Yes, sir. It was old . . . it was Mr. Castle, sir. He nearly pulled my ear off."

Travers was shocked. "Surely not! What on earth made him do a thing like that?"

"He lost his wool, sir."

"I see. He got in a furious temper, did he? And what made him do that?"

"Well, sir," began Tubby, "it was like this . . ."

As Travers knew, it was hopeless to expect Wharton back so soon from Dorking. To have gone back to the flat would have been a sort of cooped suspense and a waiting, so Travers lunched in town. Two o'clock found him home again. At half-past he was restless, and rang up the Yard. They had no information. For all they knew, Wharton was still closeted with the D.P.P. . . .

Another few minutes and Travers was prowling round restlessly. He would go down to Dorking himself—but that was sheer lunacy. Wharton might have started back already, and there were half a dozen ways from there to town. So Travers had his tea early, and then pestered the Yard again. Would they be sure to catch Wharton immediately on his arrival, and remind him that Mr. Travers wished to see him on a matter of extreme urgency?

That done, Travers became something of his old philosophical self. In due time Wharton would come. And Travers had need of his philosophy, for it was not till after six o'clock that he heard the whir of the lift, and the breezy voice of George Wharton uttering some facetiousness to the expectant Palmer.

CHAPTER XVI
THE TRUTH IS SO!

WHARTON HAD SHED most of his facetiousness by the time he entered the room. He was looking none too happy and none too sad; his manner, in fact, was a reserved expectancy.

"Tea, George?" smiled Travers.

"Had it," said Wharton.

"Then a drink of some sort?"

"Bit too early, isn't it?"

"Later then," said Travers. "And what did the D.P.P. decide?"

"Everything's still under consideration," said Wharton. "But Sir Claude came back to town— that's really what made me so late. All the same, if you ask me, I'd say Flint's for it—especially after that special information you've got for us."

"Who said I'd got special information?" blinked Travers.

Wharton laughed. "Don't I know you? And haven't you been calling the Yard?" He got himself comfortable in the easy chair. "Come on now, let's hear what it is."

"Not for a moment," Travers told him. "First of all I must know exactly the strength of your case against Flint. If we see the weak spots, that'll be the time to do repairs."

Wharton spread his hands. "You know our case. On his own admission, Flint knew all about the laburnum. He admits he was in practically all the places, and at the times, we wanted him to be. He owns up to the motive. Sandyman will give evidence, and so will Castle when it's pointed out to him. You and I know that Flint happened to be hiding up in that shrubbery—watching Godman's car—and Twirt saw him from his position where we found that cigarette. Twirt followed him in to see what he was doing there, but Flint saw Twirt, and as he came through the bushes, he got him with the hammer. And he bolted at once, didn't he? Then came back when he thought we didn't suspect him."

Travers nodded. "So that's your case."

"It is," said Wharton, "and a good one—though I say it." He gave a little chuckle. "You can't beat the old methods. It's elimination that does it. Look at all the suspects we discarded. Furrow, Godman, Vincent, Sandyman. Flint was the only one left— and he's the man."

Travers smiled. "There was even a time when you suspected Castle, wasn't there?"

"Not for long," said Wharton. "He merely came under review."

"And what would a jury think of your case against Flint as it now stands?"

"That's the D.P.P.'s job—not mine," said Wharton.

"To be perfectly blunt," persisted Travers, "that case of yours is built up on evidence that's wholly circumstantial."

Wharton tried to look hurt. "Well—why not? Don't most murderers get hung on circumstantial evidence? Hasn't it been said that it's the best evidence there is?"

Travers shook his head. "Don't you believe it! And listen to me, George. You mentioned now a list of suspects that had been discarded. Listen, George—and take me seriously. *I guarantee here and now to take any one of those suspects and build up against him on circumstantial evidence a case that shall be infinitely stronger than yours against Flint."*

Wharton laughed. "You will have your little jokes."

"Jokes!" Travers glared at him. "My God! you talk about jokes when it's a question of breaking a man's neck!" He raised his hands appealingly. "Listen, George. For the love of God, listen! I never was half so earnest in my life. Can't you see it?"

Wharton looked at him queerly, then grunted. "Well, you know best."

"Name a suspect," Travers went on. "Name the most unlikely one we mentioned. Godman, Furrow, Sandyman, Castle—" He broke suddenly off. "About Castle there's something I must tell you. When I asked him what he saw out of that window and if he saw Twirt killed, do you know what he said? I'll tell you the exact words. 'I give you my word I did not see Twirt killed. I didn't even know he was dead till I saw him lying there.'"

"Well, we knew that, didn't we?" said Wharton.

"Yes," said Travers, "but it's an added proof. I believe Castle, and I know what he said was true. Therefore he didn't commit the murder."

Wharton clicked his tongue. "What you're getting at I don't know, but you're tying me in knots. I say we *know* Castle didn't commit the murder."

"Very well then," said Travers. "That's just what I'm driving at. I said I'd prove, by circumstantial evidence, that the most unlikely suspect committed that murder. If you'll be so good, therefore as to listen, I'll redeem my promise and prove to you how Castle—as the most impossible person we can think of—did do that business with the hammer!"

Wharton stared at him. He knew only too well the uncanny workings of Travers's brain. And he saw he was in deadly earnest.

"Is it going to help?"

Travers smiled relievedly. "It's going to help more than you'll ever guess."

"Carry on then," Wharton told him.

"First of all," began Travers, "we imagine I'm prosecuting counsel. You're judge, jury and the public. Interrupt me whenever you like, but let it be only on a matter of very real importance.

"Also, everything's hypothetical. If we get that into our heads it'll save a lot of thought. But what we begin with isn't hypothetical—and that's the motives for murder that Castle had. Those motives were three, and I'll take them in order.

"Firstly he hated Twirt. I've said maybe before that it wasn't an ordinary, jealous, bodily hate. It was a hate of the soul. Every day Castle saw above him a man who was his intellectual and social inferior; a man of unscrupulous tricks and offensive manners; undoubtedly a liar, a thief, and the worst kind of egomaniac. Castle's hate came from a hurt pride.

"Secondly, Castle possessed—as you yourself assured him—a very definite public spirit. As senior master, he felt a duty to his colleagues. The removal of Twirt was the end of a real menace to the very health—spiritual and bodily—and the sanity of all the staff.

"Thirdly, we come to the question of Castle's individual profit. Life would be easier for himself, and, above all, if Twirt went, then Castle might even become headmaster himself."

"But that's the very thing he refused!" said Wharton. "He loathed the very idea of becoming Head of that school."

"I know," said Travers, "but—if you'll pardon me —I'm coming to that aspect of that particular motive, later on. We therefore pass on to the actual time of the murder. Assume it was 3.55. I will now establish the exact position of Twirt, and Castle his murderer, at that time.

"Firstly, Twirt. It has gone beyond mere hypothesis that at 3.55 he was on the strip of gravel by the main entrance, waiting to catch out Godman when he came down to his car. As for Castle, we know he was looking out of the window of Room 9. In his case, however, we must go back and appreciate the atmosphere of the room in which he was working, and review the events that had taken place prior to 3.55. There I must ask you a question. Are you really familiar with Shakespeare's *Midsummer Night's Dream?*"

Wharton smiled grimly. "My missus only dragged me off to it one night this last June. Still, I oughtn't to say that. I must admit I enjoyed it."

Travers smiled. "Well, that's going to help us a lot. Also, I needn't recall to you the Tubby Miller affair and the rag that the second fourth tried on Castle, and how Castle twisted Tubby Miller's ear. The Lion had an ox-tail on his breeks, you remember; Moonshine had an acetylene lamp. Then there was Wall. We can guess what he had. He had an old coat he'd smeared with mortar, and he had to have something in his hand. Remember his words?

> This loam, this rough-cast and this stone doth show
> That I am that same wall; the truth is so.

"But stones are none too handy in a London suburb, George, so Wall—who was our friend Tubby Miller—had provided himself with a granite block." He lifted the paper that concealed the solid rectangle of granite. "One like this, that was one of a heap where the road was up; where it lay to Tubby's hand on his way to the school."

Wharton gave him a long, intent look. But he said no word.

"That rag began," went on Travers, "and Castle soon showed the raggers exactly where they stood. He smashed the ox-tail and the lamp into the wastepaper basket, and while he was doing that, Tubby Miller tried to repent by laying the stone on the table respectfully. But it was dirty and—as we'd expect from a blundering jackass like him—he laid it on Castle's papers. That's why Castle twisted his ear. And while he was twisting his ear, another lad—also trying to help—laid the stone on the ledge of the open window where it could do no harm.

"The brief riot then was quelled. The form, in fact, was scared stiff, and it—and Castle—went on working. Which brings us to where we began; to the time 3.55, or 3.54 or whatever it was when Castle decided to have a breather at the window.

"Now try to visualize things. How does a man stand at a window when the height allows him to lean against the ledge? He folds his arms and lets them lie along that ledge, while he looks out at the scenery. Castle was about to fold his arms, when he couldn't help becoming aware of that huge stone. 'Damn the stone—and damn Tubby Miller!' That was what he thought. He would throw the stone down into Twirt's comic shrubbery, instead of having it clutter up the room, or be bothered with making Tubby take it back to the heap from which he stole it. And of course the form could not see what Castle was about to do. His back and his elongated elbows would hide the stone from the form, even if the form wished to pry—which they certainly didn't, after the twisting of Tubby's ear.

"So Castle pushed the stone away, and as he did so he saw something. He knew what it was. He knew *why* it was. It was Twirt, up to his spying tricks. The hatred, the scorn, the blinding anger all surged tumultuously in one mad moment. Twirt's head in a dead line below! Just a dropping of the stone—and life would be miraculously changed. And before he knew what he had done, Castle had poised that stone—and dropped it. Then with the awful realization, *he turned his head away.* He did not see Twirt die! He did not even know he was really dead till he rushed like a madman downstairs *and saw him lying there.* Not where you found him, George, but *there.* You see it? Castle told the truth. But so complete was the truth that it was a perfect lie."

"Yes," said Wharton with a kind of slowness, and looked steadily away across the room.

"Then when Castle saw Twirt lying there dead, he panicked. He picked up his skimpy body and stepped into the shrubbery. He moved through it to the drive. He looked out, then in a flash was across and into the other shrubbery. Some remembering of the talk beneath his window between Twirt and Vincent made him drop that body by the tree. He was heard there by Sandyman, and by a miracle regained the school while Sandyman was hidden by the wall and before Godman reached his car." Travers paused for a moment. "That's the first part of my case against Castle. I now come to subsequent actions that further establish the theory."

But there was a temporary interruption. Palmer came in with the small tray.

"The letters, sir—if you'll pardon me."

Travers looked at them, had a quick word with Wharton and examined them with more care. The two circulars he ripped open and then replaced on the tray. A small package and one letter went on the mantelpiece, and the last letter he opened. But he gave it no more than one glance, then laid it on the table. A quick look at the envelope and he screwed that into a ball and put it on the tray with the unwanted circulars.

"Those can go in the kitchen fire—if you've got one," he told Palmer. Then he turned to Wharton. "Sorry about all these interruptions, George. Where was I? Oh, yes, at events subsequent to the actual murder.

"First of all, remember that night in the Running Stag? Why didn't Castle want me to see that catalogue? Well, we'll say he didn't mind my seeing the catalogue. What he didn't want me to see in the bag was something else, which I'd have seen when he opened it—the stone which he had secreted in the common room, and which he was taking away to dispose of.

"And you know as well as I do that Castle refused to incriminate a soul over that killing of Twirt. He made no suggestions and he gave no help. He laid no false trails. He did the murder and he was prepared to pay the price—if we caught him out. And to reinforce that particular argument of mine, may I recall that on that other murder—the poisoning of Tennant—Castle had no such compunctions. He definitely suggested to me that Elsie Holl might have done it.

"Again, Castle shoo'd away old Miller that morning, as I told you. And he was far too eager to get that school closed so that Tubby Miller could be off the premises and out of the reach of possible questioning. He even gave Tubby the sack from the school.

"And just one other thing, which is really a harking back. We know now that Castle—and it's absolutely like him—refused to profit by Twirt's death. He killed him, and that was the end of it. When Ma Gedge mentioned that round-robin, he was absolutely furious, as you know. If Castle were offered the headship of Woodgate Hill County School, he'd refuse to take it."

There Travers halted. He shook his head as if in some whimsical perplexity, then drew a deep breath. When his eyes rose, Wharton's were regarding him fixedly.

"That completes my case then, George. Have I made my threat good? Doesn't Castle—on the face of things—look a guiltier person than Flint?"

"I'll be serious now," said Wharton. "Also, I'm no fool. How much of this is hypothesis, and how much real fact?"

"I think all of it is fact," Travers told him quietly. "You see, I've seen Tubby Miller, and I know what happened in that room. All except the actual touching of the stone. Naturally Tubby never saw that, but he saw, out of the corner of his eye, Castle leaning on the window-ledge, and he certainly remembered the amazing suddenness and unexpectedness with which Castle then left the room. And something else, George. This morning I rang up Castle and I told him in so many words that I knew. I invited him—again in so many unmistakable words—to write me a letter—"

"He'd never do that."

"But he has done it!" said Travers, and picked the letter up. Then he smiled queerly. "I took a risk telling you what I did, George. I don't know what's in this letter—all I know is that Castle has written it. For all I know it may prove me to be the world's most complacent fool. So you read it, George, and see."

Wharton said no word as he took it, but his eyes narrowed as he read.

My dear Travers,

So you know then? I was sure of it when you made an excuse to show me that marble game yesterday morning. All along I had the idea that you knew. Now I really know, though it's only a few minutes since you and I were talking—like two ghosts—along a few miles of wire.

I've only a few minutes because I know my train goes at—but I hadn't better tell you that. There's some money to get from the bank too, but I've already told my landlady where to send my things. She's a decent soul. Thinking of you made me think that of her.

It was the Miller boy who gave you the clue, wasn't it? I did my best to side-track him, but apparently you found out. There was a stone, as you know; a fourteen-pound lump of granite, which had been placed on the window-ledge. Your marble, in fact.

I might claim that it fell by accident—but it didn't. I know now that I squashed out Twirt's life as I'd squash a poisonous beetle. I saw him in a plumb-line beneath my eye and that stone. It was a strange shock at first, then something cracked inside me. I hardly know now what I felt, but I kept telling myself I would *not* drop that stone. I seemed to be fighting not to drop it. It was like pulling against a rope, and the rope won. My hands went out and the stone fell. At once it was as if the spell had gone and I was able to turn away.

Years of hate and repression were the rope that pulled that stone. But it was no accident. Then I remember I flew downstairs. I said, "It didn't get him. He'll be angry, and I'll let him see the curl of my lip when he has to own up that he was spying." But he lay there all right and then I went queer again. I think I had the idea that there was some sort of hole dug by that tree, and I'd bury him and come back later and complete the job. But I left him where you found him, and when it was too late I knew I'd been a fool.

By the time you get this I shall be out of England. I expect you'll catch me, and if you do, you must tell me how you first knew. But I shall give you a run for your money! Funny, isn't it? Charles Tennant used to call Twirt a tin-Cæsar. You see the point? You do if you remember the quotation:

> "O Julius Cæsar! thou art mighty yet,
>   Thy spirit walks abroad and turns our swords
>   In our own proper entrails."

I killed Twirt, in other words, and he may still be the death of me. But let's hope it will never come to that.

I wouldn't like that way out.

Good-bye, and good luck. It was nice knowing you, and it was magnificent of you to give me the hint—and my chance.

MAITLAND CASTLE.

Wharton passed it back. "Read it yourself. Or perhaps you wouldn't mind if we read it together."

So Travers read it. But there was no exultation when he had finished. He sat for a moment or two, glasses in hand, then gave a shake of the head.

"There you are then, George. Get out your hue-and-cry. Your man's away."

"Yes," said Wharton. "Apparently he is." Then his eyes opened. "What station did he go from? What's the postal district on that envelope?" "The envelope's burnt," said Travers. "Didn't you see me give it to Palmer?"

Wharton's eyes narrowed. Then his face softened. "Well, I suppose you were entitled to that much. He was your man—not mine."

Travers shook his head, then his eyes opened too. "Do you realize that Twirt was a murderer? Castle killed a murderer! And think of the case we can put up, George—I mean, the whole of that staff will be only too ready to testify to what Castle had to put up with for years. You'll get him, George, but you'd never try to hang him. Manslaughter perhaps—what do you say? Manslaughter—four years or five."

"Maybe," said Wharton laconically. "But the world's a wide place. We haven't got him yet."

He shook his head, then got to his feet. "Still, I've got to get to work—and quick. Mind if I use your phone?"

Travers waved his hand. But there was no listening to the General's voice as he gave his rapid orders. Four years—or five. *And they hadn't caught him yet.* The world was a wide place, as Wharton had said. But whatever happened, Castle would never take the coward's way out. No sword in the entrails for him. And if Wharton should get him, and the jail held him, even from such a shattering Castle would indomitably emerge, to hold to himself the finer things of life of which not even the Dead Shepherd had totally robbed him. And, as Wharton had said, Castle was his own man. However distant the day of release, he himself would be at the prison doors to hold out a friendly hand.

THE END